TRAINING THE DUKE

Suddenly a Duke Series
Book Seven

Alexa Aston

Dragonblade Publishing, Inc. is an imprint of Kathryn Le Veque Novels, Inc.
P.O. Box 23
Moreno Valley, CA 92556
ceo@dragonbladepublishing.com

Produced in the United States of America

First Edition October 2023
Print Edition

ARE YOU SIGNED UP FOR DRAGONBLADE'S BLOG?

You'll get the latest news and information on exclusive giveaways, exclusive excerpts, coming releases, sales, free books, cover reveals and more.

Check out our complete list of authors, too!

No spam, no junk. That's a promise!

Sign Up Here

www.dragonbladepublishing.com

Dearest Reader;

Thank you for your support of a small press. At Dragonblade Publishing, we strive to bring you the highest quality Historical Romance from some of the best authors in the business. Without your support, there is no 'us', so we sincerely hope you adore these stories and find some new favorite authors along the way.

Happy Reading!

CEO, Dragonblade Publishing

Additional Dragonblade books by Author Alexa Aston

Suddenly a Duke Series
Portrait of the Duke
Music for the Duke
Polishing the Duke
Designs on the Duke
Fashioning the Duke
Love Blooms with the Duke
Training the Duke

Second Sons of London Series
Educated By The Earl
Debating With The Duke
Empowered By The Earl
Made for the Marquess
Dubious about the Duke
Valued by the Viscount
Meant for the Marquess

Dukes Done Wrong Series
Discouraging the Duke
Deflecting the Duke
Disrupting the Duke
Delighting the Duke
Destiny with a Duke

Dukes of Distinction Series
Duke of Renown
Duke of Charm
Duke of Disrepute

Duke of Arrogance
Duke of Honor
The Duke That I Want

The St. Clairs Series
Devoted to the Duke
Midnight with the Marquess
Embracing the Earl
Defending the Duke
Suddenly a St. Clair
Starlight Night (Novella)
The Twelve Days of Love (Novella)

Soldiers & Soulmates Series
To Heal an Earl
To Tame a Rogue
To Trust a Duke
To Save a Love
To Win a Widow
Yuletide at Gillingham (Novella)

The Lyon's Den Series
The Lyon's Lady Love

King's Cousins Series
The Pawn
The Heir
The Bastard

Medieval Runaway Wives
Song of the Heart
A Promise of Tomorrow
Destined for Love

Knights of Honor Series
Word of Honor
Marked by Honor

Code of Honor
Journey to Honor
Heart of Honor
Bold in Honor
Love and Honor
Gift of Honor
Path to Honor
Return to Honor

Pirates of Britannia Series
God of the Seas

De Wolfe Pack: The Series
Rise of de Wolfe

The de Wolfes of Esterley Castle
Diana
Derek
Thea

Also from Alexa Aston
The Bridge to Love
One Magic Night

PROLOGUE

London—July 1807

L ADY FINOLA HONEYFIELD sat at her dressing table, staring at her image in the small mirror she held.

Would tonight be the night that Lord Crofton offered for her?

The Season would end soon. Couples were becoming engaged, left and right. She hoped she and the viscount might be one of them.

She had not drawn any suitors in her first Season, feeling much like a misfit. Her father, Lord Leppington, had passed when Finola was but eight years of age. Her mother had died giving birth to Finola, and it seemed her father had never forgiven his daughter for causing his wife's death. He called her "the afterthought" because she was so much younger than her two older sisters, who were fifteen and seventeen years her senior.

When her father died, word was sent to her sisters in Scotland. They had wed twin brothers and remained in the remote Highlands, never returning to London after their marriages. Finola had stayed with the local, elderly clergyman and his wife, waiting for months for word from her sisters regarding her fate. When it came, the message said they simply did not want her. Even as a child, their words did not surprise her. Finola could not remember anything about her oldest sister and only had a vague impression of what the other one had looked like since she had left the Honeyfield household when Finola was barely three.

Still, it was a blow to her, not to be wanted.

The village had held a meeting to decide what to do with her. After all, she was from the nobility, the daughter of an earl. Yet the Earl of Leppington had no heirs neither far nor wide and the title had reverted to the crown upon his death. Finola had sat in the clergyman's parlor as prominent citizens of the village had discussed what to do with her.

Finally, Sir Roscoe Banfield had spoken up, saying he would take her in.

She felt relief blanket the room, everyone present no longer obliged to be responsible for an eight-year-old orphan.

Finola had gone home that same afternoon with Sir Roscoe. He had neither wife nor children and told her he had no desire to wed. He loved his dogs more than people and told Finola he would teach her to do the same. Banny, as she had come to affectionately call him, had been right. Dogs never disappointed her as people had. The furry creatures became her companions and next to Banny, her closest friends.

Banny was known for training dogs, English springer spaniels, in particular. He would take them on as puppies, when they were three months or so, and teach them the basics of proper dog behavior before stepping things up and training them to be hunters. Banny had taught Finola everything he knew about training dogs and especially, hunters. She had thought it would be her life's work until he had told her she needed to attend at least one Season in London, saying due to her rank, she should test the waters of the Marriage Mart and see if a life in Polite Society, married to a titled gentleman, might be for her.

Finola had accompanied Banny to town and since he had no residence there, they had stayed with a cousin of his, Lady Nance, a dowager countess. It was Lady Nance who sponsored Finola this

Season and had prepared her to make her come-out. Lady Nance had a cold disposition and little interest in doing anything other than berating Finola, especially about her weight. She bemoaned the fact that Finola was rather plump. The dowager countess had said it was all well and good to carry a bit of weight after marriage, once a lady had given birth to one or more children, but she could not understand why Finola was so chubby at her age.

Because of this, Lady Nance severely rationed what Finola ate. She instructed at the midnight suppers held at balls that Finola was only to eat a handful of bites. At garden parties, she was to only drink tea and refrain from eating at all. The one time she had surreptitiously reached for a macaroon, Lady Nance had swatted Finola's hand with a fan, causing those nearby to stifle their giggles.

She knew the servants felt sorry for her. One maid had even taken to bringing Finola something to eat when she came in from balls, helping her to undress as Finola hungrily wolfed down whatever she could. Afraid that Lady Nance would fire the maid, Finola had finally told the girl last week not to bring her anything else from the kitchens.

While Finola, for the most part, spent her time sitting with the wallflowers at events, somehow she had drawn the notice of the incredibly handsome Viscount Crofton. He cut quite a dashing figure, tall and blond, looking like an angel. She had no idea how or why she had claimed his attention, only that he had asked her to dance once several weeks ago. After that, he had not engaged her in any more dances at balls—but he always was pleasant and kind to her at social affairs. Eventually, he asked Finola to walk on the terrace with him after supper one night. When they reached the far corner, Lord Crofton had taken her hands in his and drew them up, pressing a fervent kiss upon her knuckles.

From that moment on, Finola loved him.

Three weeks ago, Lord Crofton had whispered in her ear at a garden party for her to meet him in the gazebo, and she had done so. He had told her how beautiful she looked that afternoon and kissed her cheek, causing her to go hot all over. Two weeks ago, the viscount had stopped her as she left the retiring room at a ball and pulled her into an alcove, where he had given her a chaste kiss on the lips. Her first. She had thought she would be swept away by emotion and her love for him. In reality, the kiss did not stir her in the slightest.

Last week, while both attended a card party, Lord Crofton had asked her to take a turn about the room with him and told her how ardently he admired her, causing her to feel flush all over.

Tonight, one of Lady Nance's maids had brought a note to Finola's room from the viscount. It asked her to meet him in the library this evening during Lord and Lady Turner's ball. She just knew he was going to offer for her. Once more, she thanked the heavens for bringing such a handsome, kind angel into her life. They would have children and dogs and a wonderful life together.

Of course, she had said nothing to Banny or Lady Nance of this secret courtship, at Lord Crofton's urging. He had shared with her that his family expected him to wed a woman with a large dowry. Finola's was adequate but nothing what Lord Crofton said his family desired. Still, he pressed his suit with her, telling her to be patient. That explained why he never called on her or asked her to dance at the many balls she had attended.

It did not matter. She knew deep in her bones Lord Crofton was the man for her and only hoped she would receive an offer of marriage from him in the library tonight.

Going downstairs, she was surprised that Banny did not await her. She asked the butler if he had seen Sir Roscoe.

"Sir Roscoe is feeling ill, my lady. He will not be accompanying you and Lady Nance to the Turner ball."

Knowing Lady Nance would not be downstairs for several more minutes, Finola went upstairs and knocked gently on Banny's bedchamber door.

His valet answered the knock. "Ah, Lady Finola. Here to check on Sir Roscoe?"

"I am. Might I see him for a few moments before I leave for tonight's ball?"

The servant nodded and left the bedchamber to give them privacy. Finola stepped to Banny's bed and was surprised at how wan he appeared.

"I hear you are under the weather this evening."

He shrugged. "Just a bit of indigestion, my dear, making me uncomfortable. I probably am tiring of the city and its rich food and look forward to returning to Belldale and breathing the clean country air again." Banny paused and then asked, "Have any prospects caught your eye this Season?"

She decided to share with him about Lord Crofton. "Yes, Banny, there is one particular gentleman I favor. He has asked to speak privately with me tonight."

"Do you hope for an offer of marriage from him?"

"Yes, I do. If he does ask for my hand, I will send him to see you in the morning to ask your permission since you are my guardian. You have been like a father to me these past ten years. I know you would look after my interests with Lord Crofton, especially in reviewing the marriage settlements."

"I am happy you have found someone, Finola." He smiled wryly. "Perhaps I am also a bit blue, knowing it means I will lose you."

She placed her hand atop his. "You will never lose me, Banny. We are family. You will be a grandfather to our children."

He returned her smile. "We are family, indeed, Finola." Then he winced.

"Are you certain you are all right?" she asked quickly. "I am happy to summon a doctor."

"It is nothing. Just the indigestion. I think I will lie here and read for a bit and then retire early. We can talk in the morning at breakfast, and you can tell me more about your young man and the outcome of tonight's conversation."

Finola kissed his cheek and bid him a good evening before returning downstairs to the foyer. Moments after she arrived, Lady Nance appeared, as well.

"Sir Roscoe is indisposed, my lady. He said we are to go ahead without him."

Lady Nance's face soured. "Well, that is most inconvenient."

Finola shook her head. The woman had not even bothered to ask what was wrong or how Banny felt. All she thought about was herself.

They were silent in the carriage and then entered Lord and Lady Turner's townhouse, joining the receiving line to greet their host and hostess. Once they stepped into the ballroom, Lady Nance went to join her friends, the dowagers who sat together and watched the dancers at each ball. Finola, in turn, moved to a section designated for wallflowers. Surprisingly, she had turned out to be a good dancer, thanks to the dance lessons she had received before the Season began. Occasionally, she was asked by a stray gentleman to dance, but for the most part, Finola sat on the sidelines at every ball, her dance card empty. She would go into supper with a few of her fellow wallflowers, but even after all these weeks, she did not know much about them for there was little conversation between them. It was as if their humiliation were great enough, and they did not bother to get to know one another.

The ball began, and she danced the second set, but the remainder of her programme remained blank. She watched Lord Crofton throughout the evening as he danced several numbers. He was such a graceful dancer. She could not wait for the time when they would dance openly in public as husband and wife.

When a break occurred before the supper dance, Finola left the ballroom, not bothering to excuse herself from those seated around her, doubting they would even miss her presence. She made her way to the library and entered it. A few minutes later, Viscount Crofton joined her, closing the door. She knew if anyone walked through that door and caught them together that she would be compromised. Excitement filled her. Perhaps that was the viscount's plan—for them to be seen together and him to be a gentleman and offer for her. His family could not protest under those circumstances, Lord Crofton doing the right thing.

He placed his hands on her shoulders. "Thank you for meeting me here tonight, Lady Finola. I believe we have things to say to each other."

He bent, his lips touching hers. Her heart quickened in anticipation. Then nothing. Frustration filled her. She should *feel* something when he kissed her—but she didn't. She hoped after they wed that she would enjoy his kiss more.

Suddenly, he wasn't kissing her at all. Instead, he forced her lips apart and thrust his tongue deeply into her mouth, causing her to gag. Finola struggled against him, but he only held her more tightly. She felt as if a foreign army invaded her and tried to take her by force. She pushed hard against his chest with her palms, trying to break the contact between them and the kiss itself.

He finally did so and looked down on her, a mocking light in his eyes.

"My lord?" she asked unsteadily, looking at the face of a stranger. Gone was the kind, solicitous gentleman. In his place was a stranger.

Lord Crofton slipped an arm about her waist, and his palm went to her breast. He squeezed it tightly, causing pain to fill her. She gasped. Then his fingers pinched her nipple so hard that tears sprang to her eyes.

His mouth returned to hers in a bruising kiss. Finola wasn't enjoying this at all and struggled against him.

Once more, he broke the kiss, laughing.

"What do you think, my lady? Do you enjoy my kisses?"

Uncertainty ran through her, but she pasted a smile on and said, "Of course, my lord."

"Do you think to kiss your future betrothed?"

Her heart leaped at his words. "I would, my lord. What are you saying?" she urged, hoping to hear the words which would make her his.

He dropped his hands from her and began laughing loudly. She stood there, unsure how to react.

"You may show yourselves, gentlemen," he called.

Confused, Finola looked about the room as more laughter erupted. One gentleman stepped from behind the curtains. Another rose from behind a settee. Still a third stood from a chair he had sat in on the far side of the room.

And they all laughed loudly.

At her.

A sick feeling washed over her as Lord Crofton captured her wrist as she tried to flee the room.

"You must be wondering what is going on, Lady Finola. I will tell you. You are attending the final meeting of the Epsilon Club. For this Season, anyway."

"Epsilon Club?" she echoed.

Though his features remained angelic, the words from his mouth were those of a devil.

"You see, my lady, Epsilon stands for Enticement. The Enticement Club. We are a group of rakes who choose one unsuspecting lady each Season and see how easy it is to fool her."

"I d-don't understand," she stammered.

Crofton chuckled, his grip tightening painfully on her wrist. "We are rogues who toy with a girl making her come-out each year. We choose one who is pretty—but not too pretty. One lacking in confidence. We like young ladies who do not have many friends. The quiet ones with not many family members and lacking in social connections are simply perfect to dally with."

Tears filled her eyes. She tried to pull away, but he held her in place. Finola cast her eyes to the floor, humiliation filling her.

"We make our pick a few weeks into the Season after we have mingled with the latest crop entering the Marriage Mart."

She recalled having danced with the other three present, once each, and then they had never addressed her again.

"This was my year to play with our choice," Lord Crofton continued. "To make a chubby wallflower feel special. We knew after our reconnaissance that you would have no one to confide in. That as I paid a bit of attention to you, you would believe my lies. That I would become everything to you as you convinced yourself someone like *me* would think to be with someone like *you*."

Tears now poured down Finola's cheeks. Lord Crofton took her chin in hand and forced it upward until she was gazing in his eyes.

"Did I make you feel special, my lady? Did you go home and kiss your pillow, pretending it was me? Were your dreams of me and a life you wished to lead as my viscountess?"

He roared with laughter. "Your dreams of love and marriage are now dashed, I'm afraid. You are not special. You are not wanted. You will never be loved. Yes, I enticed you into kissing me—and I reject you now, Finola Honeyfield." His smile turned evil. "And there isn't a soul you can speak to about it without damaging your reputation. That is, if you have anyone to talk to. We have watched you. You sit among your fellow wallflowers and speak not a word. Lady Nance chastises you at the drop of a hat. And Sir Roscoe may be old—but he is not foolish enough to challenge me to a duel."

Viscount Crofton released her. "You believed the lies. You are yet another innocent fool whom the Epsilon Club has made a mockery of."

She slapped him.

It startled him, but he laughed it off, as did his friends, and he said,

"Be glad I didn't truly ruin you, my lady. I could have, you know. You believed every lie. Every sweet nothing I murmured in your ear. You would have given me anything, including your virginity. I preferred to merely reject instead of ruin you. You are far too plump for any man to ever truly be interested in you—and that includes me and the members of the Epsilon Club."

Laughing, Lord Crofton said, "Come along, gentlemen. We have dallied with and conquered yet another stupid cow."

If Finola had one of her hounds present, she would sic the dog on this man until he was ripped apart. This despicable, cruel viscount. She didn't, though, and held her tongue as Crofton and his fellow rakes left, one deliberately bumping into her and breaking into peals of laughter as they exited the library.

She ran to the door and locked it behind them, not wanting to chance anyone seeing her.

And then Finola wept.

Her sobs echoed through the empty room as she recalled every word, every touch, every glance Viscount Crofton had given her. She had been nothing but a game to them, a game in which men who were called gentlemen were anything but as they toyed with a young woman's heart. He was right—she had no one to share her story with. Even if she did, she doubted anyone would believe her. Overweight, slightly pretty Finola Honeyfield an object of desire? One led along a garden path and then unceremoniously dumped.

Humiliation burned within her, even as her face and neck flamed with embarrassment.

Thank goodness the Season was nearing its end because she did not think she could go to many more events and see Lord Crofton and his cronies pass by, laughing at her. She had been a fool to think she might attract a decent gentleman and marry. Her hopes of having a family now fled. She would return with Banny to the countryside and bury herself in her work with him, training puppies and young dogs.

Dogs were loyal and kind and loving, everything Finola now needed.

She dried her tears and sat in the library a while longer, composing herself, not knowing how much time had passed since she had left the Turners' ballroom. Going to the library's door, she threw the lock and stepped out, carefully looking in both directions. Seeing no one, she moved quickly along the corridor and heard the distant strains of music coming from the ballroom.

As she passed the retirement room, she ducked inside and remained behind one of the curtains for a long time. Finally, Finola emerged and lingered just outside the ballroom until the last dance came to a conclusion. Then she made her way to Lady Nance.

"There you are," the dowager countess said. "I did not see you at supper. Don't tell me you were off somewhere, sneaking food."

"No, my lady," she replied. "I would not do such a thing."

They went to the carriage. Inside, Lady Nance said, "Another *two* engagements were announced tonight. You have yet to have a single suitor come calling on you, Lady Finola."

"I doubt any will," she said truthfully. "I am not what the gentlemen of London are looking for. I think it is time Sir Roscoe and I returned to Belldale."

"I see." The dowager countess studied her a moment. "Did something happen to you tonight?"

Her cheeks heated, but the carriage was dim and Lady Nance's eyesight not the best.

"No, my lady. I simply have tired of the social scene in London. Sir Roscoe told me I should make my come-out and see if I enjoyed Polite Society. I have found it not to my taste at all. I prefer a quiet life in the country. If you do not mind, I think we will return home tomorrow. Sir Roscoe has mentioned how much he misses the country air."

"Do as you see fit. Polite Society is not for everyone. Perhaps you will make a match in the country. Some squire, possibly."

The carriage came to a halt, and a footman handed them down. As they entered the house, Lady Nance's butler rushed toward them.

"My lady, I am afraid I have bad news to share with you. Sir Roscoe has passed."

"Passed?" the dowager countess said, as if an inconvenience had occurred.

"Yes, my lady. When his valet readied him for bed, Sir Roscoe grew agitated and then clutched his heart. I sent for the doctor immediately, but by the time he arrived, Sir Roscoe was gone." The butler finally glanced at Finola. "I am sorry, my lady."

Finola grew dizzy and then faint. Darkness rushed up and overtook her. Even as she lost consciousness, all she could think of was she was alone.

Forever alone.

CHAPTER ONE

Spain—1 January 1813

L IEUTENANT-GENERAL CYRUS CRESSLEY slipped into the coat which Briggs, his batman, held out to him.

"Bertie should be here with your breakfast any moment now, Sir," his batman told him.

Cy had never understood why some men brought their families to war. Yes, a handful of officers brought their wives, but for the most part, it was foot soldiers whose families accompanied them to the Peninsula. Briggs had brought along his wife and their eight-year-old son. These civilians lived in camps abutting those of the military and followed them whenever they went on the march.

Cy didn't have to worry about a family. As a second son of the Duke of Margate, he had been destined from birth to go into military service, while his older brother would one day take the ducal title. Cy and Charles had never been close siblings. Charles was over ten years older than Cy and from what he had learned through the gossip of servants, their mother had a series of miscarriages and stillborn children in the decade between them. He supposed all those failed attempts at providing a spare to the heir had weakened his mother physically. The fact he had been brought to term and delivered healthy was what their cook had called a miracle.

Unfortunately, the Duchess of Margate had died shortly after birthing her second son.

His father was a cold man, with little interaction with either of his sons. Charles had been away at school when Cy was born, and Cy had very few memories of his brother because of that time spent apart. By the time he was ready to leave Melrose for school, Charles was starting university the same year. They had rarely been at Melrose at the same time over the years.

Charles preferred town and remained in London after graduation, doing whatever he did with his friends. Cy had completed public school and left for university at Cambridge, never seeing Charles once during those years and taking no trips home to East Sussex. A commission was purchased for Cy upon his graduation, and he had entered His Majesty's army, eager to take on his military duties as an officer. Being a hard worker and very disciplined man, Cy quickly rose through the ranks. He felt serving his king was a privilege.

He had gained the respect of his fellow officers by being goal-oriented and focused. In strategy meetings, others complimented him on being able to get to the heart of a matter, even as he saw the big picture of things around him. He had become used to soldiers following him without question. He would be the first to admit he was a bit stubborn and domineering, but his efforts and experience helped him ascend the ranks with ease.

His reputation was spotless, and his men adored him since they knew he was a leader both on and off the battlefield. It was the rare officer of Cy's rank who joined in the action, much less led soldiers against the enemy—yet Lieutenant-General Cyrus Cressley did this on a regular basis.

Fortunately, progress was finally being made in this Peninsular War. Joseph Bonaparte was on the run, especially after last year's Battle of Salamanca. As a high-ranking officer, Cy was able to participate in the strategy session with Wellington and knew this spring would bring a turn of the tide in the favor of Britain and her allies.

In the meantime, drills were essential to keep the men's skills at a high level, even on this first day of a new year.

"Good morning, Lieutenant-General," Bertie Briggs said, as he entered the tent with a steaming bowl of stew in one hand and a half-loaf of bread in the other.

The boy set the meal on Cy's makeshift desk.

"That's a good lad, Bertie," he told the boy. "Why don't you go back and retrieve something to eat for your father and yourself?"

"I've already eaten, sir," Briggs told him. "Bertie, you go back to your mum now. I'll send for you if I need you."

"Goodbye, Father. Goodbye, Lieutenant-General Cressley."

Bertie left the tent, and Cy picked up the bowl of stew, stirring it and seeing the steam rise from it.

"More drills today?" the batman asked.

Cy chuckled as he took a bite. "Drills are the backbone of His Majesty's army, Briggs. You know that. I hate the inactivity as much as the next man, but that is the nature of war. You know war is fought in months with favorable weather, while the rest of the time we hunker down and plot against our enemies."

"After Ciudad Rodrigo, though, I see an eventual victory for us," Briggs said.

"I do, as well," he told the batman. "Take a few minutes for yourself. I will see you on the range."

Cy finished his bowl of stew and then used the bread to mop up the juice left. He returned the wooden bowl to those men who pulled cooking duty as he made his way to the fields where drills were commencing. The soldiers constantly practiced marching, shooting, and bayoneting. He borrowed a bayonet from a private and sparred with a few soldiers, earning cheers from those around him. Cy had found a brotherhood in the army that he had never experienced in civilian life and was grateful he knew his place in the world and could put his leadership skills to good use for the crown.

He moved to where troops were practicing on the range with their rifles, slowly moving down the line as he observed. He stopped twice and demonstrated to a soldier how to better hold his weapon and what to focus on with his target.

Handing the rifle back to the private he borrowed it from, Cy then swept his bicorne from his head, using his forearm to wipe the sweat which had gathered along his brow. As he dragged his forearm across his forehead and his bicorne blocked his vision, he was suddenly knocked back, falling to the ground. Sitting there, stunned, he felt a throbbing just above his right eyebrow and realized he must have been shot. Hit by a stray practice round. He blinked as a trickle of blood dripped into his eye.

"Get back!" he heard Briggs shout.

The batman dropped to his knees next to Cy, the sound of material being ripped. "You'll be fine, sir," Briggs assured him as he wrapped cloth around Cy's head.

He recognized the signs that he was going into shock but was still aware of all happening about him. Briggs instructed men to lift Cy from the ground.

"Quickly, boys," Briggs encouraged. "But gently."

He was carried from the practice field, knowing they headed for the surgeon's tent. He hoped at least one of them would be on duty. Usually, during a battle, the tents were filled with wounded officers, crying out in anguish. Nothing came from his lips, however. It was as if he were frozen and unable to move or speak.

He sensed being placed on a table and heard Briggs shout Dr. Sheffley's name. That was good news. Sheffley was one of the younger surgeons, more skilled than most, willing to take risks in order to save a man's life.

But could Cy survive a shot to his head?

He listened as the doctor began unwinding the cloth around Cy's head. Briggs explained the accident and how Cy's bicorne had been in front of his face when the bullet pierced it.

"That may have been what saved our lieutenant-general," the physical commented. "Slowing down the velocity. A chance of surviving a bullet to the head is less than five percent. None if the bullet enters from the side. But front on, being partially obstructed, such as this? We have a chance, Briggs, of saving Cressley's life. I will operate immediately. Stay here."

Cy felt himself being brought to a sitting position and a bottle placed to his lips. He was urged to drink from it and continued doing so, the taste of sweet Madeira being poured down him to numb the pain.

"It is Dr. Sheffley, Cressley," he heard in his ear. "Drink as much of the wine as you can. The bullet is just above your right brow. Protruding, in fact. I will remove it now. Acting quickly is your best chance for survival."

He tried to respond to the surgeon, but only a mumble emerged. He supposed he finished the Madeira because the bottle was removed from his lips, and he was lowered onto his back again. Someone stuck a stick into his mouth, and he understood it was for him to bite down upon when the pain flared.

Suddenly, his limbs were stretched out and then held down by others, no time being wasted to even tie him down. The surgeon's knife cut into Cy's forehead, and he locked his teeth around the stick, grunting in agony. A surge of blood seemed to pour from him. His eyes were closed, but he could feel Sheffley dig around and then remove the ball as pain poured through him.

"This is very good," the surgeon said optimistically. "Very good, indeed."

Cy sensed Sheffley leaning over him, but he was too tired and hurting too badly to open his eyes.

"Good news, Cressley. I was able to remove the bullet—and it was intact. No fragments at all. I doubt there are any skull fragments either. I saw no damaged bone. Those would have been more dangerous than bullet fragments. I will clean and wrap the wound. You are to rest now. You will make it, man. You will live."

He drifted off, floating above the pain.

⫸⫷

CY AWOKE AND felt the dull ache above his right eye. Reaching up a hand, he touched the bandages which wrapped around his head and extended over his eyes, going to the bridge of his nose and resting there.

"Ah, you are finally awake."

He recognized Dr. Sheffley's voice and relaxed.

"Will I live?" he asked weakly.

"Briggs and your men have been asking me that same question for the last two days, Lieutenant-General. I have complete confidence that you will make a full recovery. I have already examined and cleaned the wound twice. I will do so again now. As I do, I am going to ask you a few questions. Test your memory, so to speak."

"All right," he said, sitting up with the surgeon's help.

"It's me, sir," Briggs said from nearby. "Everyone is asking about you. Don't know where the stray bullet came from. Probably never will. If I ever find out who did shoot you, I will shoot him myself," the batman promised.

Cy laughed weakly as Dr. Sheffley continued to unwind the bandages. Finally, he felt they were completely removed and opened his eyes. No, he was mistaken. There still must be bandages on them because it was dark.

Dr. Sheffley said, "All right. Let's see if we can—"

"Why haven't you removed all the bandages?" he demanded.

A slight hesitation occurred, and then the surgeon said, "I have,

Cressley. Tell me what you see."

Cy's heart sank as he uttered one word. "Nothing."

"Give me a moment," Sheffley said.

He heard whispering going on. He sensed someone moving away and figured it to be Briggs. Then he knew Briggs had returned, holding a lantern. Cy smelled the oil and then felt the heat from the lantern, knowing it was being held directly in front of his face.

"I do not see the lantern," he said dully. "I don't see anything at all."

"Don't worry just yet," Sheffley told him. "What could be occurring is temporary blindness. The force from the blow you received from the bullet could be pressing against your optic nerve. The bullet entered directly above your right brow. I am not worried about it yet."

Cy couldn't help but focus on the *yet*.

"I will test a few things," the physician said.

Dr. Sheffley proceeded to ask him a serious of questions, which the surgeon said was testing Cy's recall. He had no gaps, which Sheffley said was very good news.

The doctor then asked Cy to move various limbs. He lifted arms. Wiggled fingers on command. Twisted from side to side. Turned his head from left to right and then looked up and down as instructed.

"Your motor skills are intact," the doctor said. "Once again, excellent news. Let me ask you a few different questions now to test your reasoning. Various parts of the brain control different aspects of thinking. I want to see if you can figure out the answers to what I ask."

For the next few minutes, Sheffley peppered Cy with questions, all of which he answered without hesitation. Hope built within him.

"I see no problems in your thinking, Lieutenant-General. What I believe has occurred is that the pressure on this optic nerve has caused some swelling in your brain. It will require rest to restore it to normal."

"You are telling me this blindness will be short-lived?" Cy asked.

"I am saying it is likely to be temporary, Cressley, but doctors are not God. We can only give you our best professional opinion, based upon our experiences. I am now going to rebandage your wound and will also cover your eyes. You will need to stay prone as much as possible for the next several days and hope that the bruising and swelling within your brain will subside."

Cy sat numbly as Sheffley redressed his head wound, talking of how neat the stitches were and that the scar above Cy's right eyebrow would be minimal. Sheffley even teased him that the ladies would find the scar attractive and that he would have a good story to tell when he attended parties, entertaining the civilians present.

But Cy was a man of war—and this war with Bonaparte would not be ending anytime soon. Even if Wellington managed to defeat the Little Corporal's armies in Spain, most likely British troops would then move into France and other parts of Europe to support their allies there against Bonaparte.

He did as Dr. Sheffley required and remained flat on his back for a week, only rising occasionally to relieve himself. Briggs wanted to stay by his side constantly, but he sent the batman away, not wishing to talk to anyone. Instead, young Bertie Briggs came to keep him company. He sensed the boy's presence, and every now and then, Bertie would pat Cy on the shoulder and tell him all would be fine.

When the week ended, Dr. Sheffley had Cy sit up and removed the bandages from his forehead and eyes. He opened his eyes and looked about the tent. He could see somewhat with his left eye, though things were a bit blurry. From his right eye, however, only dark shadows appeared, shapeless blots.

"How is your vision?" the surgeon asked, concern evident in his voice.

Cy told him what he was seeing, and Sheffley said, "It may still take time."

He knew the British army didn't have time to waste on officers who could not lead. Even if his sight returned, he had experienced blinding headaches this past week, ones which immobilized him. His gut—and heart—told Cy he would never be the man he had been, and it would be best to resign his commission and retire from the army.

"Could I go and see Major-General Parker?" he asked, a lump in his throat.

Quietly, Dr. Sheffley said, "I am sorry, Cressley. I do think it would be wise if you did."

Briggs spoke up. "Let's get you to your tent, sir. We'll get you a shave and that unruly hair trimmed and then we'll go see the major-general."

Cy stood shakily, Briggs clasping one elbow and Bertie the other. They led him to his tent. He kept his eyes downcast the entire way there, not wanting to see the pity in the eyes of the men he passed. He laughed to himself, thinking he wouldn't have been able to see it even if he had baldly looked each man they passed directly in the face.

He stood as Briggs and Bertie undressed and then washed him. Bertie fetched hot water and his batman shaved Cy and then snipped away at his hair. The pair redressed Cy in a fresh uniform.

"You look fit as a fiddle, sir," the batman praised.

Yet Cy heard the false note in Briggs' voice. He had become attuned to tone in a person's voice this last week, his hearing picking up things it never had before and his brain catching the moods of others. Sharp hearing, though, would not replace the excellent eyesight he no longer possessed. Already, he had missed considerable time away from his men while they continued their training and drilling, as well as meetings with Wellington and his fellow officers. Soon, the army would be on the move again, ready to pour its heart and soul into battle once more.

With a heavy heart, Cy allowed Briggs and Bertie to lead him to his commanding officer's tent. He met briefly with Parker, giving the major-general the bad news. Parker did not try to talk him out of resigning and even said he would help Cyrus in selling off the commission. He assured Cy that a small pension would also be awarded to him since he was no longer physically able to serve.

Once again, father and son led Cy to his tent, his left eye seeing a blur and his right next to nothing. No one spoke a word to him. In the silence as he passed, he sensed others' sympathy. Pity. Restlessness. Shame poured through him, knowing he was no longer the man of action he had been and that he had let down his men. He would never pick up a sword again, nor would he lead others into battle.

The war would go on—without Lieutenant-General Cyrus Cress-ley.

CHAPTER TWO

Melrose—Late January 1813

C Y RODE NEXT to a peddler whose cart made its way toward Adderly. Bertie Briggs slept in the back. His batman's son had accompanied Cy from Spain to England, and he had told Briggs he would find a place for the boy at Melrose.

Melrose . . .

It was hard to think of going home after such a long time. Most people had fond memories associated with their homes and families.

Cy had none.

His father had been a man who had no interest in children, especially one who was not his heir apparent. Cy could probably count on one hand the conversations he'd had with the Duke of Margate. He did not take it personally, though, because he had witnessed how Charles, too, had also been ignored by their father. Cy wondered if Charles remained in town, as had been his habit, or if his brother would be at Melrose. He dreaded the meeting he would soon have with his father. Moreover, he was worried about his future.

He wasn't interested in charity and merely wanted to be useful in some capacity. A good portion of his vision in his left eye had returned, but things far away were still blurry. It was only when he was up close to something that he could truly see it. If things remained the way they were, he might try to go into London and meet with the eye surgeon Dr. Sheffley had recommended, hoping at least he might be able to get a pair of spectacles which might allow him to see things clearly at a distance. The left eye was also sensitive to light, which is why he now wore his hat low on his brow.

The right eye was covered with an eye patch. Cy had seen no progress in the three weeks since the accident that had left him almost completely blind in his right eye. The terrible headaches still crept up on him with little warning, incapacitating him. That was why Briggs had insisted that his young son accompany Cy back to England. His batman worried that one of the headaches would affect Cy so greatly that someone might do him harm or take advantage of him. Bertie was to stand by Cy's side and ward off all inquiries, protecting Cy as Bertie's father would have done.

He constantly wore the patch over his right eye, only removing it to sleep. Each morning when he awoke, he opened his eyes with a mixture of hope and dread, believing his sight had not returned, and yet still clinging to hope each morning that a miracle had occurred overnight. Only disappointment filled him and at this point, he doubted he would ever have vision restored to the eye again, despite Dr. Sheffley still being hopeful of that, telling Cy to continue to give things time to heal.

He looked down at the ill-fitting clothes he now wore. They were nothing when compared to the tailored officer's uniform he had proudly worn the past eight years. He did not feel it right, though, to continue to wear the scarlet coat and white trousers, since he had resigned his commission. He was grateful that Major-General Parker would handle the sale of his commission and direct the proceeds to Cy at Melrose, along with seeing that the small pension be awarded due to his injury. Parker did not have Dr. Sheffley's optimism and had told Cy that His Majesty's army couldn't have blind officers leading its men.

The words had cut him to the quick, but he would rather someone be honest and sting him with words than give him false hope.

He had kept his two white shirts, though, and purchased a coat and pair of breeches from a local widow before making his way to the coast with Bertie and boarding a ship bound for Brighton. The dead man had been shorter than Cy, but he tucked the trousers into his Hessians. No one would know they struck him two inches above his ankles. The ill-fit of the coat, however, could not be hidden. Cy was a large man and the coat's fabric strained against his broad shoulders and back, as well as being too short for his arms. Still, they had been the only things available in the short time he had before he left Spain for England.

He knew at first glance he made a poor impression on everyone he came across. It couldn't be helped. There was a tailor at nearby Adderly, though, the local village closest to Melrose. He would see if the man was still there and have a few things made up. For now, he focused on what he would say to his father. The Duke of Margate obviously had a steward who ran Melrose, but the dukedom also came with more estates than this ducal country seat. Perhaps Cy could be sent to one of those to manage it. If not, he would be grateful if his father allowed him the use of a cottage on the grounds of the estate. Cy was not averse to physical labor and would join the other tenant farmers if need be.

Glancing over his shoulder, he saw Bertie still asleep in the back of the wagon. He would make certain that the boy found a position at Melrose, regardless of where he wound up. Bertie could work his way up and have a career in service. Cy would make certain Bertie was cared for since the lad had done the same for him. Though the boy had admitted he missed his parents, he told Cy that he was grateful to be going home because he wanted to get as far away from the war as possible.

They reached the outskirts of Adderly, and the peddler brought the wagon to a stop.

"This is where you wished to be let off," the man said.

The peddler was traveling east after this, and Cy would go through the village and then head north toward Melrose. It would be another three miles to Melrose, but he told the peddler, "Thank you for taking us this far."

"Happy to help out, Lieutenant-General."

Cy had told the man he had recently traveled from Spain. The peddler had drawn out from him that Cy had left the army due to his recent injury, which made him unfit for duty. He knew some men in retirement continued to use their former rank as a courtesy title. His rank was a mouthful, though. Besides, those in this area would know him as Lord Cyrus, son of the Duke of Margate.

He offered the man one of his few remaining coins but was waved away. Climbing from the wagon, Cy leaned over and gently shook Bertie.

The boy opened his eyes. "Are we there?"

"We are as close as our friend can bring us, Bertie. Come. We have a bit of a ways to go."

He grabbed the boy under his arms and swung him to the ground. They both waved as the wagon proceeded to roll away.

"Where are we?" Bertie asked.

"This is Adderly, the closest village to Melrose, the name of the estate where I grew up."

"Are we going through it?"

"Actually, we need to because we head north. That means you will see all of Adderly, though there is not much to it. Melrose lies to the north three miles." He rubbed the boy's hair affectionately. "It will feel good again to stretch our legs after riding in the cart for so long."

As they walked through the village and down its only thoroughfare, Cy could see not much had changed in the years he had been absent. They passed the blacksmith's shop and heard the clang of his hammer against the anvil. They moved along and saw the bakery, where Mrs. Carroll would take pity on Cy as he stared into the window at her sweets. Occasionally, she would motion him inside and give him a treat, clucking her tongue as she did so. They passed by Mr. Simon's store, which carried a variety of items. They then passed Mr. Timmon's tailor shop, where Cy hoped he could have a small wardrobe made up.

There was no time for that now, though. It was important to get to Melrose and be settled in some fashion.

They walked at a brisk pace, Cy whistling as they went along the way. Bertie did not know how to whistle, and so he gave the boy a brief lesson.

"Wet your lips and pucker them like so." Cy demonstrated and nodded in approval at the boy.

"Now, gently blow air through your lips. Very softly. Relax your tongue and blow harder."

Bertie tried and grinned. "I heard something."

"Yes, you make different tones when you blow. You can adjust your lips. Your tongue. Your jaw. Doing so creates different tones."

By the time they reached the turnoff in the road and headed up the lane to Melrose, Bertie had a good command of whistling. He was glad the boy caught on quickly and knew wherever Bertie landed, he would do his best to learn the new position.

They saw not a soul as they walked up the tree-lined lane toward the main house. With it being the end of January, tenants would not be out in the fields. The colder months were times to do repairs, such as mending fences, re-thatching cottage roofs, and repairing tools. Beginning next month, tenants would begin plowing fields.

When Melrose came into sight, Bertie gave a low whistle, using his new skill to perfection. "This is where you live?"

"I did so many years ago as a boy. I left at age seven and went away to school, only returning for brief amounts of time between terms. My brother, too, was away at a different school and then university. I rarely saw him. My father preferred residing in town and only came to Melrose upon occasion."

Bertie's eyes widened. "You mean you lived in this house all by yourself?" he asked, clearly astonished.

"Oh, I was never alone. It takes an enormous staff to run a house such as this, Bertie. Melrose employs a butler and housekeeper, along with the staff under them, from footmen to parlor maids. Then there's Cook in the kitchens and her scullery maids. They prepare all the meals. In the stables, there is a head groom and then other grooms who care for the horses."

Bertie's eyes lit up. "I like horses. Sometimes, I would go to the pen where the officers' horses were, and one of the soldiers would let me brush the horses."

"Would you be interested in working in the Melrose stables?"

The boy frowned. "No, sir. My place is at your side."

"I know your father told you to get me here, Bertie, and I appreciate your help. Both on the ship and in England. I did promise him, however, that I would help find you a position at Melrose. If it is the stables you wish to work in, I will arrange for that to happen."

The boy's mouth set stubbornly, and he shook his head. "No. I am to stay with you."

"Then perhaps we should compromise on the issue."

Bertie frowned. "What is . . . compromise?"

"It is where one person wants one thing, and the other wants something else. They try to meet in the middle so both get a little of what they want. Shall we say you stay with me a while, then when my vision improves and I don't need to depend upon you so much, you could then work in the stables?"

Bertie thought it over and nodded. "All right, Lieutenant-General. I think I can . . . compromise," he said, saying the new world slowly.

"I am no longer a lieutenant-general, Bertie. I have resigned my commission. You do not need to refer to me in that manner anymore."

"Then what should I call you, sir?"

"Those around here will refer to me as Lord Cyrus or my lord. You should do the same."

"So, you're a lord?"

"I am the son of a duke. Using lord in front of my name is a courtesy. I am the second-born son and titles belong to my older brother. He is now designated an earl and when our father passes, Charles will become the new Duke of Margate."

"Why does he get to be the duke and you don't? You were in charge of many men in the war, my lord. I bet you would be a great duke."

Smiling, Cy said, "That is not how the laws of England operate. They favor the firstborn son. He is the one who inherits his father's title, as well as any properties and wealth."

"That's not fair," Bertie declared, with all the wisdom an eight-year-old possessed.

"Fair or not, that is the way things simply are."

By now, they had reached the front drive and Cy swallowed, nerves suddenly overwhelming him. Battle seemed tame when compared to facing his father.

As they approached the door, he said, "Let me do all the talking. The ton—that is, people who are members of Polite Society—do not wish to hear from little boys, especially if they are servants."

Bertie smiled brightly. "And I am your servant, my lord, because I help you."

He smiled fondly at the boy. "You do, indeed."

Summoning his courage, Cy rapped his knuckles against the door and waited for the knock to be answered. When it was, it was a footman dressed in full livery who opened it. His eyes glanced up and down, taking in Cy's ill-fitting clothes and then the boy beside him.

"May I help you?" the footman asked haughtily.

Hating that he had been judged and found lacking, Cy gazed into the man's eyes and in an equally haughty tone replied, "I am Lord Cyrus Cressley, returning home from the Peninsular War. I wish to see the Duke of Margate at once."

Astonishment filled the servant's face, and he stepped back, waving them into the massive foyer. Closing the door, the footman asked them to wait.

Cy looked at the lavish furnishings of the foyer, with its large grandfather clock as its focal point. It began chiming four o'clock, and Bertie raced over to it, awe on his young face.

When the clock silenced, Bertie turned and faced him. "I've never seen anything so wonderful!"

As the boy rejoined him, he said, "It is called a grandfather clock. It struck four times, which means it is now four o'clock in the afternoon. Servants wind this clock and others throughout the household every day so that time is not lost."

An elegantly dressed servant entered the foyer, trailed by the footman who had admitted them. Cy assumed this was the current Melrose butler, knowing the one who had served many years had most likely retired by now.

The servant approached him, and Cy said, "As you have been informed, I am Lord Cyrus Cressley. I have come home from the fighting in Spain. I wish to speak with the duke."

"You are not in uniform, my lord."

"No, I am not. I gave up wearing my uniform at the same time I forfeited my commission." He pointed to his eye patch. "As you can see, I suffered an injury which made me unsuitable to remain in a leadership position for His Majesty."

The butler said, "I am Arnold, Lord Cyrus. I have been at Melrose the past five years. My wife, Mrs. Arnold, serves as housekeeper here." Arnold glanced to Bertie. "And whom might this be?"

"I am Bertie Briggs," the boy said cheerfully, thinking the butler addressed him, and then looked to Cy. "It is all right if I share my name, my lord?"

"It is perfectly fine to do so, Bertie." He turned from the boy to the butler. "Bertie is the son of my batman and assisted me in returning to England. His father served me loyally for several years, and I promised to look after Bertie. He will be helping me adjust to civilian life until I am better. Then I will ask that he be placed in the Melrose stables."

"I see," the butler said. "You can take that up with His Grace and then Mitchell, who is our head groom."

Arnold turned to the footman. "Take the boy to the kitchens, and get him something to eat. Then a bath. Tell Mrs. Arnold to find him some suitable clothes, as well."

"Yes, Mr. Arnold," the footman said. "Come with me, Bertie. We will get you new things to wear and scrub the filth from you. And Cook will no doubt wish to fatten you up."

The boy glanced to Cy for approval, and he nodded. "Go on, Bertie. You could most certainly use a bath."

He watched Bertie leave with the footman and then looked to Arnold, who asked, "Would you like the chance to have a bath yourself, my lord?"

"Perhaps later, Arnold. I am wearing the only clothes I own, having purchased them as I left Spain. I am hoping to get to the village and if Mr. Timmon is still there, have him make up a few things for me."

"Mr. Timmon is still the tailor for the area," the butler informed him. "Let me take you to His Grace then. He is in the drawing room, taking tea."

They ascended the stairs, and Arnold told a passing maid to bring a second teacup and plate to the drawing room.

Tea sounded wonderful to Cy. He had missed a good English afternoon tea, with a strong brew and small sandwiches and sweets. His mouth watered at the idea of the possibility of lemon cakes being present. They were his absolute favorite, and he had not had any since his university days.

"Wait here, my lord," Arnold said, entering the drawing room and leaving Cy in the corridor.

He braced himself for the upcoming conversation with his father, the first time they would speak together as adults. The last time Cy had seen the duke was a year before he left for university. No correspondence had been exchanged between the pair during the ensuing years. Sometimes, Cy wondered if Margate even remembered that he had a second son.

Arnold appeared. "You may go in, Lord Cyrus, but I must warn you. His Grace's gout has just begun to act up. If he makes it through tea, it will be a miracle."

He had not known his father suffered from gout, a disease of wealthy men who ate rich foods and rarely exercised. Of course, Margate was close to eighty now. He had not wed until he was almost forty, quickly producing Charles and then ten years later, Cy. Idly, Cy wondered if Charles had wed or if he would repeat their father's pattern of delaying marriage and enjoying his bachelorhood for as long as possible.

Stepping inside the room, he sensed the fire burning in the grate at the opposite side of the large room and carefully made his way across its length, his gait slow because he was in an unfamiliar place after so long a time and his one eye still showing blurry shapes. His father was slumped in a chair next to the fire.

"So, what do you want?" a deep voice demanded.

Cy sucked in a quick breath as he squinted at the shape, making out the duke's familiar features, ones in which Cy did not share, having been told he took after his mother's side of the family. It was not his father, though, who sat in the chair.

Apparently, Charles was now the Duke of Margate—and had not bothered to notify Cy of their father's death.

CHAPTER THREE

C Y CAME TO stand before his brother.

Charles Cressley was grossly overweight. Cy could see so, even with his limited vision. Their father had been what was kindly termed a portly man, not very tall and one who had short, stout legs and a large, protruding belly. Charles had inherited everything from Margate's looks to his build, but had gone to the extreme. No wonder he was having trouble with gout.

"I asked what you are doing here."

Since he had not been invited to sit, Cy remained on his feet, hands clasped behind him, his posture that of the former army officer he had been.

"I have come home to Melrose, Your Grace," he said, addressing his brother as a duke for the first time. "I was hoping to make myself useful to you here or possibly one of your other properties. Of course, I was expecting to see Father."

Charles snorted. "He died years ago. Six? Seven? I cannot even recall now because his death meant nothing to me. You well know, as much as I, that Margate was no father to either of us. I say good riddance that he is gone and burning in the fires of Hell."

He did not berate his brother for not informing him of their father's death. Charles was correct in pointing out that Margate had been no parent to them. With the help of servants and tutors, the two

Cressley boys had raised themselves.

"I don't see what you think you can do around here. From the looks of it, you've lost an eye." No sympathy was present in the duke's tone. Then again, the brothers had never been close.

"I still have my eye. I was shot in the head. The surgeon who removed the bullet found it intact and said most likely there was pressure on what is called the optic nerve. For the moment, I cannot see from my right eye, but Dr. Sheffley has every hope that my vision will return soon."

Cy did not say that his left eye could only see blurred images if they were in the distance, and that it was incredibly sensitive to light. He already saw this interview would go poorly and did not wish to arm his brother with information that would only be used against him.

A maid arrived with an extra teacup, saucer, and plate, and curtseyed to the duke before offering Cy the items. He took them, and she left the drawing room.

"You might as well sit and have a cup of tea," Charles said grumpily. "Pour me some tea, as well. I like four lumps of sugar and plenty of milk in my cup."

He sat and poured out for them both, doctoring Charles' tea to his specifications and handing the saucer over.

"Make me a plate," his brother ordered. "Two of everything."

Cy looked at the veritable feast on the tray before them and assembled a plate which held a variety of items, once again passing this to his brother. He noticed both times that Charles had trouble gripping what he was given.

He then helped himself to what was before them and bit into a peach tart. It was the best-tasting thing he had eaten in a decade. He might miss the camaraderie in the army, but he would never miss the food.

"This gout will be the death of me," his brother complained bitterly. "You see, I have to prop up my leg. Gout is a sneaky thing, creeping up on you when you least expect it."

He tried to muster sympathy for his brother's condition and asked, "When did it begin?"

"I have suffered from it a good decade now. It started in my right toe. The largest one. Ached so much that I could not even walk. Could not sleep. Even the bedclothes touching it brought me the greatest agony. That first attack came from nowhere and kept me off my feet a good two days."

The duke sighed. "It has only gotten worse over the years. The suddenness of the attacks is frightening. The pain, unimaginable. I have swelling in my joints. They turn red and tender. The doctors tell me that my condition will never get better, only that the excruciating pain and frequency of the attacks will continue to make my life miserable."

Charles then rambled a good ten minutes about his gout while Cy continued to eat the delicacies on his plate. Apparently, the gout had moved to both of his brother's feet and subsequent joints. He heard of Charles' aches and pains in his fingers, wrists, elbows, knees, and ankles. His brother elaborated on how each attack grew in magnitude, often putting him to bed for weeks at a time these days.

"The toe is throbbing now. From experience, I know the pain will spread. I have already warned the servants they are to be quiet. Any noise disturbs me. This most likely will be my last tea in the drawing room for a good week or more."

"My greatest sympathies to you, Your Grace. Perhaps now that I am home, I could be of some use to you when you are incapacitated."

"You think *you* could be a duke?" Charles spewed hatefully, his rage sudden and frightening.

Quickly, he said, "Of course not, Your Grace. I was merely suggesting that while you were dealing with these infirmities that I might be able to help about the estate. No one could take your place, however, Your Grace," he added, trying to placate his brother, who seemed to have a quick temper. He wondered what else he didn't know about this man, one who now held Cy's fate in the balance.

Charles waved a hand in the air. "I have a steward. That is who manages Melrose. I have also hired competent servants who can keep my household running."

"Then might I go about on the estate, serving as your eyes and ears?" Cy inquired. "I could work with the tenants. I know this is the time of year when—"

"You know nothing about running a country estate, Cressley," his brother chided. "Why, you have been off playing soldier for what—a decade?"

Anger boiled within Cy. Through gritted teeth, he informed his brother, "I have not been *playing* at anything, Your Grace. I have been fighting our enemies on the battlefield for crown and country, so that titled noblemen such as you might be able to continue the lives you do, enjoying your holdings and wealth."

Cy sensed the tension in the air as his brother said, "Go ahead. Rub it in my face. You were always the tall, strong, handsome Cressley. The one who took after Mama and her side of the family. Well, *you* killed her."

He had always sensed some hidden animosity between them and never knew the root of it. Now, Cy understood that Charles blamed him for their mother's death.

"I am sorry that my birth caused Mama to pass. Surely, you understand, though, that she had been with child many times between your birth and mine. That she had birthed other children, stillborn babies, further weakening her."

"You still killed her," Charles said, his tone low and threatening.

"There is nothing I can do about that now, but I would like to be able to serve you and the Cressley family in any capacity I can. I know as the Duke of Margate that you have numerous holdings. Perhaps there is an estate that could use an extra bit of attention, Your Grace. I would be happy to journey there and help out."

In anger, Charles slammed his teacup into the fire, shattering the china. "I have no need of your help in anything, Cressley. I barely know who you are."

"You will not allow me to help in any way?"

"Your role in this family and society was to serve in the military. Obviously, you are half a man now and have been forced to resign your commission because you can no longer lead men into battle. If you think you will move into this house and live an easy life at my expense, think again. I owe you nothing. Absolutely nothing."

Cy rose, once again reining in his anger so he did not say something in haste which he would regret.

"I came home because Melrose *is* my home. As much as it is yours. You might be the firstborn son and hold the title, but you do have a responsibility to me, a family member, like it or not."

"I cannot look upon you," his brother admitted. "You remind me too much of Mama. While she was alive, it did not matter that Father barely noticed who I was. Once she was gone, I never felt loved."

"And I did?" Cy asked. "I was not as lucky as you to have known Mama. We both know Father ignored the both of us. I would think that would give us a bond to share." Then Cy turned the conversation. "Have you become a father, Your Grace? Have you done a better job of raising your heir than our father did?"

The duke winced, and Cy didn't know if it was from guilt or pain.

"I have yet to wed," Charles admitted. "I have thought to do so, but each time the Season approaches and I am in more and more pain, it seems beyond me."

"Well, you better pull yourself from your sickbed, Margate, and get yourself to the next Season. Find yourself a bride—else you are looking at the future Duke of Margate. I am sorry to have bothered you."

As Cy turned to leave, his brother called, "Wait."

Slowly, he turned and faced Charles again, not able to distinguish his features.

"I know what my duty is—and I *will* wed. I apologize, Cressley. The fact is, I simply cannot abide looking at you. It causes me too much pain to do so. However, I know that you are family to me, and I owe you something after your service to England. I do not want you in this house, but I will grant you the hunting lodge at the far edge of Melrose. It has not been used in a good ten or fifteen years. You can live there. It is the best I can do at this time."

At least he would not be homeless.

"Thank you, Your Grace. I will go there. If you have need of me in any way—if I can be of any service to you, personally or to Melrose in general—I hope you will send word to me. I am proud to be a Cressley and happy to serve the Duke of Margate."

A groan escaped Charles' lips. "Bloody hell. It's starting. Summon Arnold if you would. He can see to me. And speak with Mrs. Arnold before you leave today. She can help supply any needs you have at the hunting lodge."

Even with his poor vision, Cy could see his brother's face contort in pain.

"I don't mean to be cruel to you. Having you move out of my sight is all I ask."

"I understand, Your Grace."

Cy went and rang for Arnold. He then crossed the room slowly, looking to avoid bumping into any furniture, and left the drawing room to wait outside for the butler.

When Arnold arrived, Cy said, "His Grace's gout is acting up terribly. He wishes for you to tend to him, Arnold. I am to live in the hunting lodge on the far side of Melrose. His Grace said that Mrs. Arnold would be able to arrange for whatever I might need there."

The butler nodded. "If you will go downstairs, Lord Cyrus, a footman can direct you to my wife. The hunting lodge has not been used in a good number of years. It will need a thorough cleaning, as well as the larder stocked. Mrs. Arnold will be able to help with everything."

"Thank you," Cy said sincerely.

He headed down the corridor, his hands grazing against the wall to steady himself. He reached the stairs, returning to the foyer. A footman greeted him, and Cy asked that he be taken to the housekeeper.

Mrs. Arnold was in her office just off the kitchens and rose to greet him.

"It is good to meet you, Lord Cyrus," the woman said, her tone kind. "My husband told me of your arrival. How may I be of service to you?"

"His Grace has generously offered me use of the Cressley hunting lodge as my new residence," he informed her. "Arnold says the lodge has not been in use for many years and that you would be able to ready it for me."

"Yes, I can do so, my lord. It grows late, though, and I would prefer sending a crew to clean it thoroughly first thing tomorrow morning. I will supervise them myself and make certain it is stocked with the proper linens and dishes and that the larder is filled. I also will assign a maid to come and clean for you twice a week."

"That is most generous of you, Mrs. Arnold."

"If you would like, I can have a footman bring you your dinner each day from Cook."

"I would not ask for anyone to go to such trouble for me. I have been a solider for many years, Mrs. Arnold, and can make do with whatever is in the larder. If you will excuse me, I will leave now for the hunting lodge."

"Oh, no, my lord. I told you I would have staff clean it tomorrow. Why, the place will be filled with cobwebs and who knows what else? You must stay at Melrose tonight."

He hesitated and then said, "I do not believe this is something His Grace would approve of."

The housekeeper gave Cy a knowing look. "His Grace's gout is acting up. He will be confined to his bedchamber for a good week or more. He has left me in charge of the household. I run it as I see fit. You will stay the night at Melrose, Lord Cyrus. I have already had a guest bedchamber readied for you and even as we speak, water is being heated for your bath."

She glanced up and down at him. "My husband tells me this is all you have to wear. It will need to be washed. There are some trunks in the attics, filled with clothes that are a bit out of date. I am hopeful something there might suit you. It would not be fashionable, but it would be better than putting on these filthy clothes again. I merely needed to see you in person to judge your size before I went through the trunks."

She rose. "I will have a maid take you to your room now and hopefully by the time your bath ends, I will have located a few things for you to wear."

"Thank you, Mrs. Arnold. I am most grateful for what you are doing for me."

The housekeeper summoned a maid, and Cy was taken to a bed-chamber. A large tub already stood in the corner of the room and a bath sheet, bar of soap, and brush had been placed upon the stool next to it. He walked about the room restlessly, moving to the windows and glancing out, seeing the room overlooked the rear of Melrose and its gardens.

Then a brigade of servants appeared, all carrying buckets of water. The water was poured into the tub and two were left in reserve to rinse him. He was then left alone, and he stripped his ill-fitting clothes, folding them neatly and placing them on the floor beside the tub. Cy climbed in, letting out a long sigh as he sat and stretched, the hot water enveloping him. He reveled in it for several minutes and then dunked his head, scrubbing his scalp and face and then using the brush and soap to scrub the dirt from his body.

Standing, he used the extra buckets to rinse the soap from his hair and body, then dried himself with the bath sheet, wrapping it tightly around him.

Arnold arrived with a large stack of clothing in his arms and said, "Mrs. Arnold thought some of these might fit you, my lord. The boy you brought with you has been cleaned and fed and will sleep in the kitchens."

"Send him up to me if you would, Arnold. He is a long way from home and is used to sleeping on the floor next to me."

"Very well, my lord. I will send him to you after you have had your dinner. Mrs. Arnold thought you might prefer a tray in your room."

"That would be wonderful."

Cy took the next few minutes trying on the various items Arnold had brought and was surprised that a few came quite close to fitting him. He was thankful that Mrs. Arnold had allowed him to stay the night at Melrose. It would be better—safer—for him to journey to the hunting lodge in daylight. That way, he could take his time on his way there, studying his surroundings as best he could. It would also be nice to have Bertie accompanying him. He had not addressed anything about the boy's future with Charles, but knew Bertie would want to stay by Cy's side as he acclimated himself to the hunting lodge. Once he had done so—and hopefully after the vision in his left eye cleared more—he could have the boy placed in the stables under Mitchell's care.

For now, he had a home and a small amount of money to live upon until the funds from the sale of his commission arrived. Cy would be frugal as he learned to build a new life for himself, one not only on the edges of Melrose—but far from society itself.

CHAPTER FOUR

F INOLA DRESSED FOR the day in her usual attire—a man's shirt, trousers, riding coat, and boots. It was easier to go about her business of training dogs if she were dressed in such a manner. She had never known greater freedom than when she had decided to do so. Men's clothing was both extremely comfortable and practical. She had numerous pockets in which she stored treats to use in reinforcing pups' good behaviors. She did not have to worry about her hem snagging on something or worry about warmth, especially on a cold day such as today.

The boots actually were her favorite part of what she donned each day. She tucked her trousers into the Hessians, made especially for her by a Brighton bootmaker. The boots were sturdy, snug-fitting, and easy to walk in, especially across all the terrain she traveled each day. That had been something she had taken to, the walking involved in exercising her spaniels. When Banny had been alive and she had helped him, she was the one who spent more time teaching the dogs the correct behaviors and commands, both with her voice and hand gestures. Banny had taken the dogs out about the estate, walking them greater distances the older the pups became, and handling all the training when it came to hunting game and flushing prey.

After Banny's death, when Finola inherited Belldale, she had returned to the small estate, desperate for something to occupy her time as she mourned the man who had served as her father in all but name. Training dogs had saved her.

In more ways than one.

Once she added walking and hunting lessons with the dogs to her daily routine, she found the excess weight fell off her. Over the next eighteen months, she had lost a good four stones. Lady Nance had called at Belldale two years after Banny's passing, on her way to visit a distant cousin, and she had not even recognized Finola.

She glanced in the mirror now, thinking of that pathetic girl she had been during her come-out Season and saw no trace of her. While Finola was still but two inches over five feet, she now possessed womanly curves. Losing weight had changed the angles in her face. That, along with adding a few years, had seen her turn out to be quite pretty. Lady Nance had told Finola that some women grew into their looks and complimented Finola's smile and frame.

She had not seen the dowager countess again since that last meeting and doubted she ever would, since she had no desire to return to the glittering ballrooms of London. No, she had learned painful lessons there at the hands of the Epsilon Club and would remain at Belldale until her death. Thankfully, Banny's will had left Belldale to her so she would always have a home.

When the clients dried up and took their dogs elsewhere for training after they discovered Banny had died, Finola had not let that stop her. Banny had imparted to her all his wisdom regarding dogs. Training them gave Finola purpose. Instead of hoping clients came to her, she purchased two English springer spaniels, her favorite breed to train, and began raising litters from them, training the pups until they were close to a year old and then selling them to the titled nobility.

Soon, her reputation had spread and now Finola had a waiting list of gentlemen who wished to purchase one of her specially bred and trained dogs, known throughout the area as Honeyfield springer spaniels. She had retired the pair she'd mated together for five years, having studied everything she could get her hands on regarding English springer spaniels. The two dogs had each been four when she bought them and from her conversations with other breeders, she had learned the female would gradually produce fewer pups as time passed. That original pair was now retired, and she had sold them to a squire one county over, who had the pair hunt occasionally. For the most part, they were pets to the squire's three children, who lavished love on the dogs.

Finola had kept one of their pups, naming her Hera, and purchased a springer spaniel with incredible lines and a good temperament. She renamed him Zeus and had mated the pair last summer for the first time. Hera had produced a litter of eight pups, six males and two females. These were the dogs Finola now trained. She would allow Zeus and Hera to couple again this spring and had high hopes on what their second litter would consist of. So far, this first one had dogs of even, sweet tempers. English springer spaniels were known for their keen intelligence and friendly natures, and she had not been disappointed in the training of the eight.

She twisted her hair into one, long braid and then went downstairs for some breakfast. Banny had gotten along with a valet, two maids, and a cook. She had written the valet a good reference and one of the maids had gone off with him. Staying with her was Mrs. Hargraves, who served as both cook and housekeeper, caring for Finola's clothes, and Gilly, who did the cleaning and acted as scullery maid in the kitchens.

"Good morning," she told the pair as she joined Gilly at the small table in the kitchens.

She insisted the three of them eat their meals together, finding it foolish to do so separately. Banny had left her this house to do with as she saw fit. Finola simply made things easier on them all by saving the dining room for special occasions. The three took their meals in the kitchens morning and evening. The only thing that had remained the same was she had tea each afternoon by herself in what had been Banny's study. They had done so together every day from the time he brought her home to live with him, and Finola felt closer to him when she did so.

Mrs. Hargraves scooped eggs onto Finola's plate, then did the same for Gilly and herself. Gilly set a rasher of bacon in the center for them to help themselves to as Mrs. Hargraves brought a plate of toasted bread and set it down, along with a jar of marmalade. The women filled their plates and talked about what lay ahead that day.

"How is that Pollux coming along?" Gilly asked.

Of the litter, Pollux was the one who had proved to be the most curious. While he was intelligent, his curiosity had gotten him into a bit of trouble during his training. Finola was determined to pay special attention to Pollux and hoped the extra time spent with the pup might help bring him around.

"He certainly has the most stamina of his littermates," she told the maid. "He likes to walk farther than any of the others. I think I will take him and Athena out this morning for a long walk before the others get their walks in."

"Athena is very good-natured," Mrs. Hargraves said. "She is already a little mother to the others. When I feed them, Athena makes sure everyone is eating before she does so herself." The housekeeper chuckled. "And when Triton tried to muscle out Hermes yesterday? Athena swiped a paw at him, knocking him back."

"She is protective," Finola agreed. "I have seen her watching over the others. I am considering keeping her when I let the others go. I think she would make for a good mother herself in the future."

"How soon might you breed her?" Gilly asked, spreading marmalade on her bread.

"Two years old is the very minimum, I'd say. I would probably wait until she was three, however, before I tried to get a litter off her. I am not in favor of puppies having puppies. In my opinion, a more mature dog makes for a better mother."

They finished eating, and Finola slipped into her greatcoat and headed to the stable. In good weather, she kept the dogs in a run next to the barn. During these winter months, though, she wanted them protected from the cold. She had separated some of the stalls into different spaces so each dog would have a place to sleep and rest, but she also had knocked down the walls between a couple of stalls so the group could also be together and socialize. She had found socializing pups early to be key to them being a better-behaved dog and also easier to train.

"Hello, everyone!" she called as she opened the barn doors.

Gilly took care of feeding their horse and cow, while Mrs. Hargraves fed the dogs in the morning. Finola fed and bedded down the dogs at night. Since they'd all been fed already, she would take them to the dog run now. The morning was cold and crisp, but they would enjoy the play time.

"Zeus, Hera," she said in a calm voice.

The parents of the litter shared sleeping quarters and rose upon hearing their names.

"Let's take your babies out to the dog run." Opening the door, the dogs came out, and she said, "Heel."

Immediately, the pair fell into step with her, one dog on each side. Hera always favored the left, and so Zeus was happy to walk on Finola's right. She allowed the dogs to relieve themselves before opening the gate to the dog run and ushering them inside.

Returning to the stables, she took a pair at a time to do the same, finding it easier to work with the pups in pairs. With large litters, though, this proved to be time consuming. She wondered if she should hire some local farmer's boy to come and help her with the training and then selfishly decided she did not want anyone infringing on her training and time with her dogs. It was already hard enough to let the pups from each litter go once their training was complete, and they had reached an age where they could go and be productive hunters for some lord. Still, she might very well need the help in the future if she bred Athena with another spaniel. Juggling two different, large litters would be difficult on her own.

She saved Athena and Pollux for last, bringing them outside and letting them piddle before calling them to her.

"Heel," she said, calmly and firmly, giving each a treat as they fell into place beside her.

Finola started out, keeping the dogs next to her for a few minutes, testing them. Then she gave the command and let them run a bit. Athena kept within sight, doubling back every so often to be near Finola. Pollux, on the other hand, raced ahead. She whistled, and he returned.

"Good boy," she said, rewarding him with a treat pulled from her pocket.

He took off again joyfully, and she allowed him to do so. After some minutes, they reached the edge of Belldale. No fence appeared, just a copse which divided her property from that of the Duke of Margate. She had only seen the old duke, dead these past six years, once in the village. His son, the current duke, rarely entertained and never invited Finola when he did. She belonged in what was a bit of a no man's land socially. While she was an earl's daughter, at five and twenty she had no guardian and no husband. She never attended the Season in London and so did not have that in common with neighbors who did so. She was acquainted with some of the gentry and folks in the village but for the most part kept to herself. She knew she must be a topic of gossip for many in the area. Her experiences during her only Season had caused her to shy away from most people. Her dogs were her true friends.

Coming close to the thick grove of trees, she called, "Pollux!"

Waiting, she called for the dog again and still got no response. Then she worried that he had crossed into the duke's lands and feared the gamekeeper might have set a trap which Pollux had stumbled into. Containing her fear so that Athena would remain calm, Finola motioned for the dog, and they entered the copse. The day was overcast and the woods dark, little light penetrating it.

When she emerged from the trees with Athena, it surprised her to see smoke coming from the abandoned hunting lodge. She had passed by it on occasion and had never seen anyone there. Glancing about, she found Pollux—with a man and boy.

They sat in the clearing on a fallen log. Pollux was licking the boy's face, and he laughed and squirmed even as he tried to pet the dog.

It was the man, though, who drew Finola's attention. Even seated, she could tell he was a large man, likely a few inches over six feet in height. His shoulders were broad, straining against the poorly-fitted coat he wore. He had unruly, jet black hair and a strong jaw and high cheekbones. He was incredibly handsome, even with the black eye patch worn over his right eye.

But Pollux was her first concern, and she put her fingers to her lips, emitting a sharp whistle. The man and boy stilled, while Pollux glanced up with what Finola could only term a guilty smile on his face.

"Come," she said firmly. "Now."

The dog knew he was in trouble and trotted over to her. She bent and held his face between her hands.

"Come when I call, Pollux," she told him, again her tone firm—but not angry—since English springer spaniels did not do well when yelled at. "Sit," she instructed, and both dogs did so. "Stay," she commanded, leaving Pollux and Athena to walk over to the human pair, who gazed upon her curiously.

"I am sorry if my dog disturbed you," she apologized.

"He's pretty—and friendly!" the boy exclaimed. "I've never been around a dog before." The boy paused. "Is he in trouble?"

"He is because he ran off and did not come when I summoned him."

The boy frowned. "But you didn't yell at him. When I'm in trouble, my father yells."

Finola glanced to the man sitting next to the boy, figuring him not to be this boy's father by the smile the man bit back.

"No. Pollux is an English springer spaniel. They are very smart dogs, eager to please, but also sensitive ones. They do not do well if you scold them. They cower and do not learn the lesson they should. It is important to use a firm tone with them, so they understand they have done wrong. Raising your voice with them proves ineffective."

"Mum yelled at me a couple of times," the boy revealed. "But she would tell me why she was angry so I wouldn't do the same thing again."

"Ah, you learn quickly then, just as my dogs do."

"What did you say his name was?" the boy asked.

"Pollux. In Greek mythology, he was the divine son of Zeus, a god, and Leda, a mortal," she explained. "His half-brother was named Castor. He was the son of Leda and Tyndareus, the King of Sparta."

"What's a mortal?"

"A human," the man replied.

Finally, the man had spoken. Finola had kept her attention on the boy but was incredibly aware of the man during the conversation.

"Can I pet Pollux again?" the boy asked. "And your other dog?"

"Yes, if you would like. It is always good to ask a dog's owner if you can pet them. Some dogs are guard dogs and can be quite fierce. Always ask first before you touch them so that you are not injured."

Finola turned and said, "Come."

Athena and Pollux bounded over and halted before her. She patted both on the head and gave them a treat before looking back to the boy.

"What is your name?"

"Bertie."

"Stand if you would, Bertie, and come next to me."

The boy did so, and she told the dogs, "This is Bertie. Friend. Friend," she repeated. The dogs sat patiently as she told Bertie, "You may pet them now."

He moved to Pollux first and brushed his hand over the dog's head and down its back.

"See, he likes that," she encouraged. "Stroke him a few times but don't ignore Athena. We don't want her to feel left out."

Bertie did as Finola asked and then began petting Athena. Soon, he alternated petting both dogs, who looked quite content.

"If you would like, you may throw a stick for them and have them fetch it. They like that game. They also like to hold the stick in their mouths and have you tug on it."

"Thank you!" he cried, running to gather a few sticks, and tossing them.

The man, who had remained seated on the log, finally stood. His one eye was a startling green, drawing her in.

"You seem to know quite a bit about dogs."

"I breed and train English springer spaniels," she replied. "Again, I apologize for trespassing with my dogs. I live at Belldale, which abuts His Grace's land. No one has used this hunting lodge in many years. Forgive me for interrupting your day. I hope you will not share this incident with His Grace."

"Why is that?"

"I have never met him, but I would suppose a duke would be rather particular about someone trespassing on his land."

"Then we will tell him you were invited. By Bertie and me."

He did not identify himself, and she was loath to introduce herself, as well. She was drawn to him in some inexplicable way and told herself she should move on. That men were not for her. Dogs were her family and friends, all rolled into one.

"Have you lived at Belldale long?" he asked.

"Since I was eight," she replied. "Sir Roscoe Banfield became my guardian at that time."

"I have heard the name but never met the man."

"He passed seven years ago and left Belldale to me. Banny was also mad for dogs and taught me about them."

"Springer spaniels are hunters, aren't they?"

"Yes, they are. Some of the best in England. They are brave and energetic. Loyal to their owners to the point of suffering when they are separated from them. They are strong and can work in rough conditions, even heavy rains. These Honeyfield spaniels are high-spirited but follow commands well. They are not only good hunters but also serve as excellent guard dogs."

"Are these two you have bred, or do you take in dogs to train?"

"I used to accept dogs for training, but prefer now to train those I have bred and then sell them when they are a year old."

"You hate parting from them, don't you?" he asked softly.

"How did you know?" she asked, startled by his observation.

"Since I lost the sight in my right eye, I have become more attuned with my other senses. I also listen better and pick up more than I did when I was a brash, confident man leading others into battle."

"Oh! So, it is a war injury you have suffered."

"Yes. I was shot in the head."

Finola didn't know what to make of that. "I should leave you to your privacy," she said, looking to where Bertie played with Athena and Pollux.

He touched her forearm lightly, causing something foreign to shoot through her.

"Would you come see Bertie and me again tomorrow? And bring Athena and Pollux with you? The boy is starved for company other than my own. It would make him happy."

She wondered who this man was. How Bertie was related to him. But she had never been one to pry.

"All right," she agreed. "It will most likely be a new pair of pups that accompany me. I take them out in pairs when I exercise them."

He smiled—and that smile stole her breath.

"We will be happy to meet more canine friends. Please. Just come."

"I will," she promised.

Then in a louder voice, she called for the dogs to come and had them sit. Bertie ran with them and petted them both on the head.

"I will see you tomorrow, Bertie," she told him. "I will bring a few more of my dogs with me for you to meet."

"Yes!" he cried excitedly.

"Heel," she told her dogs, and they left the clearing, cutting through the copse again and returning to Belldale.

As Finola exercised the remaining dogs in pairs, she couldn't help but think about the handsome, one-eyed stranger and why he was staying in the Duke of Margate's hunting lodge.

CHAPTER FIVE

CY COULD NOT quit thinking about the woman he had met yesterday.

The one he hadn't known was a woman to begin with.

He had been caught up in seeing Bertie's pleasure and watching the English springer spaniel, which had appeared from nowhere, lick the boy's face with unbridled enthusiasm. Then he had heard someone call the dog, a low voice which he had not distinguished as either male or female. He saw a blur emerge from the copse and as it came toward him, he made out a short man, wearing a greatcoat, accompanied by another dog.

When the figure came closer, however, Cy's heightened senses picked up the scent. Her scent. The woman was dressed as a man would be, in shirt, trousers, and Hessians. She had not given her name. He had not provided his.

She had an air of calm authority about her and handled the dog, whom she called Pollux, with a quiet firmness in her tone. It had not surprised him when she said that she bred and trained English springer spaniels. He liked her even more when she allowed Bertie to play with the two dogs accompanying her. More than anything, Cy looked forward to her visit today and speaking once more with her. She had not mentioned when she would come, only that she would, and he suspected it might be near the same time as yesterday. Bertie, too, had been taken with her as much as her dogs and had talked about her upcoming visit much of yesterday.

The two of them were settling into the hunting lodge, yesterday having been their first full day in it. Mrs. Hargraves and her staff had worked a small miracle. Cy had accompanied the housekeeper and several maids to the lodge and had seen the condition it was in. By day's end, though, the place sparkled with cleanliness, and he and Bertie lacked for nothing. The lodge was isolated, though. It had been at the edge of Melrose lands, not close to any of the tenants' cottages and as far from the main house as was possible. Still, it offered Bertie and him a place to live. He had decided one way to pass the time was to begin educating the boy, teaching him to read and write. For that, they would need to go into Adderly. He needed to do so anyway because he wished to see Mr. Timmon about new clothing.

While in the village, they could stop at Mr. Simon's general store and purchase a slate and chalk, along with a basic reader or two if they were available. Since the woman they had met yesterday was from this area, she might be able to direct them regarding those purchases.

He went and stirred the porridge, which sat in a small pot now hanging over the fire, and used a thick cloth to lift the pot from its resting place. He dished out some for each of them, adding a sprinkling of cinnamon and a pat of butter to each wooden bowl.

Bertie sat at the table and picked up a spoon as Cy placed the porridge in front of the boy.

"Stir it well," he said. "It will mix the butter and cinnamon into your porridge."

"I've never had cinnamon," Bertie said after one bite. "It makes the porridge taste ever so good."

"We have Mrs. Hargraves to thank for that spice. She brought some herbs and spices for us when she filled the larder. You and I will have to learn how to cook together. We are two fine, intelligent men and should be able to figure things out for ourselves."

Bertie laughed as only a child could. "I'm a little boy, my lord. Not a man at all."

"You will grow into one sooner than you think," Cy told him. "We want you to be the best man you can possibly be. Educated. Kind to others."

He frowned. "I don't know about educated. I can't even sign my name, my lord. My mother said education wasn't for folks like us."

"I think education should be for everyone," he declared. "I will serve as your tutor, Bertie, and I have a feeling you will be an excellent pupil. You are never too old to learn. Do you wish to know how to read and write?"

Since they were seated close together, Cy could see the boy's face light up. "I would very much like that, my lord."

They finished their breakfast and washed and dried the dishes, Bertie having fetched water from the nearby well before the meal, which proved to be convenient.

"Do you think she will come with the dogs soon, my lord?"

"I hope so. I think we are both eager for some company, be it human or canine."

"What's canine?"

Cy laughed. "A fancy way to say dog."

"Rich people talk funny sometimes."

He laughed again. "I would not call myself rich, Bertie. Yes, my family was wealthy, and so I was well educated as a boy, but my army salary was modest, despite the fact officers are paid more than enlisted men."

"Do you not have any money of your own?" the boy asked, his eyes full of doubt.

"I still have a few coins, and I should be receiving the funds from the sale of my commission any day now," he shared. "I gave Major-General Parker my address here at Melrose and once Parker has seen to the sale of the commission, he will make certain those funds come to me."

"Father said you would also get money from the army for being shot."

"That is true. A small pension should come to me. I don't know if it is monthly or quarterly."

"What's quarterly?"

Cy liked how the boy asked questions when he wasn't familiar with a term and knew Bertie would make for a fine pupil when they began their lessons, full of curiosity and questions to be answered. After explaining what quarterly meant, he suggested they go outside to get some fresh air and wait for their visitor.

They moved outdoors and once more sat on the fallen log in the clearing. They didn't have long to wait. He felt the woman's presence before he actually saw a blur emerge from the woods. As she drew closer, he sensed Bertie's excitement and smelled the subtle scent of lavender wafting from her as the wind blew the smell of her in his direction. When she had come near him yesterday, it had been the same scent and he supposed the soap she used contained bits of lavender.

She was dressed similarly, still wearing the greatcoat, which was unbuttoned, revealing a white shirt tucked into dark trousers. The trousers were tucked into her Hessians. He did not know bootmakers even made boots for women. Then again, she was the first woman he had met who dressed as a man.

"Good morning," she said. "We are going to start a bit differently than yesterday, Bertie. Pollux introduced himself, but I would prefer to teach you the proper way to meet a dog you have never seen before."

He noticed that she had kept her attention on the boy and wondered if she felt any of the attraction he did toward her.

"Just as when meeting people, you do not immediately rush up. It is the same with an unfamiliar dog. Never touch a strange dog unless you have been introduced. Some have been trained as guard dogs and would either snap at you or sink their teeth into your hand if you tried to touch them."

"Pollux wasn't like that at all," Bertie protested.

"That is because Pollux is only seven months old and still in training. The proper thing to do is wait for a dog's owner to tell you a bit about his dog and then if it is acceptable, the owner will invite you to pet the dog. So, let us begin. Hello, Bertie. I would like to introduce you to two of my friends. They come from a litter of eight, which was born last summer, in late June. There were six males and two females. On my left, is Demeter, one of the females."

Cy noticed the dog perked up at hearing her name.

"On my right, is Hermes."

This time Bertie commented, "He knows his name."

"Yes, that is one of the first things in training a dog. It is to teach a dog his or her name and use it frequently as you train them, so they know you are speaking to them. Both Demeter and Hermes are friendly dogs. Even then, you never should pet a dog unknown to you. The best thing to do is hold your palm out, like this, cupped."

Bertie mimicked her gesture, and she held her hand under Demeter's nose. The pup nuzzled it.

"Dogs can smell many times greater than what humans can. They rely on their sense of smell as much as they do their eyesight. To get to know a dog, offer them your hand in this manner and let them sniff it."

Bertie brought his cupped palm to Hermes' snout, and the dog placed his nose in it, sniffing it. Then Hermes licked the boy's fingers, delighting Bertie.

"Do the same with Demeter now," encouraged the woman.

Bertie offered his free hand since Hermes was still licking the other one. Demeter sniffed it gently and then looked up at the boy. Cy could have sworn the dog smiled at Bertie before she, too, began licking his palm.

"See? You have made friends with them in the proper fashion." She turned to Cy. "Would you like to do the same?"

"I would." He turned up both palms and held them in front of him. The dogs left Bertie and came to Cy now, smelling him and obviously accepting him because they licked his fingers, as well.

"This is a way a dog makes friends," the woman said. "Now, you are free to play with Demeter and Hermes if you wish."

"Both girl dogs have brown on them, but the boy dogs are dark," Bertie noted.

"Yes, their mother Hera is liver-colored, while their father, Zeus, is dark mixed with white."

"Go on and play with the pups," Cy encouraged, and Bertie galloped away, the pair chasing after him. He turned to the woman. "Might I offer you a seat?" he asked formally but with a teasing tone.

She laughed, a rich sound which caused the hairs on his nape to stand on end.

"Why, thank you. It is nice to have furniture outdoors and take advantage of it."

He laughed, too, and they sat on the log. Cy knew little to nothing about this woman, but he did not think she would be comfortable in the presence of a duke's son. Instead of introducing himself with his courtesy title, he told her, "I mentioned to you that I was an officer in His Majesty's army until recently. You cannot see, thanks to the eye patch I wear, that I bear a scar here where I was shot." He pointed to just above his brow.

She shook her head. "I am still in awe of the fact that you lived after such a wound."

He smiled. "The army surgeon who operated on me said my odds were slim. It did affect my eyesight, however. I still cannot see out of my right eye. Dr. Sheffley believes the bullet caused a bruising—a swelling, if you will—that is pressing against my optic nerve."

"He believes you will regain your sight?"

Cy smiled wryly. "Sheffley is an optimist and tried to turn me into one. My commanding officer, however, did not believe my sight would return. An officer cannot lead men being so vulnerable."

He waved his right hand next to his face. "I have no peripheral vision and would not know if someone charged me from this side. I have agreed to selling my commission. Even if by chance my eyesight returned, who knows if I would see clearly from the eye or if my vision would be permanently impaired?"

"At least you have the sight from your other eye," she said. "That must be of some relief."

He decided to be honest with her and said, "The vision in my left eye has also been affected. I used to see things sharply in the distance. Now, however, objects are blurry to me. It is only when they come closer that I can see any detail. In fact, I mistook you for a man yesterday because of your dress."

"I have found it easier to train my dogs dressed as I am. I live alone, except for two servants, and they do not judge me for my attire."

"I hope you do not think that I judge you."

She studied him a long moment. "No, I do not believe you do."

"I am Cy," he told her. "Short for Cyrus. I do not wish to use my officer's rank now that I am a civilian. Since we are to be neighbors, I would ask that you do me the courtesy of calling me Cy."

She grew thoughtful. "You do look like a Cy to me. I am Finola."

"Finola is an unusual name, but it suits you, as well. Now, we are no longer strangers to one another."

He offered her his hand, and she took it. Cy meant to shake it, but the contact between them was electric. He froze. She gasped. Finola tried to pull her hand from his grasp, but he recovered enough to shake it a few times before releasing it.

"I am glad we are neighbors, Finola," he said evenly, his heart racing. "Thank you for bringing Demeter and Hermes to visit with Bertie. He has led a bit of a lonely life. His father came to war, bringing his wife and Bertie in tow. The boy has grown up on the move, with he and his mother following the army every time we changed locations. I am his friend now, but I know he was thrilled to meet you yesterday. You and your pups."

"Why is Bertie here in England with you if his parents are still on the Peninsula?" she asked.

"He was charged by his father to care for me because of my deficient eyesight. My batman fussed over me as if I were a helpless child and sent his son with me to help watch over me as I am healing."

"Will you send him back to the fighting eventually?" she asked.

"No, Briggs knew that was no kind of life for a boy and left him in my care, asking that I help Bertie find a new life. I knew I was coming to Melrose, and Bertie has shown an interest in horses. Perhaps the duke will allow the boy to join the grooms and be trained as one of them."

"Why did you come to Melrose, Cy?"

"I am a relative of His Grace's," he replied. "We have never been close, though. I had nowhere else to go when I left the army and came here, hoping His Grace would help find me a place. He has given me use of this hunting lodge."

"I have never met Margrave," Finola said. "The former duke rarely came to Melrose and Banny—Sir Roscoe Banfield, that is—was never asked to socialize with him. When Margrave passed and his son became the new duke, the neighborhood has seen little of him. There are even rumors this past year that he is quite ill."

"He is ill," Cy revealed, "He was not amenable to having me as a guest in his home. I am thankful, though, that this hunting lodge was available. I will acclimate to civilian life better on my own. With Bertie, of course."

"You say you are having some trouble with the eye you can see with. I have an eyewash which I use with my dogs. It might do you some good. Would you like me to make it up for you and see if it helps? It is made from chamomile flowers and rose water."

He sighed. "I would be grateful if you did so. It is frustrating to have vision from only one eye and be limited with that."

"Then I will return to Belldale and bring the herbs back with me, along with two new dogs for Bertie to meet. Since the boy lacks in human friends, I will supply him with canine ones."

Cy took her hand in his, once more feeling a rush race through him. "Thank you, Finola. From both Bertie and me."

She gazed at him, something unreadable in her face, and then stood, breaking the contact between them.

"I will see you in less than an hour's time, Cy. Put on a small pot of water to boil if you would. I will use it when I return."

Bringing her fingers to her mouth, she whistled sharply. The dogs quickly ceased their play and hurried to her side, Bertie following them.

"I must return to Belldale, Bertie, but I will return again shortly. You have already met four of my latest litter. I will bring the other four with me. It would help me greatly if you would play with them while I help Cy with something."

"I can do that," the boy said eagerly. "Maybe I could come with you and help bring them back?" he asked hopefully, glancing to Cy. "May I go?"

"If it is all right with Finola, you may accompany her."

"I would appreciate your company, Bertie." She glanced back at Cy. "We will not be long."

"I will wait inside," he said. "Simply enter the lodge when you return."

Finola called the dogs to heel, and he watched as she and Bertie disappeared into the thick grove of trees.

His instincts had sharpened with the loss of his vision, and he listened to his gut more than he had in the past. Without a doubt, Cy believed that Finola would play a large role in his present.

And hopefully, his future.

CHAPTER SIX

FINOLA LED BERTIE back to Belldale. The house was only about ten minutes from the hunting lodge. She took the boy to the dog run, where she had left the six dogs she wasn't exercising, and they returned Demeter and Hermes to the pen. She then introduced him to the four pups he had yet to meet—Triton, Apollo, Castor, and Atlas, as well as Zeus and Hera. Athena and Pollux remembered Bertie and greeted him with licks to his face, delighting the child. The pups all took to Bertie, as she knew they would. She worked with him a few minutes, telling him a few word commands which she used with the dogs, and then told him he could play with the pups while she gathered the herbs she would need.

Going into the house, Finola found the chamomile and rose petals she would use to make the eyewash for Cy's eyes. She couldn't imagine the trauma he must have experienced, having been shot in the head—and actually surviving the experience. He was fortunate to be alive, but she knew he must be hurting mentally and emotionally now. He was a large, imposing man and had an authoritative air about him, marking him as a former military officer. To have his career stripped from him must have been an incredible blow.

She still wondered how he was related to the Duke of Margate. As she had told Cy earlier, Banny never fraternized with the old duke or the current one. She was glad at least Cy had had a place to come home to after leaving the army. Still, it would be a lonely life for him, with only a small boy for company. From what Cy had said, eventually, Bertie would leave the hunting lodge and go to Melrose proper and work in the stables.

Finola was acquainted with several people in the area but didn't have any close friends. Being an earl's daughter—and yet one who earned money for her living—put her in a category that was more than unusual. Yes, she owned Belldale outright but did not truly socialize with the gentry in the area. She did go into Adderly each Sunday to worship at the local church and was known to the parishioners there, but she did not have any true friends.

Until now.

She hoped she and Cy would become friends, good friends.

And yet she had an innate sense that they might be destined to be more than friends. Much more. That thought took Finola by surprise, and she tried hard to shove it away.

Because it frightened her.

She had never felt the touch of a man since that horrible Lord Crofton had duped her, making her foolishly believe that a handsome, titled viscount might be interested in a life with her. She was no longer that naive girl, though. She was a woman of five and twenty years of age, one who had built a life perfectly suited for her. A life with no room for a man in it.

And yet she had almost melted as quickly as butter in a hot pan when Cy had touched her.

Could she be friends with a man?

She didn't know if that was possible between a man and woman. Of course, she had been best friends with Banny, even though he was her guardian. A mixture of parent, friend, and teacher all in one. Finola had learned all she knew about the care and training of dogs from Banny. They had been inseparable companions for many years, sharing their work with dogs and everything else life had to offer.

Finola promised herself not to let her fancies take flight and think that Cy could be anything other than a friend she saw occasionally. She would rein in the crazy notions flying through her head and treat him as she would anyone else. She put a generous portion of the herbs into a small pouch, intending to leave the mixture with him so he could use it daily for at least a week.

Going outside once more, she claimed Bertie and the four pups who would accompany them to the hunting lodge, allowing them to get their exercise for the day. She had Bertie give the verbal command, and the dogs heeled as asked. As they moved away from Belldale, however, she allowed the animals to run ahead and stretch their legs.

"Your dogs have funny names," Bertie noted.

"I named this litter after Greek gods. I try to give each group a theme on common names. Do you know anything of the Greeks, Bertie?"

"No. I never heard of them. Who are they?" he asked, clearly curious.

She told him a bit about ancient Greece and before she knew it, they had reached the copse and traveled thorough it, the hunting lodge appearing before them.

"Do you think you might play with the dogs while I help Cy inside? I brought a few toys for you to do so."

Finola slipped the satchel from her shoulder and opened it, showing Bertie the balls and bits of rope she used as pull toys. She also told him he could do as he had earlier and toss sticks, allowing the dogs to retrieve them for him.

"I will be right inside if you need me, Bertie."

He looked at her solemnly. "Thank you for trusting me with your dogs."

She ruffled his hair and then went to the door, knocking on the lodge's entrance and entering it. Looking about, she saw it had a small parlor to the left and a kitchen area with a table and chairs to the right.

Cy sat at the table.

"I brought the herbs I told you about, chiefly rose petals and chamomile."

He rose. "I put the water on to boil as you suggested."

"I will get it. Thank you."

As Finola worked, she explained to him how to steep the herbs and how much to use of them each time he did so. As they steeped, she asked him about where he had been stationed, and he told her a few stories of his time on the Peninsula.

"From what you say, it sounds as if you believe the tide is turning in our war against Bonaparte."

He nodded solemnly. "While I do think we will defeat Bonaparte sooner than later, there will still be dark days ahead. Battles which must be fought in order to restore the balance of power in Europe again. Men will die, a good deal of them."

"You regret not being there for your men, don't you?" she asked quietly.

"I do. I thought my future was one I was comfortable with. I trained as an officer after university and immediately went to war. I have served His Majesty the past eight years and had intended to do so the rest of my military career."

"As you said, though, we will not always be at war. Bonaparte is on the run now, or soon will be. Even if it does take a few more years to defeat him. What would you have done after the war?"

"A good portion of the foot soldiers would have returned to their homes. Officers, such as me, would have been assigned to posts throughout England and Scotland and even beyond, to places as far-flung as India. I would have continued training men under my authority and worked with the local militia on drills, as well. My future had been planned until my retirement several decades down the line."

He shrugged, a lost look now present on his face. "I have no idea now what the coming years will bring."

Finola rose and tried to lighten the mood. "I am certain you will find your place at Melrose. Give it time, Cy. You only just arrived. Think back to the beginning of your army days. It took a while, I am certain, for you to find your footing as an officer. This will be much the same. In the meantime, let's see if this gives you some relief."

She poured the steeped mixture into a bowl and dipped one of the cloths she had brought into it, soaking it.

"Would you mind removing your eye patch, Cy? I can fold this saturated cloth so that both eyes can be ministered to at the same time."

He did as she asked, slipping his eye patch from his head, and looked at her with his intense eyes. Finola demonstrated how much to wring from the cloth and how to fold it and then stood and draped it over his eyes, holding her palm flush against the cloth. Being so near to him caused her heart to flutter in the way she had supposed it should do so all those years ago when Crofton was paying her special attention. She lifted Cy's hand and slipped hers from the cloth, replacing it with his.

"Hold this against your eyes gently," she cautioned.

"For how long?"

"I would say a good ten minutes each time. Fifteen would be better."

She took a seat at the table again and said, "You might want to brace your elbow against the table."

He did as she instructed, and she told him to use the water steeped today another two times, spacing out doing so throughout the day.

"I brought enough herbs for you to place in boiled water each morning for the rest of this week. I hope it will bring you some comfort and do some good."

"Already, I can feel it soothing my eyes. Ever since the bullet entered my forehead, my eyes have been itchy and red. This concoction has calmed them—and me."

They talked as they waited the quarter hour to pass. She told him a little about the local village, and he mentioned wanting to have some new clothes made up, having left his officer's uniforms behind in Spain with a friend who fit into them.

"I also want to teach Bertie how to read and write," he shared with her. "I was thinking of going into the village to see if they had any materials I could use to do so."

"Mr. Simon does run a general store and might have some of what you need, but I have everything already and am happy to lend it to you. You see, Banny became my guardian when I was orphaned at eight years of age. He not only taught me how to train dogs for the hunt, but he also served as my tutor. I know I still have my old slates and the books we used at Belldale. We had a room dedicated as a schoolroom. It gets good light, better than this hunting lodge does. Perhaps you and Bertie would care to walk over to Belldale each morning and have your lessons there."

"Wouldn't that inconvenience you?"

Finola laughed. "Not in the least. I spend a good majority of my day outside with the dogs I train. If the weather is rainy or cold, I work with them inside the stables. Otherwise, they are in the dog run playing, and I remove them one at a time to work with them individually. Once they have mastered a certain behavior, I will take them out in pairs and train them together, as well as walk them several times a day."

"I told you that Bertie was interested in horses and that I might ask for him to have a place in the Melrose stables when I am more recovered. I wonder instead, since he seems to have an affinity for your dogs, if you might have more need of him."

She grew thoughtful. "It is interesting you mentioned that, because I have been thinking of the same thing. Not about Bertie specifically since I did not know him, but I was thinking of hiring one of the local village lads to help with the training. Bertie does seem to have a way with the pups. I taught him a few verbal commands to use before we returned here. Perhaps we can let him work with the dogs more and see if it is something he might wish to pursue.

"You could come for lessons in the makeshift schoolroom, and then Bertie could stay on and spend a few hours with the dogs and me. Would you be able to make your way back to the hunting lodge on your own?"

"I have nothing here to occupy my time, Finola. Might I watch these lessons? Or possibly even help with the dog training? I simply wish to make myself useful."

She could understand that better than most people and said, "If you are willing, I would welcome your help and that of Bertie's, too. It might help you settle in more at Melrose."

And allow me to spend time with you.

Briskly, she said, "Enough time has passed. Go ahead and remove the cloth from your eyes."

Cy did so, peeling away the fabric and looking up. He blinked several times and then said, "My eyes feel more relaxed than they have in weeks."

He slipped on the eye patch once more and looked about the room, his gaze finally settling on her. A warm feeling trickled through her.

"I do believe my vision is slightly improved than before this treatment," he declared.

"I am glad to hear it, Cy."

Then Finola thought of Mr. Colgate, who had gone off to war several years ago and returned last summer. He had been wounded in the shoulder and his leg and had come home blind, as well, but recovered his sight after a few weeks at home. Perhaps it would be good for Cy and Mr. Colgate to visit with one another. She would mention it to Cy and see if he would be amenable to such a meeting.

"Shall we join Bertie?" he asked, rising from the table and pulling out her chair for her.

He offered his hand, and she slipped hers into it, her belly flipping over once again at the contact between them. Cy did not mention it, though, and she didn't think she should address it.

They went outside, where Bertie was frolicking with his new canine friends.

Cy said, "I hear I have four new dogs to meet, Bertie. Would you do the honors of introducing me to them?"

Bertie looked to her and Finola nodded, saying, "Do as we did before."

The boy took his time, instructing Cy how to hold his hand and then calling over each dog one at a time, allowing them to sniff the man. As expected, all four accepted Cy and licked his hand, and he petted and scratched them between their ears.

"Did you know Finola named all of them after Greek gods?" Bertie asked.

"She did, did she? Tell me about them," Cy encouraged.

It warmed Finola's heart to hear the boy repeat all she had told him about each god she had used in naming this litter. He kept all of the facts straight, not confusing even one attribute of each god. Bertie was a very clever lad and would excel in both his studies and with her litter.

Bertie ended with, "And they all have the same mother and father." He frowned. "I forget those names, Finola."

"Zeus and Hera," she prompted. Turning to Cy, she added, "Bertie met the dam and sire when he came to Belldale."

"We shall be visiting Belldale on a regular basis," Cy told the boy.

She listened as Cy explained how there were books and slates that Finola herself had used as a young girl in her own education and that she was willing to share these with Bertie.

"Instead of bringing them all here, we shall go and have your lessons at Belldale," Cy said. "Afterward, Finola said she will allow you to help in training this litter."

Bertie jumped up and down, unable to contain his excitement. "Can I really? I like dogs even more than horses."

Her gaze met Cy's, and they both nodded at one another.

"Perhaps when Cy doesn't need your help, you might come and work with me at Belldale," Finola suggested.

Cy interjected. "You always have a place to live with me at the lodge, Bertie, but you could travel to Belldale each day and help Finola with her work. Would you like that better than working in the Melrose stables?"

"I think I would," said the child.

"We do not have to settle anything now," she said. "For the time being, you and Cy will come to Belldale each morning for your lessons. Then in the afternoon I will give you lessons of a different kind."

"I intend to join in those lessons you have with Finola," Cy told the boy. "It won't hurt with eight pups to have extra sets of hands. I might find I like working with animals myself."

"Then it is settled," she declared, excited about the prospect. "Bertie knows the way to Belldale now. It is less than a quarter-hour from your hunting lodge, Cy."

"Bertie and I will have our breakfast and appear at Belldale shortly after," Cy promised.

Finola already looked forward to spending some of each day with the pair. She was eager to teach Bertie all Banny had taught her about dogs—but even more keen to spend time in Cy's company.

Chapter Seven

C Y SLIPPED HIS eye patch over his right eye and rose quietly from the bed, stepping over Bertie, who insisted upon sleeping on a pallet next to Cy's bed even though there was a second bedchamber upstairs in the hunting lodge. The boy had been tuckered out after playing with all of Finola's dogs yesterday and had talked constantly about Finola and her large litter, asking him more about the names she had given the pups. Cy had told Bertie as much as he could about each of the Greek gods and goddesses and even recalled the twelve labors of Heracles, one of his favorite series of stories as a boy. As he had gone through each labor, Bertie had sat enthralled by the deeds of the hero.

Cy eased the door closed and went downstairs, where he fetched fresh water from the well and put a small pot on to boil. He had used her mixture twice more yesterday after Finola departed, and looking out across the kitchens this morning, he swore the sight in his left eye had improved slightly. The steeped herbs seemed to bring him relief, cooling his heated, itchy eyes. While no miracle had occurred overnight, for the first time since the bullet entered his head, the right eye did not seem to be as swollen or irritated. He—like Dr. Sheffley—held out hope that his eyesight would return. Maybe not as sharp as it previously been, but he would be happy to have the right eye see as well as the left one now did. If he did regain sight in it, it might be worth a trip to London to see an eye specialist and even obtain spectacles that might help him to see distant objects more clearly.

He took the pot off the fire and added the herb mixture into the water, stirring and letting it steep as Finola had yesterday. Then when it cooled, he dipped a cloth she had brought into the doctored water. After wringing the excess from it, he removed his eye patch and placed the wet cloth against his eyes.

He now had a quarter-hour to think, since he could do nothing else. What he wanted to think about was Finola. He had never been so taken with a woman, much less anticipated seeing one as he did her this morning. Like most military officers, he indulged infrequently with the fairer sex, sating his appetite with a local widow or one of the camp doxies who followed the army from place to place. Believing he was married to the army and that a woman would never permanently enter his life, Cy had not thought of his life with a woman in it. He had never pictured himself as a husband, much less a father.

Bertie was beginning to change that. The boy was bright and friendly, and Cy instinctively had a good way of handling him. It had made Cy curious as to whether he might be a good father to children of his own.

Then Finola had entered his life, and things had radically shifted. He had only known her for a couple of days, and yet it seemed he had known her a lifetime. He could not imagine her absent from his life. Yes, they were neighbors and would be seeing one another frequently, thanks to her generous offer to allow him to tutor Bertie using the materials Sir Roscoe had once used to teach her. Finola had mentioned being orphaned at eight years of age, and Cy wondered how she was related to Sir Roscoe. Obviously, the man had not wed and produced children. Instead, he had left his property to Finola, which was highly unusual. It gave her a certain independence which very few women had in English society. He was eager to see what Belldale looked like and watch and learn from her as she trained her litter of pups.

He removed the damp cloth from his eyes, realizing he had not had one of his blinding headaches for several days now. That alone made him optimistic about his future.

Going into the larder, he claimed several eggs and half a loaf of bread. Mrs. Hargraves had told him when the maid came to clean the lodge twice each week, she would bring with her items to restock the larder, including freshly baked bread from Cook. He removed a crock of butter and one of jam and placed them on the table as Bertie entered the kitchen area, rubbing his eyes sleepily.

"You should have gotten me up, my lord. I would have made your breakfast for you."

"I had to get up and make the concoction Finola wishes for me to use on my eyes," he told the boy. "I did not mind getting our food on after that."

Bertie seated himself at the table. "Finola is really nice, isn't she? I hope I do a good job learning from her."

"You would like to work with her and her dogs?"

The boy nodded as he buttered some of the bread. "I think so. But I need to stay with you, my lord, for now."

"About that, Bertie," Cy began. "I know you used to address me as *sir* when I was an officer. I think I would like you to do that when we are around Finola," he suggested.

Bertie's brows knit together. "Why?"

"We are not standing on formality with Finola," he explained. "I think it would simply be better if you referred to me in that manner."

What Cy did not express was that he thought his relationship might change with Finola if she knew him to be a duke's son. Others in the *ton* had treated him differently once they learned the rank his father held. For some reason he could not articulate, he wished for Finola to only know him as Cy Cressley, a former army officer and now resident of a small hunting lodge on a country estate.

"All right," said Bertie brightly, showing how flexible the young could be.

They ate their breakfast, and then Cy took some of the water he had heating and shaved. He encouraged Bertie to use some of the tooth powder and decided to buy the boy a brush when he went into the village. Cy thought he might do so this afternoon while Bertie was working with Finola and the dogs. Although Cy was eager to learn from her, as well, there were things he needed to accomplish in Adderly.

He reminded Bertie to comb his hair and even suggested he use a bit of water to smooth down the cowlick that sprang from the back of the boy's head.

Once they were ready, Bertie led Cy through the copse and as they emerged, the boy said, "We're on Belldale land now. That's what Finola told me. She said it's not very large, but it's all hers."

The land was very similar to that of Melrose, but obviously Finola did not have any tenants. As they drew closer to her house, he saw a vegetable garden and then a large, enclosed area which he assumed was the dog run she used during some of her training and for the dogs to run about a bit and play while she worked with individual ones.

"We should knock at the kitchen door," he told the lad, leading Bertie that way.

As they approached the door, Finola was coming out and exclaimed, "Ah, there you are! Good morning to you both."

They replied in kind and she said, "Why were you coming to the back door?"

"I realized it is still early and did not want to disturb you," Cy said. "I thought your cook might be up, however."

She laughed and he felt a warm rush run through him hearing the sound.

"We rise early here at Belldale," she told him. "We have dogs to feed, along with a cow to milk and a horse to care for, as well. Come in with me through the front door if you will."

Finola led them around to the front of the house and opened the door. No servants were in sight. As they went through the house, Cy saw it was similar in size to the dower house at Melrose but had a cozy feel to it which the dower house lacked. She led them to a small room.

"This is next door to Banny's study. It is where I took my own lessons at this very table. The light is quite good for reading, and sometimes Mrs. Hargraves and Gilly, my servants, polish the silver in here. I will make certain they do not disturb your morning lessons, though. Those tasks can be accomplished in the afternoons, when Bertie—and you, too, Cy—will be outdoors with me."

She went to the table, and he saw several books stacked upon it, along with a few slates, chalk, and rags to wipe them clean.

"I went through the cabinets after I left you yesterday and pulled some of the basic readers out. Do you know your alphabet, Bertie?" she asked.

"No, Finola. I don't know anything about reading and writing."

"That is what I am here for, Bertie," Cy declared. "We will start with the alphabet and once you master it, use it to learn simple words. We will build on your vocabulary as we go. I also wish to teach you basics in mathematics. Who knows? If you are educated, you might one day even be employed as a clerk in some office."

Bertie shook his head firmly. "No, sir, I know I want to work with animals. Either dogs or horses."

He was grateful that the boy had remembered not to address him as *my lord* and smiled. "It won't hurt for you to get the basics of an education. Even if you are working with animals. Why, you could talk to them. I always talk to my horse." He looked to Finola. "Bertie and I spoke more about Greek mythology. I think we could even do a few lessons in history and geography if he is interested."

The boy grinned. "I heard all about Heracles and his twelve labors. How he cleaned the king's stables and cut off the heads from the hydra. Those were good stories."

Finola smiled indulgently. "I am not certain that I know all those tales. You might need to tell me about these labors later today, Bertie."

Her gaze met that of Cy's, and he knew she was quite familiar with all twelve labors and merely wished to indulge the boy.

"I will leave the two of you on your own. We both have our own tasks to perform, even if they aren't as heroic as those of Heracles. Whenever you finish your lessons, come outside."

"I thought Bertie and I could work mornings and then take a short break before we came to you," he said. "Today, though, I believe I will leave things to you and Bertie. I want to go into Adderly and see the tailor and also look around in the general store to see if there is anything we are missing at the hunting lodge. I will catch up on lessons with you later."

Finola left them and Cy took one slate and gave the other to Bertie. He talked a little bit about letters and the difference between consonants and vowels, trying to draw from his own lessons many years ago. He drew letters, one at a time, and had Bertie imitated what he saw on Cy's slate. As expected, the lad picked up things rapidly and in a short time, had all the letters of the alphabet memorized and could draw them with ease. Cy thought since Bertie proved to be such a sponge that he would start with a short word and add to it.

He wrote *AT* on his slate and Bertie said, "That is an *A* and a *T*. But you wrote them close together."

"You are correct. They go together to form a word. Let us sound out the sounds they make."

Cy demonstrated, and Bertie quickly caught on. Soon, they were adding all kinds of letters in front of *AT* and within minutes, Bertie was writing and sounding out words such as cat, mat, sat, and fat.

"This is easy," the boy said. "And fun."

"I always thought learning was fun myself and am happy to hear you think the same. Let us see if you can think of another letter we can place in front of these two. Go through the alphabet and see what you come up with."

"A," Bertie said, thinking. "No. *B*." He sounded out B in front of the root word. "Bat!" he declared.

"Very good," Cy praised. "And what is a bat?"

Cy had asked for a brief definition of every word Bertie had come up with, and the boy now said, "That is part of batman."

"Yes, that is a much larger word." He wrote bat on his own slate and then added MAN after it. "That is what your father is." Covering the second syllable, he said, "This word is bat. Are you familiar with what a bat is?"

The boy shook his head, and Cy explained what a bat was and where they could be found.

"Try again. See if you can think of another word to add to our list."

"I know!" Bertie cried. He wrote an *R* with his chalk and then the *AT* after it. "Rat," he declared. "Rats are nasty little creatures that run around and should be avoided. Mum told me if a rat bites you, you can get very sick."

"That is true. One more lesson and then we will be through for the day. Sometimes, you can put two letters in front of a few to form a new word."

He took the cloth and erased his slate before writing *AT* again. Then he added *FL* in front of it.

"Sound it out, Bertie," Cy encouraged.

He listened as the boy blended *F* and *L* together and then added *AT* to it. Brightening, Bertie said, "Flat," with enthusiasm and rubbed the top of the table. "This table is flat," he said.

"I think you have done an outstanding job for your first day of schooling, Bertie. If you would like, you may go outside. I am going to put away the materials we have used. I know Finola had left them out for us, but it is important to always pick up your things and not leave a mess for others. It is especially important in this instance because we are a guest in Finola's home and do not want to leave things messy."

"I can help," Bertie insisted.

"No, go outside. I don't mind putting things away. It will help me investigate what else is here and see if there might be other things I need to order for our lessons."

The boy left the makeshift classroom, and Cy began erasing slates and opening cabinets, finding a place for everything and investigating what was there. Then he sensed a difference in the air and turned, finding Finola standing in the doorway.

She crossed the room and came to stand before him. "How did the first lesson go?"

He smiled. "Even better than I had expected."

Briefly, Cy outlined what he and Bertie had done that morning, and Finola expressed delight at how much the boy had accomplished in such a few hours.

"I suppose I should not be surprised, knowing Bertie as I do. Yesterday, he was quick to pick up on the commands I use with the dogs. He will prove to be an excellent pupil, both in the classroom and outdoors with my dogs."

"I believe you are correct," Cy said, enticed by her nearness. That faint scent of lavender, which clung to her, only increased temptation. He wanted to bury his nose against her neck and inhale her sweet scent. Kiss the pulse point at her throat. He gazed deeply into Finola's eyes, and suddenly knew he couldn't breathe another breath until he did the unthinkable. Something he had told himself he would never do—but did now.

He kissed her.

CHAPTER EIGHT

*H*IS LIPS TOUCHED *hers* . . .
Finola had not expected this when she came into the house. Bertie had appeared, and she had given him a task and then couldn't help herself. She longed to see Cy again. She *needed* to see Cy.

She had made her way into the house, deciding to ask him if he would be returning to Belldale after his errands in the village or if she should send Bertie back to the hunting lodge after they had worked together this afternoon.

Instead, she had felt the air riddled with electricity between them.

And now his mouth was on hers—and the most delicious sensations rippled through her.

Finola wasn't certain what she was supposed to do. Lord Crofton's few kisses had been light, brief, and chaste, and his body had not even brushed hers. Cy had slipped his arms about her as his lips moved over hers, his warmth enveloping her. She placed her palms against his chest and found it hard as a stone wall. She refused to wonder why he kissed her, not wishing for the doubts from long ago, which had plagued her for all these years, to ruin this magic moment. Cy's lips caressed hers, and then his tongue swept across her bottom lip, as if he tasted her. The thought intrigued Finola.

And she wanted to taste him, too.

Tentatively, she moved her own tongue along his lower lip and heard a deep groan emerge from him. He held her more tightly, and his own tongue teased her mouth open. His next move was unexpected and yet brought incredible sensations to her.

His tongue slipped inside her mouth. It swept through her mouth leisurely, exploring her without rushing. Every nerve within her body stood on alert as a marvelous tingling swept through her.

This was heaven . . .

Suddenly, he broke the kiss and moved his head from her, still holding her to him possessively.

"I must apologize, Finola," he said, his voice husky. "I do not know what came over me." He paused, his one green eye searching her face as if it hunted for some answer to a question he had yet to ask. Then he said, "No, I knew what I was doing. And I still want to kiss you."

His arms fell away from her, leaving her bereft. Desperate, she clutched the lapels of his coat when he tried to turn away from her. Their gazes met.

"I don't want you to stop, Cy. I want you to kiss me again."

Finola had never made such a daring statement and was afraid Cy would be too much of a gentleman and leave her now. She would do whatever it took to prevent that from happening. With a boldness she did not know she even possessed, Finola yanked hard on the coat she grasped, his mouth crashing down on hers. Once more, his arms encircled her, holding her flush against his hard, muscular body. He did not hide his hunger for her and in fact, celebrated it. Finola opened to him—to this unknown world—and he kissed her with a sense of desperation, mingled with desire. She knew the combination because she felt the same. It was as if she had been set adrift at sea many years ago, alone and with no hope.

Until this man appeared in her life, making her think hope still existed.

She learned from him as they kissed, mimicking what he did to her, hoping he found as much pleasure in it as she did. Finola could not have said how long the kiss went on, only that it was the greatest moment of her life. When Cy broke the contact between them, he rested his brow against hers as they both panted like one of her dogs after a long run.

She kept her eyes closed, reveling in his nearness. His warmth. His scent.

Finally, he lifted his head from hers, and she opened her eyes, smiling up at him.

"I should not have done that," he said lightly. "But I would do it a thousand times more."

His words caused her face to flush. "I would be a most willing participant for each of those thousand kisses," she told him.

Finola had always been one to keep her feelings to herself. Her father had not liked her and had been quick to anger anytime she was near him. His behavior toward her had trained Finola to contain her emotions within her. Even all those years spent with Banny, relaxing ones in which she knew she was loved, she always held back. The one time she had not done so was when she had made herself vulnerable to Viscount Crofton. Once that disaster occurred, coupled with Banny's sudden and unexpected death, she had retreated inside herself, building a wall so strong that no one would ever breach it.

Until now.

It wasn't as much as Cy had knocked those walls down as it had been her willingness to open the gates to him. To open her world to new possibilities. Still, the lessons from yesteryear lingered in the forefront of her mind, and she was afraid to voice how she truly felt to this man.

"I am going to release you, Finola," he said.

She nodded in agreement, and he did so but still remained so near to her that she could feel the heat emanating from him.

"I had hoped to be your friend," he told her. "A good friend. I hope I have not ruined that with my actions now."

She asked, "You apologized for kissing me. Do you regret having done so?"

He smiled wryly. "How could I regret the most wonderful moment in my life?"

His hand came to her face, his knuckles caressing her cheek as she absorbed what he had said.

"I do not know what the future holds for me, Finola. I cannot commit to you at this time, despite what we just did."

"I appreciate your honesty, Cy, and I am not expecting a commitment from you. I know you still need to find your place in the world. You should continue on that journey and see where it leads you. When you do find what you wish to do, then we might speak again."

He shook his head. "I should offer for you now. That would be the gentlemanly thing to do."

"No one witnessed our kiss," she assured him. "I will speak to no one of it. I meant what I said, Cy. You are at loose ends and need to discover how you wish to spend the rest of your life. Before, your future had been planned out for you, and you did not have to even think about it. Now, however, things are quite different. I will not hold you to any kind of commitment to me, other than the friendship we have established."

"You are as kind as you are beautiful." He stroked her cheek a final time and then his hand fell to his side. "You are a good and wise woman, Finola. I am blessed to count you among my friends." He sighed. "You and Bertie are my only friends now. I left behind boyhood friends years ago when I left England to go to war and haven't a clue what happened to any of them. I did make some friends among my fellow officers over the years but doubt I will ever be in their company again."

She smiled. "So, you count an eight-year-old servant and a female dog trainer as your entire circle of friends."

Cy chuckled. "I do—and I find they are the best friends I will ever have."

The mood lightened now, Finola asked, "Will you return to Belldale after you go into Adderly? Or will you go back to Melrose? I thought to ask so I would know whether or not to keep Bertie here or send him home to you."

"I will come here again once I am done if that is agreeable to you."

"I would like that," she said. "I never work with the pups once teatime arrives each day. I think it important to give myself a break from them. If you would like, you and Bertie are welcome to stay for tea this afternoon."

"I will be happy to be back from the village by then."

He took her hands in his and lifted them to his lips, pressing a fervent kiss against her knuckles. "Thank you for accepting me as I am now, Finola. A former soldier. A broken man. One who searches for who he is to become."

His words touched her deeply and she, in turn, lifted their joined hands and pressed her own kiss upon his knuckles.

"Thank you for befriending me, Cy. I have lived in this area my entire life but other than Banny, I have never truly been close to anyone. It is nice to have a friend I can count on. A friend I trust."

They gazed at one another, and Finola understood there were still unanswered questions between them. For now, though, she was satisfied with where their relationship stood. He was in no state to commit a lifetime to her, and she wasn't sure she wanted that. She would let the weeks and months unfold and hopefully see if she had a future with this man.

⤜⤛⤛

CY BID BERTIE farewell, promising the boy he would return, and went to the stable. Finola had offered him use of her horse so that he didn't have to walk into Adderly and back again. It would save him considerable time. He went into the barn and became acquainted with the horse, saddling it and noting the saddle was one a man would use and not a sidesaddle. He supposed when Finola did ride she did so astride since she dressed in a masculine fashion. The thought should have bothered him. Instead, he was more tempted by her because her breeches showed off her rounded bottom and slender legs. Cy could imagine being in bed with her, his hands cupping and kneading her buttocks, her legs locked around him.

He shrugged off the sensual image as he grew hard.

Finola needed to remain as forbidden fruit for now. Impulse had led him to kiss her. He had tried to do the gentlemanly thing and step away after the kiss, but she had pulled him to her, and he simply could not resist. The scent of lavender still filled his nostrils as he mounted the horse and turned it toward Adderly.

She had told him about the village and its residents. Guilt filled him. He should have told her he was born here and quite familiar with the area. Yet he still had a nagging feeling that Finola would skitter away like a feral cat if she learned his true identity.

He reached town and went straightaway to Mr. Timmon. Entering the tailor's shop, he greeted the man by name.

Mr. Timmon squinted at him, as if trying to establish how he knew the stranger in his shop.

"It is Lord Cyrus Cressley, Mr. Timmon," he revealed. "Have I changed that much?"

The tailor broke into a huge smile. "Lord Cyrus! How long has it been? Why, the last time I saw you, I prepared a wardrobe for you to go off to university."

"I do believe I was one of the best-dressed students at Cambridge." Then he sobered. "I have returned from the war, Mr. Timmon, and am now living at the hunting lodge at Melrose for now."

Cy held his arms out. "As you can see, I am wearing the only clothes I could find that came close to fitting me as I left Spain. I am in need of your services."

"I can certainly take care of you, my lord. First, though, we must measure you. Though I still have your previous measurements in my ledger, it looks as if you have grown even taller and broader than the last time you were in my shop. You left here a boy—and have become a man."

The tailor assisted Cy in shedding his tailcoat, and soon new measurements were recorded. Mr. Timmon began mentioning all that he would make up for Cy.

"No, I am not going to town and doubt I will socialize much here. That is far too many items. I am still waiting for the return of my commission, which is what I will be living on. I can pay you a little now, Mr. Timmon, and the rest once the sale of my commission comes in. For now, though, I need but a quarter of what you have mentioned and none of the formal evening wear."

"I see," the tailor said. "Well, I know you are good for the funds, Lord Cyrus. Let us come look at some fabrics now and see what you might like."

He shook his head. "No, that is unnecessary. I never consulted with you before because you have impeccable taste, Mr. Timmon. Make up what we've agreed upon in whatever materials you see fit. When might I stop in for a fitting?"

"I can send word to Melrose, my lord, and let you know."

"Remember, I am not staying with His Grace and have been given use of the hunting lodge. I do not wish to inconvenience His Grace or any of the Melrose servants."

"Why don't you return in a week's time, then, my lord? We can fit you for what is finished then."

"I will see you in a week's time then, Mr. Timmon. It was good seeing you again."

Cy went two doors down and entered Mr. Simon's shop, the largest in the village. He recognized the owner, who hadn't changed much and was speaking with a customer. Cy browsed the aisles, placing a few things in a basket he had claimed by the door, including a bilboquet for Bertie.

Mr. Simon completed his sale, and Cy gave a friendly nod to the woman who passed him, a curious look on her face.

As she left the store, he made his way to the counter and placed his purchases on it. "Good afternoon, Mr. Simon. I am—"

"Lord Cyrus!" Mr. Simon declared. "How good it is to see you." The shop owner frowned. "It looks as if you've been sent home from war with an injury."

"I was wounded. Shot in the head. I have lost the vision in one eye, but at least held on to the eye itself. The army surgeon who operated on me saved my life and believes my vision might return. Until then?" He shrugged. "I am the height of fashion with my eye patch."

"Always the joker," Mr. Simon said. "What have you here?" he asked, looking into the basket.

"A few things for the hunting lodge. His Grace has graciously given me the use of it."

The older man's face soured. "You are not staying at Melrose?"

"No. It was . . . inconvenient for His Grace," he said diplomatically.

Mr. Simon harumphed as he began removing items from the basket. "A toy, my lord?" He grasped the cup and tossed the wooden ball, attached to a string, up in the air, catching it in the cup.

"I have a young boy with me. My batman's son. He has been assisting me as I settle in." Cy pointed to his eye patch, not wanting to discuss the other eye's impaired vision. "I thought he might find it amusing."

"Ah," Mr. Simon said, nodding his head. "Will the boy return to his father anytime soon?"

"No. Briggs wanted a better life for his son than traipsing after the army. After all, who knows how long our war with Bonaparte will go on?"

They chatted for a few more minutes as Mr. Simon recorded Cy's purchases and gave him the total. He tried not to wince, knowing how these purchases would deplete his meager funds.

"Might I pay for half now and the other half later?" he inquired.

The shop owner smiled broadly. "Not a problem, my lord. You were an honest boy—and they become honest men. There isn't much here. I can simply include this on the monthly bill to His Grace."

"No," he said sharply, causing Mr. Simon to jump. Tempering his tone, he added, "I wish to not find myself indebted to my brother."

"Very well, my lord. Then I will establish a separate account for you. You may pay a portion of it at the end of each month."

"Let me pay you something now, and I will settle up with you in full once—"

"It is not necessary, my lord," the older man insisted, handing Cy the basket, which was full of his items. "Just bring the basket back the next time you come to shop. That is all I ask." Smiling, he added, "It is very good to have you home, my lord. I hope the boy likes his toy."

"Thank you," Cy said, moved by the shop owner's generosity.

He left the store, carrying the basket, and on his way out of the village couldn't help but stop and gaze into the window of Mrs. Carroll's bakery. He decided to step inside and purchase something for today's tea.

Opening the door, he spied Mrs. Carroll, who pursed her lips at him.

"If you hadn't come inside, my lord, I was about to go out and get you," she said, chuckling.

"Good afternoon, Mrs. Carroll," he greeted. "You were always so very good to me."

"Are you home for good, my lord?"

He pointed to the eye patch. "I am. It seems His Majesty's army doesn't need half-blind officers running about a battlefield."

They spoke for a few minutes, Mrs. Carroll catching him up on the gossip of the village, and then he said, "Do you have any of your lemon cakes? I have dreamed of those for years. I tried several different bakeries while studying at Cambridge, but no one's lemon cakes came close to yours."

She smiled, a pleased look on her face. "You are in luck, my lord. I have a few left. Baked them fresh this morning. How many do you want?"

She moved to where they were, and he saw three were left.

"I will take all three," he declared, thinking each of them might have one during tea today.

"Anything else?" Mrs. Carroll asked.

"Not today." He grinned. "But I will back for lemon cakes—and more—in the future."

She wrapped and handed them over.

"How much do I owe you?"

"Nothing," she proclaimed. "It is my welcome home gift to you."

"Ah, Mrs. Carroll, you have given me far too many free sweets over the years. Let me pay you for these now. The boy I was did not have the funds to do so, but the man I have become did earn a salary from His Majesty all these years."

"No," she said, crossing her arms before her. "I am just happy to have you home, my lord." She grinned. "Besides, I know one bite of my lemon cake, and you'll be back. I'll get my money from you on a regular basis."

They both laughed, and he thanked her, exiting the bakery and placing the cakes in the basket he carried. Cy returned to his horse and mounted it, taking up the reins and balancing the basket on his thigh.

It had been good to be back visiting with the people of Adderly again. He hadn't realized he had missed them. They were a link to his past, a fond one.

He turned the horse in the direction of Belldale, looking forward to sharing the lemon cakes.

And being in Finola's company.

CHAPTER NINE

FINOLA WATCHED CY ride off toward Adderly and then turned her attention back to Bertie.

"Cy told me how well you did at your lessons this morning. Are you ready for a different kind of lesson?"

"Like before? When you taught me different words to say to the dogs?"

"Yes, that's exactly right."

The boy grew thoughtful. "But don't they already know all the things you're going to teach me?"

She couldn't believe how perceptive the boy was for one so young. "That is true, but with dogs—especially pups such as these—reinforcement is the key not only to learning and then mastering a behavior. It is essential to making certain that behavior is never forgotten. Even if you were not here with me, I would be going over the same voice commands with the litter on a regular basis."

He nodded. "That makes sense. What do I need to do?"

"Banny taught me there are five commands that are considered the basics, ones which you teach a dog before anything else. Then you continually use those commands, giving them praise and reinforcing their good response to those commands with treats."

She went to the satchel that lay nearby on the ground and opened it, removing a sack with a strap upon it. Taking it to Bertie, she slipped it over his head so that the strap fell diagonally across his body, and the pouch hit him between his hip and knees.

"You'll wear this whenever you are working with the dogs. Inside, you will find tiny treats for them. They are what you use to encourage good behavior. And what is the one thing you never do when you are working with an English springer spaniel?"

Quickly, he said, "Don't scold them. They don't like that."

"That is correct. You may ignore them if they've behaved poorly. But dogs, especially this breed, never respond well to a raised voice. If you berate them and shout at them, they will grow fearful of you and withdraw."

"I promise I won't lose my temper, Finola."

She didn't think this sweet-natured boy could ever do so. "Just do your best. Now, what do you think are the basic commands we want our dogs to respond to?"

"Well, I know you've taught them their names, and they should come when you call them. That's one. And sit and stay are two and three." He paused, thinking a moment. "Heel. You always use that when we begin to walk. But that's only four. What's the other one?"

"You left out down. Some trainers use lie down, but I have had more success keeping with one-word commands."

Finola went to the dog run and called for Athena and Apollo. They were the brightest of the litter and caught on quickly to commands. The two came running, and she let them out from the pen.

"Call them to you, Bertie."

The boy did so, and she followed after them. "These two are very smart. Walk several paces away from us and then call for one of them. Take them through the five commands."

He did so, summoning Athena, who quickly responded to each command. Bertie rewarded her and Finola called the dog to her so that Bertie could work with Apollo. The pup responded to Bertie well, and she led Athena over to the pair when Bertie had gone through all the commands.

"Nice work!" Finola praised. "I actually have a sixth command that I teach after those five. It is a very hard one to teach and difficult for a young pup to master. These two have, however."

Quickly, she explained the principal of leave it, where a treat that appeals to a dog is placed on the ground—and they are commanded *not* to touch it.

"This is a very difficult behavior for a pup to learn, Bertie. They want that treat more than anything and have to sit and look at it. Do you like sweets?"

He grinned. "Mum says I've got a sweet tooth. I'm mad for anything with a bit of sugar in it."

"Then think of your favorite sweet sitting on the table in front of you. It is close enough for you to pick it up. The smell wafts to your nose, tickling and teasing it. Your eyes focus on it. Would it be hard to simply sit in front of it and not grab it?"

"It would, Finola."

"It is the same for these pups. Shall we try that behavior?"

She called Athena to her side and motioned for Bertie to test Apollo. The boy placed a treat next to his foot, and the dog inched toward it.

"Leave it," Bertie said, never taking his eyes off the dog, just as Apollo was focusing on the treat less than two paw lengths away from him.

"Leave it," the lad said again when Apollo grew twitchy and wiggled his bottom.

"Good, Bertie. You saw him moving and anticipated. That takes instinct and practice."

Keeping his eyes on Apollo, Bertie asked, "How long to I have to make him wait?"

"Long enough to test him. A minute at this age. No longer than that. It is almost that now. Pick up the treat, and place it in your palm."

Bertie did as requested.

"Tell him he's a good dog and award the treat."

The boy stroked Apollo's head with his left hand, and said, "Good dog," as he offered the treat in his right. The pup gobbled it down, and Bertie praised him again. Bertie's way with the dogs wasn't something that could be taught. The boy simply had a natural instinct on what to do and say. A person could be taught how to train dogs, but Bertie's gut would take him far. If he chose to work with Finola after he finished caring for Cy, she believed he might become one of the premier dog trainers in all of England.

But she wouldn't push him now. His loyalties lay with Cy. When the time came for the boy to make a decision, though, she would encourage him to work with her.

"Try now with Athena," she suggested.

Bertie went through the paces with Athena, who gracefully nibbled the treat from Bertie's hand when she was allowed to do so.

They then took turns removing dogs from the dog run and letting Bertie work with each of them on the basic commands. All but Pollux and Triton successfully demonstrated all six behaviors correctly. Triton almost mastered leave it, but snatched the treat seconds before Bertie gave him the command to do so.

"That's all right," she assured the lad. "Triton merely anticipated what you would say. That is not necessarily a bad thing at this stage."

As for Pollux, his natural curiosity did not allow him to even think about leaving the treat alone. Bertie was frustrated and turned his back as Finola suggested.

"Ignoring Pollux will hurt him far more than you shouting at him," she said. "Of all this litter, Pollux is the most inquisitive—and the one who can get his feelings hurt more than the others."

The pup came around to Bertie and bumped the boy's leg several times.

"No, do not look at Pollux," she warned. "Being indifferent to him will teach him."

Although the boy ignored Pollux, Finola could see it was difficult for him.

"Speak to him gently now. Have him heel, and place him back in the dog run."

Bertie did as asked, Pollux happily sticking close to the boy's leg. He placed the dog inside the pen.

"How did the training go?"

She turned and saw Cy approaching. Immediately, Finola's mouth grew dry, and her heart slammed against her ribs in anticipation. She could still feel his mouth on hers. His tongue stroking hers. His rock-hard body flush against her soft one.

Swallowing, she waved. "Very well, Cy." Looking to Bertie, she said, "I think we are done for the day. We can wash up at the water pump over there."

Bertie ran to Cy. "I have to wash for tea. Finola says we are through training now."

"Very good. I cannot wait to hear about your adventures with the pups."

Finola joined Cy. "You have a full basket."

"I did a bit of shopping. I even stopped at the bakery for lemon cakes that we can have for tea."

"Oh, Mrs. Carroll makes the most heavenly lemon cakes. Thank you for bringing them, Cy. I haven't had one in some time."

"Thank you for the loan of your horse. I rubbed him down and fed him a bit of oats just now. Riding him saved me a good deal of time."

"Were you able to see Mr. Timmon and be measured for some new clothes?"

He eyed her. "Are you saying you are tired of seeing me in what I now wear?"

She realized he was teasing her. "As a matter of fact, I am. I hope your new clothes will be made up soon."

"I am to return in a week's time for a fitting."

"Mr. Timmon does excellent work."

"I will take Bertie with me to my fitting. I want the tailor to create some things for him, as well as for me. I would have had Bertie accompany me today, but he was so eager to be with you."

"You mean the dogs. He did a wonderful job, Cy. He has good instincts and an even temperament. If he chooses to do so, he would make for a fine dog trainer. Here, let me wash up, as well, and then we can go inside for tea."

She did so and they went into the house and to Banny's study. She still thought of the room as her guardian's, despite the fact he had been gone seven years now.

"Oh, I didn't think. There are only two seats in here. I have my tea here every day. We should go into the parlor. I so rarely have guests, I suppose I am out of practice with entertaining."

They accompanied her to the parlor, and Cy handed over the wrapped cloth with the lemon cakes inside.

Finola accepted them and said, "I will take these to Cook so she can include them in the tea she is preparing for us."

Going to the kitchens, she passed the baked goods to Gilly and asked for them to be part of the tea which would be served in the parlor.

"Ooh, Mrs. Carroll's lemon cakes," the maid said as she un-wrapped the cloth. "They make my mouth water."

"Since there are three here, take one and you and Cook split it for your tea."

"Oh, thank you, my lady."

Finola stilled as Gilly addressed her. She had not used her title with Cy and wondered if he might think differently about her if he knew she was the daughter of an earl, one who worked for her living. It shouldn't matter. Either they would stay friends, or they wouldn't. She couldn't help who she was and what her origins were, much less the fact she needed to earn her living in order to pay for Belldale's upkeep and her two servants.

Still, she waited in the kitchens as Gilly and Cook placed items on a tray, and then Finola offered to take the tray in herself, sweeping it up.

"I can do that, my lady," the maid protested.

"I know you can. Stay here an enjoy that lemon cake while I go entertain my guests."

She had told her two servants that a former army officer and his young servant would be using the schoolroom in the mornings for the foreseeable future. She had not introduced the pair to Cy and Bertie, though.

Entering the room, Cy leaped to his feet and met her, taking the tray in his hands.

"Where do wish me to put it?"

She indicated a table. "Here will be nice. We can gather around it."

Bertie's eyes grew large. "Look at all the food!" he exclaimed.

"I have a rather hearty tea each day," she admitted. "I am always so hungry after a day's work with the dogs. Tea is really my biggest meal. At night, I usually have soup and bread, and that is enough to fill my belly until the next morning."

Finola poured out for them. She thought Bertie might like a cup of milk and had brought one for him, but the boy said he preferred tea.

"Mum says tea soothes the soul. I like the tea in England. We had tea in Spain, but it didn't taste like this."

"Make up a plate for yourself, Bertie," she encouraged. "Have as much as you'd like. You, too, Cy."

He took a plate and began placing items on it, then he frowned. "I only see two lemon cakes. I could have sworn I had bought three."

"You did. I gave one to Cook and Gilly to split for their tea."

His gaze met hers, and she saw approval.

"You are indeed extremely kind, Finola. Why don't the two of us split one of the lemon cakes? That way we both can have some—and Bertie will not have to share."

"Oh, I have had Mrs. Carroll's lemon cakes before. I want you to take it all."

An odd look crossed Cy's face. It was there for but a moment and then gone.

"If you insist," he said quietly.

They filled their plates and had a most enjoyable tea together. Bertie told Cy all about the five crucial commands and how he had practiced them with each pup. Then he explained the sixth one and how two of the dogs had yet to master that behavior.

"They will," he said, nodding to himself. "They are good pups and will learn to listen to Finola and me."

She was touched that Bertie already thought of them as a team, working together just as she had apprenticed under Banny. She looked to Cy and saw that he, too, was aware of the same thing.

Cy then told them about what he had done in the village, leaning down to the basket and producing a bilboquet.

"I found something you might like at Mr. Simon's store. I had one of these as a boy and enjoyed playing with it."

He demonstrated to the boy how to hold the cup and toss the ball into the air, catching it in the cup.

"Thank you, sir. Thank you so much."

Cy handed over the toy, and Bertie asked if he could play with it now.

"Away from the tea things," Finola cautioned. "Move over to the center of the room."

Bertie did so, joyfully tossing the ball up in the air and trying to catch it.

"That was very thoughtful of you, Cy."

"I spent hours playing with mine when I was a child. I have never seen Bertie with a toy. When I spotted it as I browsed the general store, I knew I simply had to buy it for him."

"A toy and dogs. What more could a boy want?" she asked, smiling as she watched Bertie.

A sudden pang hit Finola. She had never thought to have children of her own. Never thought she would pass down the skills she had learned from Banny. Now, though, a deep yearning filled her, one which asked to be filled. To have children, though, she must first have a husband. She had shied away from the thought of marriage after Lord Crofton had made an utter fool of her, along with his rakish friends.

Yet here with her now was a good man. A quiet one. One who was damaged from his time at war. Could she help make Cy whole again? Would he truly consider a life with her?

Just as patience was required in dog training, Finola would need to exercise massive amounts of it now, especially after her last conversation in private with Cy. He still had much to work out, becoming accustomed to a life that was unfamiliar with him. But the kisses she had shared with Cy had made her heart sing. The thought of spending a lifetime with this man, loving him, bearing his children, made her almost weep.

Finola blinked away the tears forming in her eyes and turned to him. "More tea, Cy?"

CHAPTER TEN

A WEEK HAD passed. It had been the happiest of Finola's life. She had always found her work with her dogs rewarding, but had not realized how solitary a life she had led ever since Banny's passing. Being around Cy and Bertie made her look forward to each day. The boy was simply joyful in every task he took on and was a delight to teach and work with. She had moved on, teaching him hand commands after the voice ones. Now, all it took was a raised hand from Bertie and a dog would stay, or two claps and the dog would come to him.

They had continued working on those basic commands with the litter but had progressed to things such as agility training, which required conditioning, concentration, and a sense of teamwork between human and canine. This type of training built up a dog's endurance, which would be useful when they began hunting. They had great success with fade the lure, as well. The pups were getting old enough now to work on their eventual roles of flushing game and retrieving it for their masters. It was extremely helpful that she had others to help train this litter. The pups caught on faster because they spent more time with an individual. This first group produced by Zeus and Hera would be the most successful to date.

As for being around Cy, just looking at him brought happiness to Finola. Not only was he excellent with the dogs and Bertie, but he was a pleasure to be around. Interesting. Funny.

And extremely nice to look at.

She had spent hours thinking about the kisses they had shared and wondered when the next might come. She had even done what Lord Crofton had accused her of so many years ago, taking her pillow and kissing it, pretending it was Cy. She had dreamed of him almost every night this past week, awaking with her body flushed with heat, aching to be held in his arms once more.

Today they had reversed their schedule, and Cy and Bertie would be working with her and the litter this morning because he was scheduled to return to Adderly this afternoon for a fitting with Mr. Timmon. He wanted to take Bertie along to have new clothes made up for the growing boy.

When Bertie had been told of the outing, he begged the two of them to allow him to skip his lessons in the schoolroom just this once so that he wouldn't miss out on working with the pups. Cy had readily agreed, citing Bertie's progress as nothing short of amazing. He told Finola how Bertie knew both his upper- and lower-case letters and drew them with precision on his slate. Bertie's vocabulary was growing, and he was learning to form many one-syllable words, such as can, man, and ran. Yesterday, Cy had stressed blends with him, and the boy had moved from words such as mop to drop, flop, and stop. Finola had even sat in for an hour of their lessons and was thrilled at the progress Bertie made.

Cy's lessons continued outside the schoolroom, as well. While Finola was teaching the child and man what she knew of dogs and how to handle them, Cy continued his job as tutor when they went on the long walks. With three of them, they would take out the entire litter of eight pups and even Zeus and Hera at the same time. On these excursions, Cy would talk to Bertie about history. She had chimed in when she could when the lessons were about Greek mythology, which had been a favorite topic of Banny's.

Cy's lessons went far beyond her knowledge, though. He had shared history and philosophy of the ancient Greeks on these walks, along with facts about ancient Rome. He had also started teaching the both of them the history of England and the British Isles. How it had started with the prehistoric era, including the Bronze and Iron Ages and the changes made when the Romans came to settle it. He talked of Hadrian's Wall and she longed to see it someday.

Yesterday, he had described in detail the invasion of the Normans into England and the crowning of William as the first Norman king of England. He said that line had died out, replaced by the Plantagenets and followed by others. She was shocked to learn in the previous century when George I came to the throne, he was not an Englishman, but a Hanoverian from a German state. Since Finola had never had any lessons in history, she was soaking up the information as much as Bertie. She hoped to hear more history today.

Finishing her breakfast, Finola went outside, finding Cy and Bertie already here, allowing the pups to leave the dog run two at a time to piddle after their breakfasts.

"Good morning," she called, and they returned her greeting.

Finola outlined what they would be working on this morning as she always liked them to have an overview of what the day's training sessions would involve.

Before they could start the dogs' lessons, however, she spied a carriage in the distance. As it approached, she saw it was the finest carriage she had ever seen and assumed it must belong to some duke.

Cy came to stand beside her and asked, "Did you have visitors planned for today?"

"No, I did not. Most likely, it is someone wanting one of my Honeyfield spaniels. This litter is spoken for, however, and there is even a waiting list for the next one."

Finola was not telling the entire truth. The current litter only had six of the pups reserved for members of the nobility. She had learned over time that sometimes pups were stillborn or they weren't strong and did not live beyond a few days or weeks. Once she knew the number of a litter, she kept two of those pups in reserve in case there was a death among them. Hera's first litter had been exceptionally hale, however. While she planned to keep Athena and breed her in a couple of years, it still left one of the pups available to be sold.

"I will go see what our visitors want."

She told Cy and Bertie what to work on during her brief absence and then headed toward the carriage. She wished to meet the carriage alone because she knew the visitors would refer to her as Lady Finola. She could not say why she was still hiding her social status from Cy and fully intended to reveal more of her background to him when the proper moment occurred.

The footman on the vehicle's back jumped to the ground and approached her, a folded parchment in hand.

"I need to deliver this to Lady Finola Honeyfield."

"I am she." Finola held out her hand for the parchment.

The footman's eyes swept up and down her, obviously noting her manner of dress, but he recovered quickly.

"Of course, my lady."

She broke the seal and read the contents.

My dear Lady Finola –

I have heard marvelous things about your Honeyfield spaniels and wish to purchase one immediately. I would ask that you come to Stonecrest at your earliest convenience and bring one of your dogs with you. Normally, my wife and I would come to you—but she is heavy with child and due to give birth in late April. Although we live but ten miles from you, I do not wish for her to be jostled about in a carriage in her delicate condition.

If you would be so good as to let my footman know when you might visit us at Stonecrest, we will send a carriage for you and eagerly await your visit.

Finola knew the Duke of Stoneham's name and had heard a bit of gossip about him. Stoneham had not come from the gentry. In fact, he had been a shopkeeper when he learned he was a duke. She did not know the entire story since Stonecrest was ten miles from Belldale and its inhabitants did their shopping in Gramsby, the village closest to them, not Adderly.

She owed this duke nothing and looked to the footman, saying, "My current litter is spoken for, as well as half of the next. Please inform His Grace that I will write to him in the future, once that litter is born, and see if he is still interested in one of my Honeyfield spaniels. Thank you," she said dismissively, turning around to return to her dogs.

She heard the carriage door opening and a deep voice called, "Wait!"

Turning, she saw an imposing man leap to the ground and stride toward her. As he drew near, she was drawn in by his ice-blue eyes and dimple in his chin.

"I thought you might say that, Lady Finola. That is why I decided to come in person and hope to sway you. I am the Duke of Stoneham."

He might be elegantly dressed, but there was an air about this man, as if he were still rough around the edges, showing his working-class roots. He looked extremely strong. Not from boxing at Gentleman Jackson's but from physical labor. She actually liked him more for it.

Suddenly, Cy appeared at her elbow and asked, "Is there something I might help you with?"

The duke turned his gaze to Cy and said, "I am Stoneham. From your ramrod posture, I gather you have served in His Majesty's army."

"I did," Cy said bluntly. "I was Lieutenant-General Cressley."

"It is a pleasure to make your acquaintance, Cressley, and I thank you for your service to our king and country."

"Why are you here?" Cy demanded, his tone neutral and yet threatening at the same time.

"My duchess carries our first child," Stoneham said, his voice softening as he spoke of his wife. "She has always longed to have a dog and wants to bring up our children with dogs in the household as pets. I came here because Honeyfield spaniels have the best reputation far and wide. Not only as excellent hunters of game and fowl, but as dogs with pleasant dispositions."

The duke turned back to Finola. "This dog will not be a hunter. Instead, it will be a family member." He grinned, his harsh features softening, making him even more handsome. "I am sure my duchess will pamper the beast. I know Honeyfield spaniels are also good guard dogs. I want my children always looked after and kept safe."

Finola found herself liking this man quite a bit. "I would like to meet Her Grace if I could."

The duke gave her a wry smile. "You want to inspect the both of us? I believe we will pass muster. Nalyssa charms everyone she meets. Even a rough and tumble character such as me."

The love for his wife shone in this man's eyes, and Finola knew that her pup would go to a good home.

"I may actually have one dog in the current litter which is unspoken for. Although I do have a list of waiting names, Your Grace, it is for hunters and not pets."

"Might I persuade you to accompany me now so you could meet my wife? I do not expect you to bring the dog with you. I want you to meet the two of us and see our household before you commit to us."

She looked to Cy. "Would you and Bertie continue with this morning's training while I accompany His Grace to Stonecrest?"

"I can do so—or I can go with you."

She liked that he felt protective of her. "I think your time would be better spent with Bertie and the pups."

"If that is what you wish." He turned to the duke. "It was an honor to meet you, Your Grace."

"Likewise, Lieutenant-General Cressley."

Cy shook his head. "It is plain Cressley now, Your Grace. My military days are long behind me. If you will excuse me."

Finola watched Cy stride away, and she turned to the duke. "If you will give me a few minutes, Your Grace, I will change into more appropriate attire."

"That is unnecessary, Lady Finola. In fact, Nalyssa will be delighted to see you dressed in such a manner. Come with me now and meet her—and I will have you back with your dogs by noon."

"All right," she agreed.

She accompanied him to his grand ducal carriage. Seeing them coming, the footman quickly put down stairs, and the duke handed her up, joining her inside the vehicle.

"I have heard nothing but good things about you, my lady, and the dogs you train. One of my neighbors has a Honeyfield spaniel. That is where my duchess got the idea of having a guard dog and companion for our children."

"You are certainly planning ahead, Your Grace, since your firstborn has yet to arrive."

The duke smiled broadly. "Oh, we plan to have many children. And they will be brought up in love. My mother raised my sister and me. You might have heard some of the local gossip. I do not hide the fact that we came from the working class. Mama and Pen owned and ran a millinery shop, while my haberdashery was next door and catered to gentlemen of the *ton* and even those of the middle class. I only recently became the Duke of Stoneham, which was quite the surprise to me. Nalyssa worked with men such as me—clerks, doctors, and others outside of the *ton*—who suddenly found themselves members of it. I learned quite a bit from her."

His smile softened. "And that included learning I could not live without her."

Finola sighed inwardly. "I do believe that is the most romantic thing I have ever heard, Your Grace."

"Nalyssa has brought things out in me that I never knew were hidden within. I do know that life is better with love in it. She is my soulmate—and I will love her until the end of time."

The duke's words moved her. Finola wondered if she were capable of such an all-consuming love. Thinking of Cy, she decided she definitely was—and only prayed when he found himself that he, too, could imagine a life with her by his side.

CHAPTER ELEVEN

A s THE DUKE of Stoneham handed Finola down, she saw that
Stonecrest was a handsome property, the house the largest she
had ever seen. Then again, she had yet to catch sight of the Duke of
Margate's home. Perhaps one day Cy might walk her and Bertie about
Melrose so that she could get a glimpse of his relative's ducal seat.

Stoneham led Finola inside, where they were greeted by a butler.

"Her Grace is in her sitting room, Your Grace," the butler informed his master.

"This way, my lady," the duke said, taking her to the sitting room
and gently knocking on the door before entering.

"My love, I have brought Lady Finola Honeyfield home with me,"
he announced, leading Finola across the room to where the duchess
sat in a large chair, her feet propped upon a padded footstool.

Stoneham bent and brushed his lips not against his wife's cheek
but her lips, causing Finola to blush. She was unused to seeing any
affection between married couples of the *ton* but thought it a good
thing.

Even seated, it was obvious to see the duchess was a tall woman.
Her auburn hair was gathered on the sides with jeweled combs, which
kept her hair away from her face, showing off the woman's excellent
bone structure. Her sapphire eyes were vivid, and Finola thought
immediately that their children would all have some shade of blue

eyes.

The duchess smiled up at her husband. "You are a miracle worker, Pierce. I had no idea you would bring Lady Finola home with you." She smiled at Finola, offering her hand. "I am delighted to meet you, my lady. Please forgive me for not rising. It takes forever to stand these days, and I am so comfortable right now."

"No apology is necessary, Your Grace," she said, taking the duchess' hand. "I understand you will give birth soon."

"Late April is what the midwife tells me, so about ten weeks." Rubbing her belly, the duchess added, "I hope she is wrong and that this little one comes sooner. We are so eager to meet him."

"Or her," interjected the duke. To Finola, he said, "I am hoping for a girl. My duchess thinks, though, that she carries a boy."

Again, this duke surprised her. Most titled men, especially dukes, wished for their firstborn to be male and their heir apparent.

"We truly wish for a healthy babe, male or female," Her Grace said. "If it is a boy, then hopefully I will produce a girl the next time."

The duke laced his fingers through his wife's. "I am going to leave the two of you to chat. Lady Finola and I had plenty of time to do so in the carriage."

He lifted his wife's hand and kissed it, his eyes burning with hunger. Finola found the couple to be infinitely fascinating.

"Shall I have tea sent up?" the duke asked.

"Yes, darling. Please do so."

Once Stoneham left, the duchess said, "Oh, please, have a seat, my lady. I did not mean to leave you standing. Sit in that chair if you would. I can see you better that way."

She took a seat, and the duchess said, "You look so comfortable in the clothing you wear. I envy you for fitting into breeches like that. Is it easier to train your spaniels dressed in such a manner?"

"It is why I dress this way, Your Grace," she replied. "I can move with ease. Bend. Sit on the ground and play a bit with my pups."

"Tell me about them," the duchess urged.

Finola shared how her current litter was the first for Zeus and Hera and how she had named each of their offspring after Greek gods and goddesses.

"They are seven months now and have mastered their basic behaviors. I have started their additional training recently, teaching them the things they will need to know to become good hunters of both fowl and prey."

"How long have you been training dogs?"

"Almost my entire life."

She explained how she had been orphaned at a young age and had come to live with Sir Roscoe Banfield, who trained dogs for a living.

"He was the best of guardians, educating me in academics and the care and training of dogs, as well. I lost him seven years ago and have continued his work. Banny used to train various breeds, but I have chosen to exclusively work with English springer spaniels because of their nature and intelligence."

"Yes, we have heard of Honeyfield spaniels, my lady. You have quite the reputation." The duchess paused. "Might you have any pups that we could take on at present? I would love to do so before our child arrives. I would like the dog to have time to acclimate to us and Stonecrest before the babe comes."

"His Grace said you were looking more for a pet, one whom your children could play with, and a dog who would protect them."

"Yes, that is correct. Pierce has never hunted a day in his life. He was a laborer for several years, saving money so that he might open his own haberdashery. It is a long, convoluted story, but he actually became a duke a little over a year ago. I was hired to train him, so to speak. It was what I did for a living."

"You *earned* your own living?"

Her Grace smiled confidently. "I most certainly did. You see, my father, the Earl of Starling, was a gambler. A charming man who lost his entire fortune and couldn't face what he had done—so he killed himself."

Finola gasped. "I am sorry," she apologized, a bit taken aback by the openness of the duchess.

"No need to be. We were not close. Unfortunately, *his* scandal became my own. Polite Society rejected me—until I turned my cousin, the new Lord Starling, into proper *ton* material. Suddenly, I had a reputation to uphold, and I earned my living preparing men who had unexpectedly come into a title, training them and polishing their ways so that they might take their place as a member of Polite Society."

She could have listened to the duchess speak all day. The woman's voice was cultured, and she was most charming and down-to-earth.

"I was all about business, Lady Finola. A practical woman who had no room for love in my life. I never let others grow close to me. I was focused and direct. A survivor. I had to be—because I had no other choice."

The duchess paused when a maid brought in a tray of tea, pouring out for the two of them and then leaving the room. The duchess picked up her story.

"Then my life changed radically. I met a quick-witted, intelligent man who didn't suffer fools. He was loyal and loving to his family and did not trust outsiders. He was a most reluctant duke, one who did not wish to join the *ton*." She smiled. "Pierce absolutely stole my heart. I polished him as one would a diamond in the rough and thought he would make an excellent match with a well-bred lady of society."

"But he chose *you*," Finola said, her heart telling her that the pair was meant to be together.

The duchess sighed. "I like to think we chose one another."

If she'd had any doubts before, this woman had dispelled them.

"I think you and His Grace are perfectly suited for one another and will make for excellent parents."

"Thank you, my lady. I have had a late start, marrying at my advanced age. I will turn thirty this year, and we are hoping to have as many children as we can. I have come to love the country and see us spending a good deal of our time here. I wish for my children to have dogs. Not hunting dogs but ones they can love. Dogs who will be their companion and best friend."

"I believe I have the perfect pup for your family, Your Grace. His name is Pollux. He is a very smart dog and quite playful and affectionate. He is curious, though, so you will have to keep a close watch on him at first in order to keep him from mischief."

"Pollux sounds lovely," the duchess declared. "He will spend most of his days with me for the time being. I don't go far afield."

"He will need to be exercised regularly, Your Grace."

Finola detailed how often and how far the pup should be walked each day, sharing how Pollux excelled at the commands he had been taught and how he was eager to please.

"Pierce will enjoy walking Pollux. I will join him once I am able to do more than waddle," the duchess teased. "When might we claim Pollux?"

"How about tomorrow morning? His Grace said that he would send a carriage. I could bring Pollux to you, along with a few toys. It would give me time to write out detailed instructions as to his feeding and care. I will also make a list of commands he is familiar with and has mastered. I use both voice and hand gestures and hope you will keep to those. I could demonstrate them when we arrive tomorrow."

"Oh, this sounds wonderful, Lady Finola. I cannot thank you enough for giving us the opportunity to raise Pollux." She smiled, mischief in her eyes. "Perhaps we can add another dog to the household every time a child is born."

Finola laughed. "We should see how you do with Pollux, Your Grace. One Honeyfield spaniel might be enough for your family."

They talked another half-hour about a variety of topics. She liked how easy the other woman's manner was.

"It feels as if we are old friends," the duchess noted. "I cannot remember the last time I felt such a strong connection with another woman. You are not that far from us, Lady Finola. I do hope we will see each other on a regular basis."

Tears stung Finola's eyes. "I would like that very much, Your Grace."

The duchess grinned. "We are far from the social restraints of London. Why don't you call me Nalyssa?"

"That is a beautiful name, Your Grace."

"I hope it is one you will use often."

"Then you must call me Finola."

"I shall. Another very pretty name. Perhaps you can help me come up with a good name for our child. Do not tell Pierce—but I *do* believe I carry his daughter. I tease him all the time that it is a boy simply because he wants a girl this first time."

"I will work on male and female names, Nalyssa," she promised. "I am already used to coming up with names for each litter. I try for a theme, as this time with Greek gods and goddesses."

"What is next? Will you breed Zeus and Hera again soon?"

"I plan to do so and will start later this week. I am also keeping Athena from this litter. It will be two years before I can breed her, but she is even-tempered and highly intelligent, as well as the pup who has nurtured the others from their beginning. I think Athena will make for a wonderful mother when her time comes."

"Then I hope our second Honeyfield spaniel comes from Athena's first litter."

By the time the duke returned, they were laughing and chatting as old friends.

"I promised I would have Lady Finola home by noon," Stoneham said. "We should leave now if I am to keep to my word."

Finola reached over and took Nalyssa's hand. "It was a great pleasure to meet you."

The duchess' eyes misted. "I feel the same, Finola. I will see you again tomorrow morning."

"Ah, so we have a pup coming, do we?" the duke asked.

"We do," his wife assured him. "His name is Pollux, and you will be walking him twice a day."

"As long as I do not have to hunt with him. I enjoy getting out and walking for exercise. I look forward to having Pollux as my walking companion."

He bent and gave his wife a lingering kiss and then looked to Finola. "Ready to return to Belldale, my lady?"

"Yes, Your Grace."

The duke accompanied her outside and said, "My driver will take you home now. When would you like for my carriage to call for you in the morning?"

"Eight o'clock will do, Your Grace. You will both need to make yourselves available so I may demonstrate all of Pollux's behaviors and commands. It won't take long for you to catch on to things. And Pollux himself will help you."

He took Finola's hand. "Thank you, my lady. I see my duchess has taken to you. She could use a friend."

"As could I." She hesitated a moment and then said, "We have agreed not to stand on formality and address one another by our Christian names. While I do not expect to call you anything but Your Grace, I would ask that you call me Finola."

The duke nodded. "I will do it on one condition, Finola."

"What?"

"That you call me Pierce."

"Oh, I could not—"

"You most certainly can. I get enough of Your Grac-ing as it is. Frankly, I grow weary of it. If you are to be friends with my wife—and I believe you will be good friends—then please do not stand on ceremony, Finola. Would you agree to my request?" He smiled

112

charmingly. "After all, I am a duke. I believe dukes are supposed to get what they want."

Finola burst out in laughter. "Yes, I will stop Your Grac-ing you if you stop my lady-ing me."

His smile was genuine as he said, "My name is Pierce. Use it."

The duke handed her up and closed the carriage door. "Until to-morrow, my lady." He motioned to the driver and the vehicle began to roll.

Finola decided it would be fine now to bring Cy and Bertie with her tomorrow. It would be a good test of Bertie's growing skills. She would have the boy demonstrate the correct voice and hand commands for Their Graces. And it would give her an excuse to spend more time in Cy Cressley's company.

Without him worried about her being a lady.

CHAPTER TWELVE

C Y GAVE UP trying to work with the dogs and watched Bertie put them through their paces. He was having trouble concentrating because he could not stop thinking of Finola. He didn't like the fact that she had gone off with the Duke of Stoneham. Yes, she earned her living training spaniels for men such as Stoneham, but he was unhappy she'd had him stay behind. He couldn't help but feel protective of her.

That's when he knew that he loved her.

Obviously, he couldn't tell her he did so. He couldn't ask Finola to commit to him. Not in the current state he was in. Although his brother had loaned him the hunting lodge, for all intents and purposes Cy was homeless. He needed Parker to sell his commission and get the funds to him. He wished to take care of Finola and couldn't do so as a penniless, half-blind ex-soldier. They had left things between them after they'd kissed, both agreeing he needed to find himself.

He had done so. In a quiet way. Basking in the glow of happiness that Finola brought to him. Cy had thought he would need to regain his eyesight before approaching her again. Find a new occupation and purpose. Now, he realized it didn't matter if he could only see her with one eye. Being with her and working with her Honeyfield springer spaniels brought him satisfaction, more than even being an officer had.

Of course, even if Finola did agree to wed him, most likely she would wish to continue living at Belldale. He didn't know how he felt about being a kept man, while his wife was the homeowner and supported the two of them. He wanted to protect her not only physically—but financially. He had no idea how much she earned from her dog training. Still, if he could contribute to the household expenses with his income—pay the servants, purchase food and other necessities—then he would not mind staying at the manor house. Belldale was a small, beautiful property, and he would not want to take Finola from her home of so many years.

The more he thought about it, the more Cy realized that he did want to spend the rest of his life with Finola. But was that fair to her? He believed she could do much better than a broken-down man, injured physically and emotionally battered by his long years at war. Yet there was something between them. Not just the spark of physical attraction—but something that led him to believe they were soulmates. Cy determined to see the doctor today when he took Bertie into Adderly to see if the physician might spy something Dr. Sheffley had missed. If his eyesight could be restored, he might feel more like the confident man he had once been.

And more worthy of Finola.

He heard the carriage before he saw it, and his heart sped up in anticipation of seeing Finola again. He watched the ducal coach drive up to the manor house and stop. Cy began walking in that direction to meet Finola. She descended from the carriage with the footman's help, and Cy realized that Stoneham had not accompanied her back to Belldale. Relief washed through him. He didn't know why he had not wanted her in the duke's company—and then realized he knew exactly why he did not.

Jealousy.

The feeling had been previously unknown to him. He chided himself silently, knowing the duke was wed and had no interest in seducing Finola. Feeling ridiculous, he tamped down the jealousy, hoping she would never learn he had felt it.

Finola gave a wave to the driver, who shouted down, "I'll be back tomorrow at eight o'clock, my lady."

Hearing her addressed as my lady caused Cy to pause. Then he realized it was mere courtesy on the coachman's part, and he picked up his pace to meet Finola.

Looking at Finola Honeyfield was like breathing in clear, crisp, fresh morning air. He found it hard to believe a creature such as this could be interested in him.

"How was your visit to Stonecrest?" he asked.

She smiled, and the warmth from her smile filled him to the brim with happiness.

"It is a grand house. An absolutely lovely estate. More importantly, the duke and duchess are very gracious people."

"So, you found Her Grace to your liking?"

Her cheeks flushed. "I most certainly did. In fact, I believe we will become friends. Good friends. She envied me wearing my shirt and breeches and wished she could wear them herself. The duchess isn't anything like what I thought a duchess would be."

"What did you think she would be like?" he asked.

Finola shrugged. "I didn't truly know. I have never met a duchess before. She was a practical woman. Friendly. Amusing." She paused, a slow smile spreading across her lovely face. "In fact, she actually earned her living before she met the duke."

Inwardly, he gasped, thinking the duchess one of those rare, manipulative women—such as an actress—who sank her claws into a wealthy man of the *ton* and refused to let go. Concern filled him, and he did not want Finola to be on friendly terms with a woman such as this.

"She is like me," Finola continued. "Whereas I train dogs, she trained men."

Her remark puzzled him. "How so?"

"Nalyssa was touched by a bit of scandal."

Finola briefly explained the duchess' background and how she had lost her reputation through no fault of her own, but through the scandal her father had created with his suicide.

"Then she made a silk purse out of a sow's ear and turned her most unsuitable cousin, her father's heir, into a dignified member of Polite Society. Thus, her career was born."

"I am not certain I understand."

She laughed. "It seems that sometimes the most inappropriate men gain a title for themselves. Her husband is the best example of that situation. Nalyssa took men who had inherited titles and knew nothing of the ways of Polite Society and tutored them. Taught them, much as I train my pups, to fit into a certain place in a new world. She polishes them until they know the ways of the *ton* and can blend in effortlessly. This time, though, she fell in love with one of her clients."

"Stoneham."

"Yes, His Grace. Apparently, he was a most reluctant duke, and Nalyssa had to do everything she could to cram lessons down his throat, wheedling and cajoling him into behaving properly. She must be quite good at what she does, though, because Stoneham is a gentleman through and through now."

"You refer to the duchess as Nalyssa," he said. "I am curious as to why you do so."

Her cheeks filled with color, making her look quite appealing to him.

And kissable.

Cy shoved that thought deep into the recesses of his mind, swearing not to act on impulse again as he had before when he kissed her.

"It is most unusual, Cy, but we formed a lovely connection between us. Nalyssa does not stand on ceremony at all and begged me to call her by her first name. I think both of us were searching for a friend, whether we knew it or not."

"So, you like her enough to hand over one of your spaniels to her?"

"Yes, I have decided it will be Pollux. He is bright and inquisitive and very affectionate. I do not know if his tender heart would allow him to be a true hunter. I do believe he will make an excellent guard dog and companion to the Stoneham children, though. I am to take Pollux to Stonecrest tomorrow morning when the carriage returns for me at eight o'clock. I know this disrupts your tutoring schedule, but I would like for you and Bertie to accompany me to Stonecrest. I want Bertie to be the one to put Pollux through his paces and teach the duke and duchess the commands to use with their new dog. Would you be willing to move your schoolroom lessons to tomorrow afternoon so that the two of you might accompany me?"

"I would be happy to oblige this change, Finola."

"Good. Let me tell Bertie of the plans, and then I know you and he need to leave for Adderly."

They went to the boy, and Finola explained what she was asking of Bertie the next day. Excitement lit his face.

"I know this is a lot of responsibility, but I believe you are ready for this, Bertie," Finola told the lad.

"I'd be happy to show Their Graces how to handle Pollux." Then his face fell.

"What's wrong?" Cy quickly asked, attuned to the boy's moods.

Bertie sighed, and Finola put an arm about the boy. "This is the hardest part of what we do. Eventually, you have to let the pups go. Usually, I do so when they are about a year old, and so I have more time with them. Since Pollux is not to be a trained hunting spaniel but a companion to a family, he is certainly old enough to leave us."

She ruffled the boy's hair. "The good thing is that we know Pollux is going to an excellent home. Also, we are not that far from Stonecrest, and perhaps one day we might be able to visit Pollux in his new home."

"I'd like that, Finola. How do you do this, though? Let them leave?"

"It is difficult, but I thoroughly investigate the owners my Honey-field spaniels are to be sold to. Besides, it is the way I earn my keep. Banny left me Belldale, along with a small inheritance, but I must continually perform upkeep on the house and property. I must also pay my servants and purchase the food and the necessities we use. At least I am fortunate enough to be doing something I love."

She smiled. "Besides, there is always the next litter to train. New pups to name and get to know and work with. I find that highly rewarding. Now, you and Cy need to be on your way. I will take over from here."

Cy and Bertie walked the two miles to Adderly, Bertie clamoring for a new lesson in history as they went. Cy was reluctant to do so because Finola seemed to be enjoying their lessons on English history.

"Why don't we shift to modern times and talk a little of the current war? Of Bonaparte and the geography involved?"

"All right," said Bertie amiably, ready to learn no matter what the topic.

As they made their way toward Adderly, Cy talked a little of the French Revolution and the death of Louis XVI and his family. He spoke of Robespierre and the Reign of Terror and then how Bonaparte rose from the chaos, bringing order into the lives of Frenchmen. By the time they had reached the village, Cy was to the point where the British had become involved in fighting the Little Corporal and told Bertie he would pick up the story on their way home to Melrose.

They went straightaway to Mr. Timmon's shop, where he introduced the boy to the tailor. Timmon had three tailcoats ready for Cy to try on, along with two shirts and two pairs of trousers. Only a few adjustments were needed, and Mr. Timmon made notes in his ledger of them.

"I will finish the last bit of your wardrobe, my lord, and I also have something to show you."

The tailor excused himself and returned with a beautiful, gray greatcoat.

"I did not ask for this to be commissioned, Mr. Timmon."

"No, you didn't, my lord, but you will need one all the same. Here, try it on, and let us see how it fits."

Cy slipped into it. The greatcoat fit him as a well-made glove did a hand.

"No more being chilled, my lord," Timmon said with a twinkle in his eyes. "I should be through with the remainder of your things in two days' time. Shall we say three to be on the safe side? You may come in then to claim the rest of your things."

"I brought Bertie along with me today because I wish for him, too, to have a few new things to wear." He looked to the boy. "His sleeves strike him above his wrists, and his pants have grown too short in the time since we left Spain. I have promised his parents that I would look after him. That includes seeing him properly clothed."

"Well, then, Bertie, we shall get you measured and see what his lordship wishes for you to wear. Perhaps some type of uniform?"

"No, that is not necessary. Just a neutral shirt and breeches. A vest and a dark tailcoat. Bertie is growing like a weed, so I only wish two outfits to be made up for him. He can alternate between those."

"Ver well, my lord."

Once the tailor had taken Bertie's measurements, he told Cy to make it another week before they returned to the shop and that everything would be ready at that time. Cy thanked the tailor and then asked, "Who is the local doctor these days?"

"That would be Dr. Addams," Mr. Timmon replied. "He is young—just past thirty—and took over the previous physician's practice recently."

"If you would be so good as to give me directions to him, I told my army surgeon that I would seek out a doctor when I returned to England."

The tailor did as requested, and Cy and Bertie set off through the village again. Before they left, though, they called at Mrs. Carroll's bakery, purchasing two cinnamon buns for them to eat later.

Bertie told Mrs. Carroll, "Your lemon cake was the best food I have ever eaten."

"Well, let's wait and see what you think of this cinnamon bun, lad. You will have to stop by and let me know what you thought of it."

"We will!" cried Bertie enthusiastically, causing both adults to chuckle.

They left Adderly and went a quarter-mile, coming upon a tidy cottage. Cy rapped on the door and moments later, a servant answered.

"Here to see the doctor?" the woman asked.

"I am," he told her.

"Well, come on in, sir. You and the boy may wait here." She indicated a bench against the wall. "Dr. Addams is with a patient and will see you shortly."

Ten minutes later, a door opened and a middle-aged man came out, wearing a sling, his right arm cradled to his chest. A second man, much younger, smiled and said to the first, "I will see you in a week. Remember, leave the arm in its sling, and do not take it off until I see you next. Even if it begins to feel better, it still needs more rest."

"All right, Doctor. Thank you."

The man left and Dr. Addams came toward Cy and Bertie. They both rose.

Cy said, "Good afternoon, Dr. Addams."

"You must be Lord Cyrus Cressley." The physician smiled. "The villagers are all abuzz about your return to England and Melrose. I am glad you stopped by for us to visit a bit."

"It is more than a get-acquainted visit, Doctor. I promised the army surgeon who operated on me in Spain that I would find someone to work with upon my return home."

Cy turned to Bertie. "Wait here. I will return shortly."

"Come with me, my lord," the doctor said, ushering Cy into an examination room. It had a high table and two chairs. Adams indicated for Cy to take one of them.

"Tell me about your war injury, my lord, and what wounds you had that needed to be operated upon."

Cy ran through his medical history from the time the bullet struck him, Dr. Addams occasionally asking a question. He even mentioned the eyewash he did three times a day and the herbs he used, mentioning how it gave him much needed relief.

After Cy finished, he was asked to sit upon the table, and the physician removed the eye patch.

"Hmm."

"Is that a good or bad remark?" he asked lightly.

"The eye is looking quite good," Dr. Addams declared. "Surprisingly so. And you say you cannot see a thing out of it?"

Depression blanketed him. "No. I cannot. But I do believe my vision is improving in my left eye. I can see things clearly now at a greater distance than previously."

"The eyewashes may have helped. Also, you might have less pressure on your optic nerve than previously. From when you say the wound occurred, the swelling has gone down on your brow and should be doing the same internally."

Dr. Addams stepped back. "I wish to bring something up to you, my lord. I have heard of this condition and actually saw it in a Mr. Colgate, who lives about five miles outside Adderly on a dairy farm with his daughter and son-in-law. Mr. Colgate was wounded and also struck with blindness. He was discharged and returned to England several months ago."

The doctor paused. "He survived his wounds—and he is no longer blind."

"Was it a case of pressure on his optic nerve, as Dr. Sheffley said of me?"

Dr. Addams shook his head. "No, not at all. Mr. Colgate was shot in his shoulder and stabbed with a bayonet in his calf. Neither wound was life-threatening."

Puzzled, Cy asked, "Then why was he struck blind?"

"That was the riddle. Naturally, the army released him, and he came home to Adderly. I saw him upon his return. His blindness continued and then suddenly vanished. He literally woke up one morning and could see again."

"I am hoping for something similar to happen," he admitted.

The physician looked uneasy. "I am going to say something that may offend you, my lord. Yes, you might have had swelling which pressed against your optic nerve. But after six weeks, that swelling inside should be long gone. You should be seeing now without any problems."

"Then why I am not?" Cy asked, a trace of bitterness in his voice.

"It is what I and another doctor friend of mine are calling *hysterical blindness.*"

"What? I have never heard of such a thing. Frankly, it sounds like the hysteria delicate women suffer from. I am highly insulted." He rose from the table, ready to leave.

"Sit, my lord," Dr. Addams barked. "You will sit—and listen to me. Because this is your life we are talking about. The quality of your life, post-military. I am assuming you wish to live one to the fullest."

Thoughts of Finola filled him. Cy sat.

"Thank you, my lord. Now, back to my friend. We have seen this in a few men. Men who have returned from the war. Men *not* injured anywhere near their eyes."

"But I was," he insisted. "I told you the bullet entered just above my right eyebrow. You can still see the small scar I bear."

"You were—but I still believe you show similar characteristics to these other cases I have referred to. Dr. Mills and I have come to believe that a severe emotional trauma can cause blood pressure to surge, making fluid leak into the capillaries, which are behind your retina. Even after the fluids stop leaking or the swelling recedes, the emotional stress is manifested physically."

He frowned. "You are saying I suffered emotional trauma. That emotional stress is causing a physical problem."

The physician smiled. "Yes, you have grasped the situation quickly. The brain is a marvelous, mysterious thing. We learn new things about it each year in medicine. Dr. Mills and I believe the strain you have been through—that trauma from both fighting in the war and being shot in the head—has caused a type of stress-induced blindness. Your brain is dealing with this trauma by converting it into something physical. Either that or fluids have built up around the membranes in your skull, increasing pressure against the nerve endings or in the optical canal. That, too, could contribute to temporary blindness."

He sat a moment, taking in what Dr. Addams had told him.

"You believe I truly can see? Or will be able to see one day soon?"

"I do, my lord. Once you truly feel safe—comfortable being back in England—I have every belief that the blindness will subside. It did for Mr. Colgate."

Shaking his head, Cy said, "But I was an officer. I went into battle a countless number of times, leading my men. I wasn't even shot during the fighting, but during drills being conducted."

"It doesn't matter, Lord Cyrus. You have suffered a great trauma. You are among a handful of men who have been shot in the head and survived it. Your body needs time to heal, as does the emotional and mental parts of you."

He nodded to himself. "You actually think this will end?"

"Yes, I do. When you know you are secure in this life, I have faith that your vision will be restored. In the meantime, continue the eyewashes thrice a day. Relax. Take time to walk. To think. Savor the air you breathe and each bite you take. Do what makes you happy.

Pass your time in ways which please you. When you are truly content, I think your body will relax, as will your brain."

Cy grinned. He could think of something that pleased him greatly.

Kissing Finola . . .

CHAPTER THIRTEEN

INOLA ROSE, HER heart heavy. Today would be the day she would
have to let Pollux go. All her pups were special to her, but none
more so than this first litter produced by Hera and Zeus. These were
true Honeyfield spaniels in every sense of the word, and she would
miss Pollux and his sweet, curious nature. Still, she knew he was going
to a loving home, one which would be filled with children.

The thought of children brought a smile to her face. She had a lot
of love in her heart for her dogs and knew it would increase a
hundredfold if and when she gave birth to a child of her own. She only
prayed that Cy would be the man to father them. She had enjoyed
working with him since his arrival at Melrose, as well as Bertie. It was
the boy as much as the man who had let her admit what was in her
heart—that she loved Cy and wanted to spend a lifetime with him.
Bearing his children. Living and loving together.

She made her way down to breakfast and ate quickly so as to have
extra time to spend with Pollux before Pierce's carriage arrived. She
went to the barn and took the pups out in pairs in order to allow them
to piddle and then placed them inside the dog run to play. Pollux and
Castor came last and once they had relieved themselves, she placed
Castor with his littermates and held Pollux out. Finola sat on the
ground, and Pollux climbed into her lap. She stroked him, telling him
that he was going to a fine home, a place where she would be able to

visit him.

As she petted him, she said, "You are going to be so happy, Pollux. Nalyssa and Pierce will take such good care of you. They are loving people, and you will become as a family member to them. I will even come and see you on occasion."

She caught sight of Bertie running in the distance and a chill rushed through her.

Something was wrong with Cy.

Quickly, Finola rose and placed Pollux in the dog run. He took off, racing to rejoin his littermates as she closed the gate and hurried to meet Bertie. By the time she reached him, the boy was out of breath. He stopped, placing his hands on his knees and bending over as he panted, trying to catch his breath. She tried to remain calm, not knowing what the situation was.

"Deep breaths, Bertie," she encouraged.

He pushed himself upright and said, "We cannot go with you today to deliver Pollux to the duke and duchess. He's in a bad way, Finola."

"What does that mean, Bertie? Are Cy's eyes troubling him?"

"No, it's one of those headaches. He hasn't had one since we arrived at Melrose. They're awful, Finola. He just lies in the bed and moans, holding his head. He sent me to you to tell you he couldn't go today."

Tears formed in the boy's eyes, and she enveloped him in her arms. Bertie started to cry, and Finola felt herself tearing up.

"He says I'm supposed to go with you today. That he wants me to."

Bertie raised his head and met her gaze. "But I can't leave him, Finola. I just can't. I know you were counting on me to show Their Graces what to do and how to handle Pollux. My father sent me to take care of—"

The boy's voice broke, and he began sobbing. She held him to her again, stroking his hair.

"It is all right, Bertie. You don't have to leave Cy today. In fact, Pollux won't be going anywhere until both of you can come for his sendoff. I will come with you now to help."

Just then, Finola heard the rumble of a carriage and told the boy, "Let me go tell the coachman we will need to arrange for Pollux to be delivered on another day."

She released Bertie and went to meet the carriage. As she reached it, the door swung open and Pierce emerged, surprising her.

"Good morning, Finola. I thought I would . . ." His voice trailed off. "What is wrong?"

"It is Cy," she said.

"Cressley? What happened?"

"I wanted Cy and Bertie to accompany me to Stonecrest today. I thought it would be good for Bertie to be the one to teach you and Nalyssa the various voice and hand commands to use with Pollux. Bertie just arrived and told me that Cy is experiencing a debilitating headache. They have plagued him since he was shot in the head."

"In the head? Good God!" Pierce exclaimed. "No, Pollux must come another day. Shall I go for a doctor?"

"That would be so helpful, Pierce." She gave him directions to where Dr. Addams lived and then added, "I am going to go and collect some herbs which may benefit Cy. I will meet you at the hunting lodge. Why don't you take Bertie with you? He can help facilitate things for you."

"I will do so and see you there," Pierce told her.

Finola waved Bertie over and said, "I am going to collect the herbs which may help Cy's headache. I want you to go with His Grace and fetch Dr. Addams to the hunting lodge. Can you do this for me, Bertie?"

The boy nodded, his eyes still filled with tears.

"Very well. I will see you soon. Be a good boy."

She hurried away and entered the house, going to her stillroom, just off the kitchens. Quickly, Finola gathered the herbs she thought would be helpful in treating Cy's headache, along with the herb mixture she had already prepared for him. He had told her how much relief the eyewash had brought to his eyes and how much better he could see from his left one since he had been using it. She had already intended to send these herbs home with him today.

Placing the herbs she had wrapped in handkerchiefs inside a small satchel, Finola left the house and made her way across Belldale and through the copse to where the hunting lodge stood. She did not bother to knock, and entered the abode. She found a bucket and took it to the well, drawing water and returning to set it to boil in order to steep the herbs she would give to Cy. Moving up the staircase, she heard his moans before she saw him. Turning to the left, she entered a bedchamber and saw Cy lying in the bed. He was bare to the waist— and took her breath away with his sleek muscled physique.

She went to his bedside. The heels of his hands pressed against his temples as he grimaced in pain.

"I am here, Cy," she said softly, doing her best to concentrate on his pain and not his body.

He opened his eyes, and she noted he was not wearing his usual eye patch. He was a handsome man in it, but without the patch obstructing part of his face, she could see just how handsome he truly was. She cupped his cheeks and pressed a kiss upon his brow.

"Why are you here?" he asked. "You need to be on your way to Stonecrest now."

"And leave you here when you are aching so badly? Never," she assured him.

"No, Finola, I want you and Bertie . . . to go." He winced.

"And I am my own person and have decided to stay with you. I have already sent His Grace and Bertie for the doctor. They should arrive shortly."

He gave her a crooked smile, which touched her heart. She released his face and took his hands in hers.

"When did the headache start?"

"A few hours ago. I have experienced blinding headaches since I was shot. They usually come out of nowhere. The pain is fierce and unrelenting."

"Dr. Addams may be able to give you something for it. I have also brought some herbs for you to ingest."

"I hate to be such trouble to you," he said.

"You are no bother at all, Cy."

They sat in silence until she heard the door opening and voices downstairs.

"Dr. Addams is here," she told him. "Let me go down and speak with him. The water I put on to boil may also be ready, as well."

Finola bent and pressed a soft kiss against his sensual lips, bringing a weak smile to them.

She left the room and went down the staircase, finding the duke, the local doctor, and Bertie.

"I have been sitting with him, Dr. Addams," she began. "I have also brought some herbs to use."

Briefly, Finola told the physician what she was going to do, and he said he would visit with his patient and return shortly.

Once he left, Pierce asked, "How is Cressley?"

"I won't lie to you. He is in a bad way." She turned to Bertie. "How long do these headaches last?"

"Usually, a few hours. But none of them seemed as bad as this one today."

"You did the right thing in coming to me, Bertie." She looked back to the duke. "I am very sorry I cannot bring Pollux to you today. I take pride in the training my pups undergo. It would not be right to give him to you without you being instructed in how to handle him properly. Please excuse me to Nalyssa. Hopefully, we can have Pollux with you soon."

"The pup is the least of my concerns," Pierce said. "I simply hope Cressley will be on the mend soon."

"I hope so, too," Finola said.

"Even if the headache leaves him today, he will be weak. Let us give him tomorrow to recover, and then I will return the day after to see if he is able to accompany you to Stonecrest. Is there anything else I might do for you, Finola?"

"No, you have done enough. Thank you for fetching Dr. Addams."

Pierce nodded, "Then I will leave things to you."

She went to her satchel and removed the herbs. Bertie showed her the container which held the mixture for Cy's eyewashes, and she added her herbs to what little remained. Then she divided the water she had boiled into different bowls, one for the eyewash and two others for his headache. If she could bring relief to his eyes, that might help calm the pain in his head.

Just as she had finished, Dr. Addams appeared.

"He is in severe pain at the moment but said it is now subsiding. I have laudanum for him to take but did not give it to him because I know how effective herbs can be. What are you using?"

"I have brought yarrow, which I am steeping by itself. The other is a mix of lavender and chamomile. They blend together well and have used them to soothe headaches I have experienced myself."

"Then let him sip on what you have made. I agree that the eyewash might benefit him. Once he has ingested the herbs, however, give him some of the laudanum. Sleep is restorative, and it will help him to gain his strength again."

"Thank you for coming, Dr. Addams," she said, noting Bertie had slipped up the stairs to be with Cy.

"I was happy to do so, my lady. I had just seen him yesterday, and we had discussed his eyesight and these headaches. He shared that he had not had any since his arrival at Melrose."

"Do you think they will end? Or that he will regain his sight in his right eye?"

"I think it is a good possibility, but only time will tell. Time is the biggest gift he can give himself now." The doctor smiled. "That—and patience. I will call tomorrow morning and see how he is."

The physician left the hunting lodge, leaving the laudanum behind and telling Finola how much to give Cy. She waited for the herbs to finish steeping and then took everything upstairs on a tray she found, placing the wet cloth over his eyes, and having him sip the yarrow first and then the lavender and chamomile combination.

"Dr. Addams also left some laudanum for you to take now," she informed him. "It will help you sleep."

He reached for her hand and squeezed it. "The headache is finally subsiding. Just give me a touch of the laudanum. I have used it before, and it makes my thinking fuzzy for a good day after." He paused. "Will you stay with me until I fall asleep?"

"I will stay with you for as long as you wish, Cy."

She stood and signaled for Bertie to follow her. They returned downstairs, and she began mixing a small portion of the laudanum with some of the boiled water.

As she did, she said, "Bertie, I know you wish to stay with Cy, but I could use your help with the pups today. Would you return to Belldale and work with them? Exercise and train them? I will have Cy drink the laudanum. He should fall asleep shortly after he does so. I can stay with him."

Bertie nodded thoughtfully. "He likes you. He would want you to be with him. I will go to the pups and take care of them all day."

"You have been a huge help to me in training them, Bertie. When the day comes and Cy no longer needs your help, I hope you might consider coming to work for me."

He brightened. "Really? Do you mean it? It's what I want to do, Finola. I have since the first day when I met Pollux and Athena."

"Then count on it. However long it takes, you have a place with me when you finish fulfilling your commitment to Cy."

The child threw his arms about her. "Thank you, Finola."

The gesture touched her. She knew Bertie would make for an excellent dog trainer someday. Already, he had learned so much. Coupled with his natural instincts, she believed he would go far in this business.

She saw him out the door and then brought the laudanum upstairs, helping Cy to sit up and drink it.

"You will feel sleepy soon," she told him. "Bertie has gone to exercise the pups, while I stay here with you."

He cupped her cheek. "Will you lie on the bed with me?" He asked. "I know it is unorthodox, but having you near brings me comfort."

"Of course."

She lowered Cy again and placed the dampened cloth against his eyes before she brought the bedclothes over him, admiring his magnificently muscled chest before she covered him.

Finola climbed upon the bed. Cy slipped an arm about her and she turned, resting her cheek against his shoulder, his warmth enveloping her, bringing comfort to her when she wished to comfort him. She placed one hand on his chest, against his beating heart.

They lay there for some minutes until his breathing slowed and he fell asleep. Still, Finola stayed next to him. She told herself she was afraid if she stirred it might wake him. In truth, she cherished being near him and fell asleep herself.

Chapter Fourteen

C Y AWOKE AND was aware of two things. The headache had gone. And a warm woman lay next to him.

Finola . . .

He lay still, the subtle smell of lavender in the air. Lavender would always remind him of Finola.

The woman he loved.

Cy needed to tell her this. He needed to see if she felt a tenth of what he did. He lifted the cloth that still rested against his eyes and placed it on the table beside the bed. His hand touched Finola's hair, stroking her head. She stirred against him, igniting the desire within him.

Then she was awake. He sensed it in her breathing. And the way her body changed and became aware of him.

Finola?" he whispered.

"I am here, Cy."

He continued stroking her hair, and then his hand moved to her cheek, cupping it, his thumb caressing it. The bedclothes slipped downward, and her hand touched his bare chest. It felt like fire, branding him.

"I want you to be mine," he told her. "I am already yours. In body and in soul."

She stilled, not saying a word for a long time. He didn't know if he had made a mistake telling her how he felt.

Then she said, "I have always been yours, Cy. I always will be yours."

He turned her in his arms and gave her a slow, lingering kiss. He took his time, brushing his lips against hers, every fiber in his body screaming her name. Still, he didn't know how far he should take the kiss.

It was Finola who changed things. Finola whose tongue ran slowly against his bottom lip. Back and forth until he opened to her. Tentatively, she pushed her tongue inside his mouth and slowly explored each crevice within. His arms tightened about her. His hand began stroking her long, slender back.

They kissed leisurely for a long time, and then he deepened the kiss. Her fingers now stroked his bare chest, the heat overwhelming him.

Breaking the kiss, Cy said, "May I touch you? Intimately?" he added.

Her eyes widened at his request and then a slow smile curved her beautiful mouth. "Yes. If I may return the favor, as well."

A rush of heat rippled through him at her words, and his mouth came down on hers, hard and demanding. His hand moved to her breast, kneading it. She let out a small sigh, and he began teasing her nipple.

Finola gasped, and Cy knew he needed his mouth on her breast. He broke the kiss and sat up, pulling her with him. She still wore the bulky tailcoat, and he eased it from her shoulders. It was not fitted as tightly as a gentleman's and came off easily. She helped him, and he tossed it to the floor. She wore a man's shirt beneath it, tucked into her breeches, and Cy pulled at the material until he freed the shirt. Unbuttoning and then lifting it over her head, he again tossed it to the floor. She was now bare from the waist up, and her breasts were a thing of beauty.

Cy eased her back onto the mattress, following her, his mouth fastening on one breast, sucking hard. A low moan escaped from her, and he couldn't help but grin. He savaged the nipple with teeth and tongue, Finola squirming beneath him, making the most delicious sounds. When he finally lifted his head, their gazes met, and he saw her flushed with desire.

"I cannot neglect your other breast," he said, and soon he feasted on it as he had the first.

His lips finally left her breasts, returning to her mouth. As they kissed, his hands glided across her skin of silk. But Finola was also learning, and her hands brushed against his chest, enflaming Cy. Then she pushed against him, and they switched places, her now hovering over him with a wicked smile, Finola bent and flicked her tongue across his nipple. He gasped.

She lifted her head and smiled. "What is good for the goose is even better for the gander," she told him, mischief flashing in her hazel eyes. She returned to the nipple, teasing it with tongue and teeth, causing him to grow rock-hard.

Finally, she paused and he pushed her down until she lay sprawled against him, his hands roaming her back.

"I want more of you," he said huskily. "You do not have to give it to me just yet, but I want you to know how much I need you. Desire you."

Raising her head, she said, "I need you, too. Not just here and now—but always. I have kept my feelings to myself, wanting you to have the time you needed to come to understand your place in the world. But I can no longer keep silent, Cy."

He placed two fingers against her swollen lips. "Please, let me be the first to say the words aloud, Finola. I love you. I don't know how I have lived these nine and twenty years without you. But I want to share a lifetime—and beyond—with you."

Her hand took his, moving his fingers from her mouth. "I love you, as well, Cy. I have never felt such happiness as I have being in your company."

A wave of tenderness filled him, and he softly brushed his lips against hers. The kiss was one full of unspoken promises to her. He knew he was meant to spend the rest of time with this kind, generous woman.

Her hands began moving urgently over him, taking him in. He broke the kiss and moved his lips to her throat, nipping at it feverishly.

"I want you, Cy," Finola called out, desperation in her voice. "I want to couple with you."

He paused, lifting his head until their gazes met. "We are not yet wed."

"We are in my heart," she replied. "I will marry you whenever you wish—but for now? I pledge my body, my heart, and my soul to you."

Cy kissed her again, boldly now, knowing he belonged as much to this woman as she did to him. He tossed aside the bedclothes and kissed his way down her throat, along the valley between her breasts, and down to her belly. As he kissed her, he unbuttoned the breeches she wore.

He raised his head and said, "I will stop if you ask me to. I can wait if you wish us to do so. I know how you have not done this before, Finola."

Her eyes held nothing but trust. "I love you, Cy. I want to be with you in every way possible."

He pushed himself up and climbed from the bed, hearing her gasp, realizing he wore nothing, and it was the first time she had seen a naked man.

Standing before her, he asked, "Are you pleased with what you see?"

The wonder on her face told him she was. Then mischief lit her eyes, and she smiled at him. "I am very ready to explore you."

He grabbed her ankles and quickly turned her in the bed, hearing her laugh with abandon. He removed the boots she wore and then tugged her breeches over her hips and down her legs. She was half-on and half-off the bed, her legs dangling, the most tempting morsel he had ever seen. Cy knelt, taking her thighs in his hands and kneading them, their gazes locked upon one another. He saw the trust and love in her eyes, and it almost undid him.

Still looking at one another, he allowed his hand to slide up her thigh to where her legs joined. He stroked along the seam of her sex and heard her breath hitch. Still connected, his fingers stroked and explored her. When he pushed a finger into her, Finola's eyes grew large, her mouth trembling. He caressed her lovingly, bringing her to the edge, and then she tumbled over it, her hips bucking as she cried out his name, the orgasm tearing through her. When she stilled, she grinned at him, her satisfaction obvious.

"I enjoyed watching you come," he said roughly, his hands gripping her thighs again. "Let us try this and see what you think."

Confusion filled that lovely face of hers, and he hated that he would not be able to watch her this time. His head bent, his mouth finding her core. She wriggled beneath him, protesting as he licked her. Then the protests died and delicious sighs replaced them.

Cy worked Finola into a frenzy, his tongue invading her, exploring her, possessing her until she orgasmed once again. When she lay limp and told him she could not move, he grinned wickedly at her.

"You do not have to move a single muscle. Let me take care of you."

He lifted her, placing her head back on the pillow, and then climbed atop her, his body covering hers. He was already thoroughly aroused from having watched her come and placed his cock against her. He had never taken a woman's virginity but knew he should not prolong it and quickly pushed into her.

She mewled a protest but by then, he was deeply seated inside her. Cy forced himself not to move and said, "Become accustomed to me first."

Finola nodded and said, "The pain is no more. It was fleeting."

"Now, it will only be pleasure for you."

"I trust you, Cy. I know we belong together."

Slowly, he withdrew from her and then pushed into her once more. This time, her gasp was one of pleasure instead of pain.

"Ooh, that feels marvelous."

"We can do better than marvelous, my love. I plan to take you straight to the heavens."

"Is that a promise?" she asked, her tone teasing.

He laughed, threading his fingers through hers and bringing them to where they rested on each side of her head. Cy began moving again, and Finola caught on to his rhythm and their dance of love. He had never felt the physical sensations he did now and knew it was because of his emotional connection to this woman.

"I love you, Finola. Now and forevermore."

Cy covered her mouth with his and pumped away, love pouring through him into her. They climaxed together, and he fell atop her, driving her into the mattress. He kissed her again and again, until they were both breathless, and then he rolled to his side, bringing her with him, their bodies still joined.

"That was . . . indescribable," Finola said, wonder in her voice.

"There is more," he promised. "Much more. We will have a lifetime to explore one another and decide what pleases each other. My commitment to you is unbreakable. I may not bring a wealth of worldly goods into our marriage, but know that my love is the biggest gift I can offer you."

He kissed her tenderly.

"Will you allow us to live at Belldale?" she asked quietly.

"It has been your home for many years, and I would not take you from it or your dogs. My commission will bring in some income for us to live on, but you will need to continue training and selling your

Honeyfield spaniels."

"*We*," she emphasized. "We will train them together. Perhaps we should rename them Cressley spaniels."

The thought left a sour taste within him. Cy wanted no association with his brother or father touching their union.

"No, they are to remain Honeyfield spaniels. That is what they are known as. It will be your lasting legacy—that I am more than happy to continue to help you in this work."

She touched his cheek, stroking her fingers against it. "Bertie will be happy about this turn of events."

Cy chuckled. "He will, indeed. And speaking of Bertie, where is he? I know he cannot be here."

"I sent him to Belldale to work with the dogs today so I could stay with you."

He kissed her softly. "Maybe he should stay there so I can keep you here."

She laughed, the sweetest sound in his world. "I look forward to all of us being at Belldale together. But we should dress. Or at least I should. You should remain in bed. I cannot believe I haven't asked you how your headache is."

"It is totally gone."

"I had no idea how debilitating it could be. I was very worried about you."

"Dr. Sheffley said the headaches, like my eyesight, are results of the bullet entering my head and the swelling and stress that resulted from that. I hope if my sight returns that the headaches might end."

Finola had risen from the bed and was redressing. Cy definitely enjoyed watching this process.

"Dr. Addams will return tomorrow morning to check on you."

"What of Stoneham? And Pollux? When do you plan on delivering the pup to him?"

"He knows I wanted you and Bertie to accompany me. He said he would send his carriage again the day after tomorrow, hoping you would be fully recovered by then."

She bent and pressed a kiss on his brow. "I will go home now and—"

Cy snagged her by the waist and yanked her down, kissing her again until they were both breathless.

He released her. "I would make love to you again, but you will be sore as it is, come tomorrow." Taking her hand, he brought it to his lips for a tender kiss. "When will you wed me?"

"I suppose in three weeks. It will take that long to call the banns."

"There are other ways to speed things up," he told her.

"You mean for us to go all the way to Gretna Green?"

He chuckled. "No, Scotland is much too far away. I knew of an officer who obtained a bishop's license before he left for the war. It doesn't give quite the freedom a special license does, but that cost is a little too rich for this retired soldier's blood. With a bishop's license, we can avoid calling the banns. We could then wed in the local parish church during morning hours between eight and noon."

Cy kissed the tip of her nose. "Would you like me to pursue one of those?"

"I will share the costs with you," she said. "After all, we are both getting married."

Since he had no idea how much a bishop's license cost, he almost agreed to her proposal. Still, his masculine pride would not allow him to do so.

"No, I should be the one who provides the license. I will ride into Chichester tomorrow and meet with the bishop. That is, if you will lend me the use of your horse."

"Will you feel well enough to do so?"

He laughed and kissed her soundly. "I feel on top of the world, my love. I am to be married to the woman I love. One who loves me in return, despite my being blind in one eye and homeless."

"I don't care about those things." She paused. "Will you seek permission from His Grace to wed?"

He frowned. "I *am* going to see His Grace, the Bishop of Chichester, Finola."

"No, I meant your relative, the Duke of Margate."

"No. I am a grown man," he said harshly. "I have no need of his permission." Seeing the surprised look on her face, he softened his tone. "We are related but have never been close. I will let him know when I vacate the hunting lodge but beyond that, I owe him nothing."

What he did owe Finola, though, was the truth. It was time she learned exactly who he was.

"I need to—"

But he heard the door open downstairs and knew Bertie had arrived.

"Get back under those bedclothes," she said, hurrying to the other side of the bed and sitting in the chair there.

Cy pulled the bedclothes to his neck. Moments later, Bertie entered.

"Hello, Bertie," Finola called brightly. "Cy is awake now and no longer has his headache. I was just going down to put on some water to boil for his next eyewash, and then I will leave."

"I can do that, Finola," the boy said, always eager to please.

"All right," she agreed. "We are to go to Stonecrest the day after tomorrow and take Pollux to the Duke and Duchess of Stoneham."

"I have business to conduct tomorrow," Cy added, "so you are to skip lessons again and work with Finola."

"Shouldn't I come with you?" Bertie asked.

"I will be fine. Finola is lending me the use of her horse again." He glanced to her, and she nodded. "We will have to make up the lessons that we are missing. Is that understood?"

The lad nodded and then said, "On the way to Stonecrest, you can tell us some more of the history of England."

"I will do so with pleasure," Cy told them.

"I am glad you are feeling much better," Finola said, rising from the chair. "Bertie, I will expect you tomorrow morning. In fact, come and have your breakfast with me, and then we will begin our work for the day with the dogs."

She turned to Cy. "I will see you the day after tomorrow, Cy. Be ready for our trip to Stonecrest."

"I look forward to it, Finola."

Cy watched his new fiancée leave. He would have to speak with her privately after he returned from Chichester and let her know exactly who she was marrying. He didn't think it would make a difference now because they loved one another.

Still, the sooner she knew he was the second son of the deceased Duke of Margate, the better.

CHAPTER FIFTEEN

FINOLA WAS ALREADY waiting outside when Cy and Bertie appeared. She had brought out all the dogs, and they were now in the dog run, including Pollux. She left the pup to play with his littermates until the last minute. Still, Athena seemed to understand something had changed and followed Pollux about, nuzzling against him and then pawing him playfully.

She greeted the pair as she saw Pierce's carriage arriving.

"If you will get Pollux from the pen, Bertie, I will collect his things."

Bertie raced off and Cy said, "What do you have for the pup?"

"Just a few toys for him to play with and some treats. A small blanket that I let him and Athena sleep upon last night, which can be placed next to him as he sleeps in his new space. Athena's scent will remain on it for a while. That should be a comfort to him."

"Pollux will miss you," Cy said.

She chuckled. "I believe he may miss Bertie more."

Cy looked to the boy coming toward them, Pollux heeling nicely beside him. "Bertie will certainly miss Pollux."

She lifted the satchel, and Cy took it from her. The trio made their way toward the carriage and the coachman called out a greeting as the footman set down the stairs and opened the vehicle's door. They climbed inside, Cy sitting next to her and Bertie across from them. The boy held the pup close to him, his eyes bright with tears.

As they started up, she said, "Remember, you still have seven other pups to work with. And Athena will definitely be staying with us. I also will let Zeus and Hera try for a second litter soon. That will give you something to look forward to."

"What will you name them?" Bertie asked. "Like all these have the names of gods and goddesses."

"I have already been thinking on that," she said. "I may aim for a litter of Viking gods. How would you like to work with Thor, Freya, Loki, or Odin? Or we could think about English kings and queens since Cy is teaching the two of us about England's history. Edward. Henry. Mathilda. Elizabeth. Eleanor."

"Harold," Bertie added. "Mary and Lady Jane. I like both ideas, Finola." He thought a moment. "Could we keep with the Viking names this time? I like the sound of them."

"Then we shall save English monarchs for another litter. The next shall be Norse gods and goddesses," she said. "We will make a list, separating the names into male and female. Once the litter is born, I will let you choose the name of each pup."

"You will?" Bertie asked, surprise on his face.

"I think it would be a good reward for all the hard work you have put in with this litter. I also think by the next time Hera's pups are born, you will have come to work for me."

They had not spoken about when to tell Bertie their good news. For now, Finola would keep silent until at least the bishop's license had been purchased.

The child quickly turned to Cy. "Would that be all right with you, sir?"

Cy chuckled. "As long as you let me come and help. Hopefully, Finola will continue to allow us to use her schoolroom and supplies in the mornings and then we can help train the pups in the afternoons."

"There will be a bit of a break when they first arrive," she said.

"They are incredibly small. Their eyes won't even be opened. They will do little but eat and sleep. I do like to be around them at that age, though. I think picking them up and holding them, talking to them, helps you to create a bond with them. That bond comes into play later during their training."

"So, a little more schooling while the pups are young then," Cy said. "And a little less once they are older and ready to be trained."

They reached Stonecrest, and she watched as Bertie brushed his lips against Pollux's head. She understood exactly how he felt. Other than Banny, her dogs had been more companions to her than people. She loved them and lived for them.

But now she had Cy. Her love for him was boundless. She was eager to ask how his trip to Chichester had gone, hoping he had been able to obtain the bishop's license. They also needed to talk about when they would marry. Finola assumed there would be a time limit on the marriage license. Even after the banns were called, couples had a timeframe in which they must wed, else the banns had to be called again. She wondered what the parameters were of the bishop's license he had acquired.

The door opened, and Cy bounded out, handing her down and then swinging Bertie and Pollux to the ground. She turned and saw both Nalyssa and Pierce standing there to greet them and was touched by the effort the pair made.

"Good morning," Nalyssa called, coming and embracing Finola. She then looked to the man and boy. "My husband tells me you were unwell, Mr. Cressley. I am sorry to hear that."

He bowed. "I am much improved, Your Grace." He indicated Bertie, who also bowed, causing both Finola and the duchess to smile. "This is Bertie Briggs, who has been helping me ever since I returned from the Peninsula."

"Bertie also has begun working with my Honeyfield spaniels," Finola added. "He has promised to come and work with me once Mr.

Cressley is more settled. In fact, it will be Bertie today who will take Pollux through the commands and teach them to you."

Nalyssa moved to Bertie and petted Pollux. "My, aren't you a darling boy? I hope you will like living with Pierce and me."

The duke had joined them. He reached out and scratched Pollux between his ears, and the dog closed his eyes in bliss.

"Ah, I see he likes that," Pierce said. "Well, shall you come inside? Or should we stay out here to learn how to handle Pollux?"

"The morning is not nearly as cold as I had thought," Nalyssa said. "Why don't we go to the lawn in the rear of the house? There are seats there in case I tire and still plenty of room for Bertie to show us how to be good dog owners to Pollux."

By now, Bertie had set the pup on his feet and said, "Heel." Pollux stood close. As they began to walk, Bertie and Pollux fell into step behind the duchess, who led the way into the house and through it, exiting out the back.

Finola and Cy took seats and turned over things to Bertie. She was incredibly proud of the boy as he first asked the duke and duchess to sit and then told Pollux to do the same. Bertie explained the daily regimen they should follow with the pup, from when Pollux should be fed and allowed to relieve himself to the times the dog should be exercised.

"Exercise is important," Bertie told them. "Pollux will feel his best when he's walked twice a day. Honeyfield springer spaniels have a lot of energy. Walking helps tire them out. Pollux will be calmer and quieter because of these walks. They'll also help him keep at a good weight and help his growing muscles."

The boy thought a moment and then added, "Walking and playing isn't just good for movement. It helps Pollux to think. For his mind to grow. It will give him confidence and keep him from getting into trouble." Bertie grinned. "I'd say Pollux is a little like me."

The four adults chuckled.

He explained how important a routine was to have and how Pollux would look forward to their walks if they kept him on a schedule of walking and playtime.

"He's to be fed twice a day, in the morning and the evening. And he'll need to piddle soon after he eats. On walks, let him smell things. Spaniels see with their noses as much as their eyes. He'll want to sniff everything."

The lad looked to her. "What else should I tell them, Finola?"

"About his ears."

"Oh, yes." Bertie lifted Pollux's ears. "See how long and floppy they are. You need to check his ears each week. If he's rubbing his head on the ground or scratching them, he might have something in them." He explained how to clean them.

"How long do they live?" Pierce asked.

Bertie looked to Finola, who replied, "Usually an English springer spaniel's typical lifespan is twelve to thirteen years. If you don't have any further questions, Bertie can now show you the commands Pollux knows."

Over the next hour, Bertie demonstrated each of the basic commands and had both the duke and duchess repeat them several times. He started with voice commands, as Finola had done with him, and then moved to hand gestures.

"You're both very smart," the boy praised. "You've learned the commands quickly."

Finola saw the pair bite back smiles, the duke even coughing into his hand, stifling a laugh.

"I hope you think we are worthy to have Pollux come and be a member of our family, Bertie," Nalyssa said.

"I'm sad to see him leave the litter, but I think he'll be happy here."

Bertie then demonstrated how to use the various toys and then his stomach rumbled loudly.

"Why don't I send you to the kitchens with Pollux, and he can keep you company while Cook gives you something to eat?" Nalyssa suggested.

Pierce motioned to a footman who had stationed himself at the door, asking for the boy to be taken to the kitchens. Bertie told Pollux to heel, and they accompanied the servant inside.

"Oh, he is a delight," Nalyssa declared. "So bright and sweet. I mean the boy—but Pollux is also the same."

"I had questioned my wife's intentions in bringing a dog into our home, but Pollux has certainly changed my mind," Pierce said.

"The pup may test you a bit," she warned. "Once we are gone, because we are all he has known. He will be in a new place with unfamiliar people. Simply keep to the training Bertie taught you—and shower Pollux with lots of love."

"Why don't we go inside?" Nalyssa suggested. "I could stand to have my feet propped up and a hot cup of tea."

Her husband leaped to his feet and helped Nalyssa from her chair and then swept her into his arms.

"I am perfectly capable of walking, Your Grace," she said lightly.

"And I am perfectly happy carrying you, Your Grace," Pierce replied.

As they approached the door, the duchess said, "Why don't you show Mr. Cressley your new horse, Pierce? That way Finola and I can have a long talk."

"As long you promise to say only good things about me," the duke teased. "Let me see you settled in your sitting room."

She and Cy followed the duke, who led them to the same room Finola and Nalyssa had visited in last time. Pierce eased his duchess into a chair and lifted her feet onto the footstool.

"I will tell Cook on our way out that tea is to be sent to you." He brushed his lips against hers. "Come along, Cressley. I am only beginning to learn about horses, but even I can tell what a beauty I have."

Cy accompanied the duke downstairs, and they stopped in the kitchens, where Stoneham requested tea be sent up to the sitting room. Bertie was eating a ham sandwich, and he and Pollux were being fussed over by two scullery maids.

As they left the house and made their way toward the stables, Stoneham said, "I know you know nothing of me, Cressley. I was a haberdashery owner. The only time I had anything to do with the members of Polite Society was when one of them entered my store five miles outside Bristol. I wasn't given anything in life. I worked years at manual labor, saving enough to open my shop. Mama and Pen, my sister, were milliners, and their store was located next to mine. This whole thing of being a sudden duke was a bloody surprise.

"And I couldn't have done it without Nalyssa."

"Finola mentioned to me that she worked with men, such as you, helping acclimate them to a life in Polite Society."

The duke chuckled. "She did, indeed. She is still training me how to behave in certain circumstances. I'm taking riding lessons from my groom since I had never had the opportunity to get on the back of a horse."

By now, they had reached the stables and entered. The duke waved off an eager groom, telling him they were just here to see the new horse. Going down a long aisle, they finally reached the stall. Immediately, Cy saw why the duke was so excited by his new horse.

He whistled, low. "What a beauty."

"She is as smart as she is beautiful. Just like my duchess," the duke said proudly.

They entered the stall, and he ran his hands over the horse's flesh. "Whatever you paid for her was worth it," Cy told the other man.

"She was expensive. Spirited. Affectionate. I have enjoyed learning how to ride her."

Cy was stroking the horse between its ears when the duke said, "How long have you been in love with Finola?"

He started. "What would make you say that?"

Stoneham's wicked smile spread. "Because I am a man in love with his wife, man. I recognize all the symptoms. You are me. I am you. Have you told Finola how you feel?"

"I did two days ago. Yesterday, I rode into Chichester and purchased a bishop's license." He did not add that it had taken all the money he had to do so.

The duke slapped Cy on the back, offering his hand. "Good for you, Cressley. When is the wedding?"

"We have yet to discuss that. Soon, though. The license is only good for fourteen days."

"I hope you will consider inviting us to the wedding."

"It will be small. Held at the village church in Adderly."

"Just send word, and I will be there. I cannot guarantee Nalyssa's presence. You see how round her belly already is. I have no wish to see her jostled about in a carriage. I would be happy to attend your nuptials, though."

"We will let you know what our plans are." Cy hesitated a moment. He didn't know this man, and yet he decided to seek his opinion.

"Do you think if you would have been a mere haberdasher that Her Grace would have wed you?"

Stoneham grew thoughtful. "I would like to think so. Of course, if I were, then I never would have met Nalyssa. If you are thinking she wed me because I am a duke, let me assure you that is not the case. We are soulmates and recognized it. Why do you ask?"

"Because I haven't exactly been honest with Finola." He saw the duke's eyes spark with anger. "No, I have not deliberately lied to her. Yes, I am Cyrus Cressley, and I served as a lieutenant-general in the Peninsular War. Yes, I was wounded and told I must sell my commission and return to England."

"But?" the duke pressed.

"I am *Lord* Cyrus Cressley, second son of the deceased Duke of Margate and brother to the current duke. Margate and I are years apart in age and were never close. In fact, when I returned from Spain, he did not even want me residing in his house. The best he offered was the use of a small hunting lodge on the edge of Melrose. The lodge is only a short distance from Finola at Belldale."

"Why would you not share this with her?" the duke asked, clearly puzzled.

He shook his head. "I had a sense from the beginning that the closeness which sprang between us rather quickly would be lost if Finola knew I were a duke's son. She is an orphan and raises her Honeyfield spaniels not only because she loves dogs, but she must work for her keep. While her guardian left Belldale to her, she has shared that no income accompanied that legacy and only a small amount of funds was included. I believe if she knew I held a title, even if it is a courtesy, she would view me differently."

The duke studied him a moment. "I think the two of you should be completely honest with one another. The sooner you both share your secrets, the better your chances are of having a successful marriage."

"I love her. I know she loves me," Cy insisted. "Yet I am filled with dread at having to tell her who I am."

"Do it as quickly as possible, my lord. Else I warn you that things might become distant between you."

He sighed. "You are right. I will tell her when we reach Belldale today." Cy offered his hand, and the duke took it. "Thank you for your advice."

As they shook, Stoneham said, "Let me know how the situation plays out."

Cy hoped it would be nothing of consequence and that Finola would accept him. Love him. Marry him.

Determination filled him. He would talk with her today.

No more excuses.

CHAPTER SIXTEEN

THEY REACHED BELLDALE and thanked the coachman for returning them. Finola hurried to the dog run, the pups jumping and barking, eager to see her. Cy wanted her full attention for the conversation they would have and knew now was not the right time. She would want to devote the entire afternoon to her dogs.

Immediately, she began releasing the dogs from their pen and told Bertie and him that the pups were due for a long walk since they had not been exercised this morning.

"I like when we take all of them out," Bertie said happily.

Cy was glad to hear Bertie sounded in good spirits since he had looked a bit glum during the carriage ride home from Stonecrest. He knew the boy couldn't help it. Pollux was the first pup Bertie had lost and a very special one, at that.

Finola let the dogs run about for a few minutes before calling them to her, and then their entire party set out. Cy decided to pick up with where they had left off in the English monarchy and began telling them about the charming but feckless Stephen, who violated his oath by seizing the throne, and how this action caused Matilda, the rightful heir, to plunge the country into civil war.

After they had traipsed about Belldale, they reached the copse, and Finola said, "We should let you go to the hunting lodge and soothe your eyes with one of the eyewashes."

He had come to appreciate the relief the eyewashes gave him and agreed. They led the dogs to the copse, and Finola gave them their heads, allowing them to run ahead until the dogs reached the hunting lodge. As the humans emerged from the wooded area, he saw a footman nervously pacing in the clearing. Relief broke out on the servant's face as he hurried to meet them. Cy had not waited this long to tell Finola his identity, only to have it ruined by one of the servants from Melrose.

He turned to his companions. "Wait here," he said firmly, hurrying off to meet the footman.

When Cy reached the servant, he said, "What is wrong? Speak quietly if you would."

The footman glanced over Cy's shoulder and then met his gaze. "My lord, His Grace is quite ill. He has asked to see you. Hours ago. When you were not here, I hurried back to Melrose and informed Mr. Arnold."

He recognized the name of the butler. "Go on."

"Mr. Arnold sent me here to wait for you, no matter how long it took. We must go immediately to Melrose."

"Go without me," he instructed. "I will follow you shortly. I promise."

"Very well, my lord."

The footman rushed away, and Cy returned to Finola and Bertie.

"His Grace is asking to see me. The footman said the duke is ill." Looking to the boy, he added, "Bertie, you are to stay at Belldale until I come for you."

The boy shook his head. "No, sir. My place is with you."

He saw the stubborn set to the boy's jaw. Although Bertie was a servant, he had become much more to both Cy and Finola. Even if he ordered Bertie to remain at Belldale, he knew the lad would disobey those orders. Cy was not willing to set up the boy for failure.

"All right. I will go to Melrose and see what His Grace wants. You stay with Finola and the pups until the usual time, and then you are to return here to the hunting lodge. I will get here as soon as I can."

Bertie nodded in agreement and then left, returning to the dogs to throw sticks for them to retrieve.

Cy looked to Finola, who asked, "Do you know what His Grace wants with you?"

"I haven't a clue. The footman merely said the duke wished to see me. His moods are quite mercurial. By the time I get to Melrose, he will probably have forgotten he even sent for me."

"Then I will send Bertie home at the end of our training. He can have your supper waiting for you."

Cy regretted not being able to speak to Finola about what was in his heart. He took her hand and squeezed it. "I have things we must discuss tomorrow. They have been put off long enough."

She smiled at him, a sweet smile that made him want to gather her up in his arms and never let go.

"If it is a wedding date you wish us to choose, I am ready to do so, Cy. I will see you tomorrow morning."

He released her hand and gave a wave of farewell to Bertie before turning and following the Melrose footman. With his long strides, Cy came within sight of the servant but saw that the footman trotted along, wanting to reach Melrose as quickly as possible.

When Cy got to the main house, he did not have to knock. The butler was waiting for him outside.

"His Grace is gravely ill, Lord Cyrus. The doctor is with him now. We are all fearful of the outcome."

The news took him aback. Yes, Cy had seen his brother was in pain during their visit upon Cy's arrival at Melrose. He had not thought Margate ill to the point of death, however.

"Is it His Grace's gout which is acting up again?"

"The gout is a large part of his woes, my lord. Each attack seems to get stronger, and its effects last longer. His Grace also has a fever which set in. He cannot seem to shake it."

Arnold turned and led Cy into the house, where he saw Dr. Addams descending the stairs. He waited for the physician, who came to him, a worried look on his face.

"I assume you have been summoned by His Grace," the doctor began.

"Yes, I am told that he asked for me."

"The gout will never kill him. It merely makes his life miserable. All his joints are hot and swollen, tender to the touch. This latest attack's pain is the most severe case I have seen. It has reached a point where the disease has progressed so much that His Grace cannot move his joints in a normal fashion. He cannot hold a cup to drink from or cut anything with a knife."

Dr. Addams raked a hand through his hair. "It is the fever which has now struck him that worries me."

Cy frowned. "It is that serious?"

"It is more than serious, my lord. I fear His Grace may not survive it."

Cold fear pooled in his belly. He had never cared for his brother but had also never envied Charles for being the heir apparent and now Duke of Margate.

What if Charles died—and Cy became the new duke?

"I will go to him now."

"I plan to return tomorrow morning. Send for me if I am needed before that."

"I will."

Cy mounted the stairs, dread filling him at the prospect of Margate dying. If he did so, Cy's world would turn upside down. He shrugged off that terrifying thought and made his way to the duke's rooms. He had never been inside them, though he had been brought up in this house. His father was rarely at Melrose and when he was in residence, he didn't want to see his sons, much less in his private quarters. Cy could remember being a young boy and coming to stand in front of the door now before him many times, wanting to open it and go inside. Fear had ruled him then. He had been frightened of the duke and had never invaded his father's space.

He did not bother to knock, knowing there were two outer rooms before the bedchamber, thanks to servants' gossip, and he doubted any servant would be present to answer his summons. Cy pushed open the door and closed it quietly. He found himself in a study, complete with desk, settee, and two chairs. He didn't know of anyone outside the family who had been invited into this private sanctuary and went through the open door to another room. It was a sitting room for the duke's use alone. Ahead, he saw another door and assumed his brother lay beyond it.

Cy went and tapped on it lightly, thinking Margate's valet would be with him. He was right, as a servant answered the knock.

"My lord, thank you for coming. I am Hunt, His Grace's valet. His Grace has been asking for you all day."

"I had left Melrose and only recently returned."

The servant nodded. "I will give you privacy with His Grace and wait in the corridor. Call if you have need of me." Hunt left the bedchamber.

With trepidation, Cy stepped over the threshold and closed the door behind him. Turning, he saw how enormous the room was. The curtains were drawn, however, leaving the bedchamber dark. A lone candle burned at the bedside table, and he crossed the room to where a huge bed sat. Margate was lying in it, pillows propped behind him. The bedclothes were bunched at the foot of the bed, and his brother was naked except for a cloth draped across his loins. Cy could see the immense rolls of fat and how pale his brother was—except for his face—which was flushed a bright red from the fever.

He stood at the foot of the bed, studying Margate for a moment. The duke's eyes were closed, and he whimpered softly.

"I am here, Your Grace," he said quietly.

The duke's eyes fluttered open, and he grimaced. "It took you long enough," he grumbled.

Leave it to Charles to start the conversation with a complaint.

"I was not at Melrose when the footman came to fetch me. But I am here now, Your Grace. What can I do for you?"

His brother's face scrunched in pain, and he groaned loudly.

"I am sick and tired of this evil disease dominating my life," Margate said, bitterness in his tone. "I cannot even have the bedclothes touch me. My joints are so enflamed that even the feel of them brings me to tears."

"Dr. Addams said it was not only your gout acting up. That you also have a fever."

"Yes, that young fool has told me the gout cannot kill me. It only brings me bloody misery."

Margate began coughing violently as Cy stood helplessly watching him.

"I hated him, you know. I think we both did."

Cy understood his brother spoke of their father.

"He was the most selfish man I ever encountered. And yet I wanted to be just like him. I looked like him. I spoke like him. I merely wished to be a better version of him. Instead, I followed his same path, reveling in my title and bachelorhood. He did not wed until he was almost forty, you know."

A bitter smile crossed Margate's face. "I thought I, too, could enjoy my newfound wealth and live a debauched life until it was time to settle down and produce an heir for the dukedom."

The duke fell silent. Cy had nothing he could say.

Finally, Margate said, "I waited too long. I have wasted my entire life. I have been a terrible duke and ignored my people and my many responsibilities." His gaze pinned Cy's. "Tell me that you will be better at this than I ever was. Promise me you will make the Cressley name stand for something good again. Assure me that you will wed quickly and produce an heir. That you will raise him well and teach him right from wrong. That you will shower him with the love our father never bestowed upon either of us."

Margate's eyes closed. Cy did not reply. Instead, he moved to the side of the bed and sat upon it, placing his hand over his brother's for the first time ever.

He kept vigil beside Charles for a few hours, listening to his labored breathing and moans of pain. Then the breathing became even more erratic and suddenly ceased. He knew there was nothing Dr. Addams could have done to prevent this death. Cy only hoped that his presence had comforted Charles at his end. With a heavy heart, he rose and exited the bedchamber. He passed through the sitting room and study and opened the door to the corridor, where he found the valet and butler waiting together.

"His Grace is gone," Cy said softly. "I sat with him and held his hand until the end. His Grace was not alone when he passed. He had family at his side to comfort him. Do what you must now to prepare him. I will send a message to Dr. Addams and the local clergyman and consult Mrs. Arnold as to mourners returning to Melrose after His Grace's burial."

"Of course, Your Grace," Arnold said, addressing Cy with the title that now hung about his neck like an albatross, much as the suffering sailor from Coleridge's famous poem.

He was the Duke of Margate. Nothing could change that.

Cy only prayed this change in his life would not cost him Finola.

CHAPTER SEVENTEEN

FINOLA AND BERTIE brought all the dogs back to Belldale. She thought the boy a bit distracted, which would not do well in training. She knew he was not only sad and missing Pollux, but he was worried about Cy.

"You know what, Bertie? I think you and I need to go into Adderly."

"Really? Why?"

"Sometimes, it is good to give your dogs a day off from their training. The rest is good for both you and your pups, and it also will see if they have mastered what you have been working on, taking a slight break. They have gotten their exercise for now, and I think we should go into the village. We could see if Mrs. Carroll has any lemon cakes available."

That did the trick because Bertie broke out into a huge smile. "Could we, Finola? I really liked those lemon cakes. And we also got some cinnamon buns from her the other day when we went to the tailor's shop. They were also very good."

"Let's put the pups into the dog run, and then we can go into town."

They called to the dogs, who had been frolicking, and led them into the pen, seeing them safely inside. Finola secured the gate and then asked if Bertie would care to walk or use the cart to go into the village.

He pondered it a moment. "Do you have shopping to do, Finola? If you do, we should take the cart and put your goods into the back of it."

"I do have a few things I could pick up for Cook," she told him. "Let's go to the barn then."

She showed the lad how to hitch the horse to the cart, and they set out for Adderly. On the way, she decided to have a talk with Bertie.

"Things are going to be changing some," she began. "You see, Cy and I have decided that we will wed."

Bertie beamed at her. "I knew it! I told you that he liked you, Finola." He thought a moment. "Will you come live at the hunting lodge with us?"

"No, His Grace has only lent the use of it to Cy. I own Belldale, both the land and the house. The house is much bigger, and so we can live there."

"Can we keep training the dogs?"

She laughed. "Of course. It is the way I earn my keep. I hope you and Cy will keep helping me in this work. I know you like horses, too. You could help care for mine, even if it is only the one. You also might help out by milking our cow. Gilly does that twice a day now."

"I could learn how to milk," Bertie said eagerly. "When are you going to get married?"

"It is something we will discuss tomorrow when things get back to normal. You and Cy can continue to hold your morning lessons, and we will work with the pups in the afternoon together. Perhaps we'll discuss the wedding plans over tea tomorrow and arrive at a day and time. Of course, we will need to check with the Adderly clergyman to see when it would be convenient for him, as well. We could stop by the vicarage while we are in Adderly."

They arrived at the village and stopped in front of Mrs. Carroll's bakery. She asked Bertie if he would stay with the horse and cart while she went inside the bakery.

"I'm happy to watch the horse, Finola. What is his name?"

"It is Autumn," she said as they both climbed from the cart.

Bertie went straight to the horse, stroking his side, as Finola collected one of the baskets she had brought sitting in the cart's bed. She entered the bakery, the sweet scent invading her nostrils as she inhaled deeply.

"Ah, Lady Finola. I haven't seen you in a good while. How are your pups?"

"They are coming along nicely, Mrs. Carroll. Thank you for asking. In fact, I just delivered one this morning to the Duke and Duchess of Stoneham."

The baker pursed her lips in thought. "He's the one who owned that haberdashery, isn't he?"

"Yes, he is. Both Their Graces are lovely people."

She glanced about the bakery, taking in all the goods.

All business now, Mrs. Carroll asked, "What can I get for you today, my lady?"

"I spy lemon cakes and simply must have them. I see you have four. I will take all of them—and try not to eat one on the way to Belldale."

They both laughed and Finola moved about, pointing out a few more items, including some tarts she thought they might have at tea tomorrow afternoon. Mrs. Carroll wrapped up the goods, and Finola handed over the basket she had brought, allowing the baker to place the items into it.

"It was good seeing you, Mrs. Carroll."

"Come anytime, my lady."

Finola exited the bakery and saw Bertie in conversation with Autumn. She felt the boy was much like her, befriending animals and trusting them more than people. It had taken her years to get past the cruel trick Lord Crofton and his friends had played on her, but she was glad she had opened her heart to Cy. She knew Banny would have liked the former army officer very much and been relieved that Finola had found someone to love.

Bertie looked up as she placed the basket into the back of the cart. "Were there lemon cakes?"

"There were. I was even able to get enough for Gilly and Cook. Each of us will have one of our own, and no one need to share. Shall we go down to Mr. Simon's store now?"

"I don't know where it is. I haven't been there before. We only went to the tailor and the bakery."

"You may walk Autumn the few doors down if you like," she said. "It is on the right."

The lad took Autumn's bridle and led the horse as Finola walked alongside them. She pointed out which was Mr. Simon's store and this time had Bertie bring the horse to a stop.

"I will be back in a few minutes. I just have a few things to get."

She entered the general store and greeted the store's owner, picking up more tea and a small bag of sugar, placing both on the counter. She went back to a section and found a ledger, thinking it was time for Bertie to graduate from his slate to writing with a quill in hand.

After chatting briefly with Mr. Simon, he placed the goods in the basket she had brought inside. Finola returned outside and placed the basket into the cart's bed, next to the baked goods.

She heard the beating of horse's hooves and looked up as a rider raced down the main thoroughfare of Adderly. He wore elegant livery, and she guessed he came from Melrose. Again, she wondered what the duke wanted with Cy. Rumor had it that His Grace was in poor health since he was never seen, and she thought for a moment that the duke might be dying. She wondered who was next in line to assume the dukedom and would ask Cy about his visit to his relative when she next saw him.

As they climbed into the cart, Bertie said, "I know him. He's a footman at Melrose. He took me to the kitchens and got me something to eat when we first arrived."

"Do you mind if we stop now at the vicarage?"

"Not at all. I like seeing new places."

Finola took up the reins and flicked her wrists and Autumn started up. She drove the length of Adderly, reaching the end of the village where the graveyard stood. Next to it was the church and beyond that, the vicarage. She had not been to visit Banny in some time and felt the sudden urge to do so. She had noticed the horse that had passed them now stood tied to the post in front of the vicarage. Its rider was nowhere in sight. That meant he was inside delivering his message to Reverend Hall. It would give Bertie and her time to go and see Banny before calling upon the clergyman.

"Would you mind if we visited Banny's grave first?"

"No, Finola. Should I stay in the cart?"

"Why don't you come with me? I would appreciate your company."

They secured the horse and walked through the graveyard, straight to Banny's burial place.

"This is his headstone. Sir Roscoe Banfield was his name."

They paused, and she touched the stone, saying, "It's me, Banny. Come to visit you and introduce you to Bertie Briggs. He is helping me in training my Honeyfield spaniels."

Bertie looked at her wide-eyed. "Do you always talk to him?"

Finola smiled. "I do. Banny and I came to be a family of two when I was but eight years of age. We always talked to one another about everything. I feel close to him when I come here and like to have a conversation." She grinned. "Even if it is one-sided."

The boy laughed. "I miss talking to my parents—but I don't miss being around the war. So many people died or were hurt. Mum and I were always picking up and following the army. I like being in one place. I like learning how to read and write and how to train dogs."

"When the war ends someday, your parents might come to Melrose. Would you like that?"

He nodded solemnly. "I'll let you finish talking to Banny, Finola."

Bertie turned and left the graveyard, leaving her alone. She looked down at the headstone.

"Banny, you will not believe it—but I am going to be wed soon. I have found the most wonderful man in the world. We understand each other." She paused. "I love him. And he loves me. I will bring him here so he might see your final resting place. Cy knows how important you are to me. I just wanted to tell you how happy I am, Banny. We'll live at Belldale and continue training the dogs. Oh, you should see this latest litter."

Finola told Banny about each of the pups and then bid him farewell. She returned to Bertie, who stood at the gates of the graveyard, waiting for her.

"The rider came out of the vicarage and is gone, Finola. In case you wanted to stop in and ask about a wedding date."

"Let's do so. That way, I can tell Cy what days and times are available when we speak tomorrow."

They walked back to where Autumn stood, and Bertie took up a spot beside the horse. She went to the door and knocked.

Mrs. Hall answered the knock, her face flushed with excitement. Where Finola liked Reverend Hall and found him to be a humble, unassuming man, his wife was another matter. She was always the first to bring up and spread gossip. Finola did not enjoy being in the woman's company.

"Ah, Lady Finola, you're coming when we have a bit of excitement going on."

Reverend Hall appeared in the doorway behind his wife. "Hello, my lady. What brings you to see us? I am afraid I do not have time to visit with you now. I must get to Melrose at once."

Mrs. Hall stepped aside in order to allow her husband to pass and before Finola could excuse herself, the woman took Finola's elbow and said, "Come in, my lady."

"I only wanted to visit with—"

"Nonsense. You must come right in. I can get you a cup of tea."

She did not want to be there for as long as it took to brew and consume a cup of tea and said, "No, I really do need to get back to Belldale. I only wanted to ask Reverend Hall a quick question. I can do so at a later time."

Trying to look important, Mrs. Hall said, "Well, my husband will be busy the next few days." She paused, waiting for Finola to ask why and when she didn't, the clergyman's wife blurted out, "His Grace is gone. Dead, he is. Just like that."

She had suspected there was a reason Cy had been summoned to Melrose. Then she recalled that the footman had said the duke wanted to see Cy at once.

That could only mean the Duke of Margate had died while Cy was at Melrose. The rider they had seen—the footman Bertie had recognized—had brought the news of the duke's death to Reverend Hall. He must now be going to Melrose to discuss details regarding the funeral. She wondered if Cy might help with the arrangements.

"I am sorry to hear of his passing," she said politely. "I never met His Grace."

"Well," the woman said, "it is most convenient that Lord Cyrus returned when he did."

A cold chill ran through Finola. "Lord Cyrus?" she asked weakly.

"Yes, His Grace's younger brother. There were only the two of them. I am surprised you have not heard of his return. Some war injury, and he was booted from the army. I heard His Grace gave his brother the use of the hunting lodge on the estate. They weren't close, you know. The new duke won't be needing that now." Mrs. Hall chuckled. "Not with a house as grand as Melrose."

Nausea washed through Finola. "I must leave, Mrs. Hall."

"Why, my lady, you do not look well at all. Why don't you sit a few minutes and let me get you that cup of tea?"

"No," she protested, shaking her head vigorously. "I must go. Now."

Rushing to the door, she threw it open and went through the doorway, not bothering to close it behind her. She raced toward the cart.

"Get in," she shouted, scrambling into the cart, and taking up the reins.

"What's wrong, Finola?" Bertie asked, clearly puzzled by the abrupt change in her as he left the horse and climbed up beside her.

She urged the horse on, turning the cart and returning the way they had come. She did not speak until they had left Adderly behind. Once they were clear of the village, she pulled to the side of the road and drew up, bringing them to a halt.

Looking at Bertie, she asked, "Is Cy *Lord* Cyrus Cressley?"

His eyes grew wide, and he nodded.

"He is the brother of the Duke of Margate?"

Again, the lad nodded.

"Why do you not address him as Lord Cyrus then?"

"He asked me not to do so. I have always called him sir, Finola." Bertie swallowed hard. "It's what my father called him. Lord Cyrus asked I do the same when we were in your company."

Bitterness filled her. He was just another man who had toyed with her. She had fallen in love, thinking she could trust Cy implicitly. Now, she learned of this horrible betrayal.

She could never wed a man who had lied to her.

Who had used her . . .

Finola had given her virginity to this man. To a liar. She doubted he even wished to marry her. It had all been a game to him, one even more cruel than the one Viscount Crofton had played upon her. No, worse—because she had never loved Lord Crofton.

And she loved Cy with all her heart.

She took up the reins, and they traveled to Belldale in silence. When they reached the barn, Bertie climbed down and said, "I can help you rub down Autumn."

"No," she said sharply. "Return to the hunting lodge and wait for His Grace to come." When Bertie gasped, she said, "Yes. He is now the Duke of Margate. That is what Mrs. Hall told me. His brother died today. That is why Reverend Hall did not have time to speak with me."

Sadness filled the boy's face. Finola hated to hurt a child, but she could not be around Bertie—because that meant being around Cy. No, His Grace. He would never be Cy to her again. He would only be a stranger. She would not allow him to have any sway over her. In fact, she never intended to see or speak to him again.

"Do not return to Belldale, Bertie. Tell His Grace the same. I want nothing to do with either of you."

Tears flooded Bertie's eyes, and he looked as if he wanted to protest. His gaze met hers, and the boy realized she meant what she said.

"Goodbye, Finola." He turned and walked away, his head hung in sorrow.

She unhitched Autumn from the cart and brought him into his stall, where she rubbed him down.

Then Finola sat in the stall and wept a river of tears.

CHAPTER EIGHTEEN

W HEN CY RETURNED to the hunting lodge, it was close to seven in the evening. He had meant to send word to Bertie so the lad wouldn't worry. That good intention had been forgotten, though, as he was pulled in every direction. He met with the Arnolds to discuss the funeral arrangements. They were familiar with the surrounding community and knew more about the kind of service which should be held and who should be invited to it. Mrs. Arnold had opinions on what to serve to mourners when they returned to Melrose after the burial.

He finally told them he would open the service up to anyone who wanted to attend—tenants, servants, neighbors, and villagers alike. Cy didn't know how many people might show up. He didn't know any of his brother's friends and thought it useless to place an obituary in the London papers. The city was dead this time of year and would only come to life in spring once the Season began. He decided he would place a death notice then so that the members of the *ton* would know the Duke of Margate had passed.

By opening the funeral to the public, he realized some would come out of curiosity. Some would like the chance to say they had attended the funeral of a duke. He worried if he didn't, though, the turnout of mourners would be small enough to count on one hand. Though he and Charles had never been close, he hated the thought of there not being a goodly number of people present at the service.

Cy had sent a rider to Dr. Addams and Reverend Hall with the news, asking both men to come to Melrose at their earliest convenience. The Arnolds had then helped compose a list of prominent neighbors in the area that should be invited. Word of mouth would do for the rest. He composed brief notes to send to the local gentry, with all but the time and date of the funeral listed. Arnold was dispatched to speak to the Melrose steward, who would get word to the tenants on the property. Cy also dashed off quick notes to the people in the village he'd had contact with since his return—Mr. Simon, Mrs. Carroll, and Mr. Timmon. He would count on them in spreading the word that the funeral would be a public one, held in the church at Adderly.

Dr. Addams was the first to arrive and asked to examine the body. Hunt was in the middle of washing it and stopped so the physician could see the deceased duke. Dr. Addams returned to Cy and offered his condolences just as Arnold informed Cy that the blacksmith had finished with the coffin and was ready to bring it into the house. Arnold suggested His Grace be laid out in the downstairs parlor, and Cy agreed to the request.

By then, Reverend Hall had arrived. He was new to Cy, as the doctor had been, and a calming presence. The three men retreated to the study, Cy taking his place behind the desk for the first time. They discussed an appropriate day and time for the funeral and settled on the day after tomorrow at ten o'clock. Reverend Hunt said his wife and her ladies' guild would handle preparing the church.

"I am happy to speak during the service, Your Grace, but would you like to do so, as well?"

He thought of getting up in front of a large group and trying to speak kind words about a man he hadn't truly ever known.

"No, I will leave the eulogy to you, Reverend Hall."

They discussed the hymns to be played, and then the two men

stood to take their leave. Cy asked the clergyman to wait a moment. Once Dr. Addams was safely out of the room, he closed the door.

"I have one other matter to discuss with you," he began. "In fact, I was coming to see you about it tomorrow. Of course, things changed today. My life drastically has altered its course."

"Of course, Your Grace. You have experienced many changes recently, I am sure."

Cy knew the clergyman referred to Cy's vision and nodded brusquely.

"I was planning to wed and had gone to Chichester, where I obtained a bishop's license. I was told it was good for two weeks."

The older man nodded. "Yes, Your Grace. A bishop's license allows a couple to wed on the day of your choice, as long as the ceremony is performed inside a church and occurs between the hours of eight o'clock and noon. Did you have a specific day in mind?"

"No—and I feel others might believe it highly inappropriate if I wed so quickly after my brother's death. I have never had to take into account public opinion regarding my actions and decisions, but my new title says otherwise."

Reverend Hall shook his head. "I can subtly put out the word that the marriage was already planned, Your Grace. That the two of us had already spoken and arranged the details of the ceremony. No one will think less of you going through with your plans, especially now because it is important for you to wed in order to produce an heir."

"Unlike my brother."

"The previous duke was . . . shall we say . . . not one who was interested in Melrose or its people. I already have a far different impression of you, Your Grace. Perhaps it is because of your service to crown and country, but I believe you will take your duties as the Duke of Margate seriously."

"I plan to," he said, determined to do as Charles had asked and be a better duke than his father or brother had been.

"Since the funeral is set for Thursday, would you like the wedding ceremony to be performed on Friday morning? The church would already be filled with flowers for the occasion and need no further decoration."

"Yes, that would be satisfactory. Could we say eleven o'clock?"

He hoped Finola would not mind that he was going ahead and scheduling their wedding without her input. Still, he knew she was as eager as he was to cement the bonds between them and become husband and wife.

And it would give him time to tell her how their lives were about to be transformed in ways neither of them could imagine. Cy was only glad that they would make this transition together. Having Finola by his side would breed the confidence he needed to lead as the Duke of Margate.

"I won't speak of this for now but when the time is right, I will certainly put out the word that we already had these plans in motion."

"I am grateful, Reverend."

"Think nothing of it, Your Grace. I do hope we will be seeing you and your duchess every Sunday morning. I will also expect you on Friday morning with your bride. Might I ask who she is? Perhaps a childhood sweetheart?"

"No, I left no sweethearts behind when I went away to war. In fact, I had not thought to marry at all, being married to the army and my service to His Majesty. As for my bride? She is a local who is well known for raising her Honeyfield spaniels."

The clergyman smiled. "Ah, Lady Finola. She is a delight."

Lady Finola?

The older man's brow creased. "Is there something wrong, Your Grace?"

"No," he said, trying to hide the shock that rippled through him.

Reverend Hunt sighed. "Lady Finola is quite a lovely young woman. She has a sweet nature and is kind to everyone she meets. She is also a hard worker and dependable. I believe Lady Finola will make for a fine duchess."

"I know you are new to the area. At least since I left it for university and the army. Do you know how Lady Finola came to be here?"

"Oh, that was long ago. From what I recall hearing, her father, Lord Leppington, died with no heir, and so his title reverted to the crown."

"And Lady Finola had no family?"

Looking sheepish, the clergyman said, "None that would take her, Your Grace. She stayed with my predecessor for months while she awaited news from her family. When they refused to take her, a local gentleman stepped up."

"Sir Roscoe Banfield," Cy supplied.

"Yes, I believe that was the name. An agent of the crown sold Lord Leppington's estate. I don't know if the king ever awarded the earl's title to another or not."

He did not recall a Lord Leppington, but then again, he hadn't left Melrose other than to visit Adderly on rare occasions. Cy would have been away at school when Finola was orphaned. His heart ached for her, waiting all those months, only to be told no one wanted her. But why had she hidden the fact that she was an earl's daughter?

Then guilt rushed through him, knowing he had also kept from her that he was a duke's son.

And now a duke.

The clergyman told Cy what time to have his servants bring the coffin to the church on Thursday morning and then excused himself. Cy quickly filled in the date and time of the funeral on the notes he had previously written and then slipped the signet ring from his finger to seal them with the Margate seal. Hunt had sent the ring to Arnold, and the butler had given it to Cy earlier.

Ringing for Arnold, he asked that the butler send out riders to deliver the messages and informed the servants when the funeral service would be held.

"Have Mrs. Arnold and Cook decided on the menu for the mourners?"

"They have, Your Grace. Your rooms have also been prepared. All traces of the previous Duke of Margate have been removed. Shall I have servants go to the hunting lodge to pack your things?"

"Not until tomorrow morning, Arnold. I will spend a last night there."

Surprise flickered in the butler's eyes, but he kept his opinion to himself. "Very well, Your Grace. When would you like for the servants to arrive?"

"Nine o'clock," he said crisply. "I may not be there so have them come inside and gather everything. Make certain one is Maisie. She has done an excellent job cleaning the lodge since I took up residence there."

"Certainly, Your Grace."

The butler left with the notes to the neighbors, and Cy sat in the chair behind the desk once again, needing to absorb what he had just learned.

Finola was an earl's daughter. She was Lady Finola. Of course, he should have realized it by the way she conducted herself. Her posture. Her gracefulness. Still, he worried about why she had held the knowledge from him. She must have had her reasons, as did he. He wondered if he should let her know he knew of her origins and then decided he wouldn't mention it. What was important was for him to share that he was now the Duke of Margate—and that nothing had changed between them—other than the fact they would not live at Belldale, as planned. Instead, they would move into Melrose after their wedding.

He left the house and returned to the hunting lodge, seeing the lamp glowing through the window. When he entered, Bertie jumped to his feet.

"There you are, my lord. What kept you?"

"Sit, Bertie."

The lad took a seat, and Cy did the same.

"His Grace has passed. I am the new Duke of Margate."

"I know," the boy said quietly.

Fear seized him. "How? How do you know?" he demanded.

"Because Mrs. Hall told us. She's the clergyman's wife." Tears filled Bertie's eyes. "We went into Adderly this afternoon. Finola wanted to buy lemon cakes to cheer me up. And she told me . . . that you were to wed. She stopped at the church to ask about days you might be able to get married."

Bertie began sobbing. Cy reached for the boy and brought him into his lap, whispering comforting words to him.

"She acted funny when we left. And then she asked if you were Lord Cyrus Cressley." Bertie raised his tearstained face. "I had to tell her, my lord. I mean, Your Grace."

"Of course, you did," he assured the boy.

"She was so angry. She didn't even look like Finola. And she told me never to come back to Belldale. You—or me. She doesn't want to see us again."

Bertie began to bawl, and Cy rocked the boy, even as tears formed in his own eyes.

He had not had the chance to be open with her. He had not been able to tell her he was Margate's son.

And now *he* was the Duke of Margate.

Cy pulled a handkerchief from his pocket and handed it to Bertie. The boy blew his nose into it and mopped his eyes. He wriggled from Cy's lap.

"What are you going to do, Your Grace?"

Grim determination filled him.

"Whatever it takes to win her back."

CHAPTER NINETEEN

FINOLA BAWLED AS a lost sheep for a long time, curled into a ball. Finally, she forced herself to sit up and angrily swiped at the tears. Tears were good for nothing. She had cried copious amounts in the past, and they had been for naught. She remembered crying nightly in bed after her father's death. Not because she missed him—but because she was worried about her future. Even at the tender age of eight, her gut had told her that her sisters in Scotland would not want her—and she had been right. If Banny had not stepped up and volunteered to take her in, she didn't know what would have become of her.

She had also cried a river of tears after the cruel trick played on her by Lord Crofton and his cronies. That experience had led her to becoming untrusting of all men.

Until Cy had appeared.

She knew now that he lied just as other so-called gentlemen did. She had fallen for his lies. His sweet words of love. Finola had given him the most precious gift she had to give.

All for naught.

She could forgive herself for thinking she had a future with Viscount Crofton. She had been young and foolish and hadn't known any better. What hurt now was that she had not learned from that previous experience and been caught in Cy's web of deceit. That's what hurt now. He had made her fall in love with him. With Lord

Crofton, she had not had the emotional investment.

But with Cy, damn him to Hell, she still did love him. Or at least love the man she thought he was.

None of this did her any good. Finola understood she was not meant to love or be loved. That her life was to be a lonely one. Yes, she would have her dogs, but even then, she could not become too emotionally invested in them because they, too, would always leave her one day.

Pushing to her feet, she swiped at the remaining tears on her cheeks and pulled herself together. She collected the two bags from her visit to the village and returned to the house, entering through the kitchens.

"I have lemon cakes for you," she said brightly.

"Lemon cakes!" squealed Gilly, her joy apparent. "Oh, thank you, my lady."

Cook studied her wordlessly as Finola handed over what she had bought at Mr. Simon's store.

"I feel a bit of a headache coming on," she told her servants. "I hope some tea and a lemon cake might help, but I would like a hot bath afterward."

"I will put the kettle on, my lady, as well as water for your bath" Cook replied, handing over the ledger Finola had purchased for Bertie. "This must be for you."

"Thank you," she said, accepting it.

Going to Banny's study, she placed the ledger inside one of the desk's drawers and sat, forcing her mind to stay blank until the tea and cake arrived.

"The water's on for your bath, my lady," Gilly said. "I do hope you feel better soon."

Finola smiled weakly and sipped the tea. She tried to force down the lemon cake unsuccessfully. When she finished her tea, she returned her things to the kitchens and then entered the stillroom.

Cook was pouring water into the tub. Finola never made her servants bring the tub and hot water to her. Instead, the three of them used the same tub, which was kept in the stillroom since it was just off the kitchens.

"I'll leave you to it, my lady," Cook said, exiting the room.

She stripped off her clothes and stepped into the tub, sinking until the water came up to her chin. The scent of lavender surrounded her, and Finola knew Gilly had added some of the oil to the bath.

She couldn't help it. The tears came again and she let them, hoping this would be the last time for them. She would have to put on a stoic face to the world, but for now, she allowed herself to wallow in pity.

Finally, she scrubbed herself and stood, rinsing away the soap and then drying off with the bath sheet Gilly had left for her. Wrapped in the bath sheet, Finola returned to her bedchamber and dressed in her night rail, placing her dressing gown over it, and belting it at the waist. She brushed her hair and left it undone.

Going to the parlor, she removed a book from the shelf as the grandfather clock, Banny's pride and joy, chimed eight times. The household went to bed early since they rose well before dawn each morning. Usually, Cook and Gilly were asleep by eight, while Finola would read until half-past eight and then head to bed. Tonight, though, the book remained opened and unread in her lap. She decided to seek refuge in her bed although she knew sleep would most likely not come for hours.

As she replaced the book on the shelf, a loud pounding sounded on the door.

Cy.

It could be no one else.

Gathering her courage, she stepped from the parlor and saw Gilly come into the foyer.

"Go back to bed," she ordered. "I will deal with this."

The servant hesitated. "Are you sure, my lady?"

Finola nodded and Gilly left.

The pounding continued, and she moved to the door, steeling herself before she opened it. Cy stood there, a lantern in one hand, wearing a look of desperation.

"Finola."

"I suppose you did not understand the message I gave to Bertie, so I will say it to your face, Your Grace. I want nothing to do with you. I have nothing to say to you. I wish never to see you again. Please do not call at Belldale again."

She closed the door. Or at least tried to. Cy had stuck his booted foot so that the door would not shut. Opening it again, she slammed her palm into his chest, forcing him back. Finola closed the door behind her, not wanting lurking servants to hear what she had to say.

"I did not think you to be so thick, Your Grace. You are no longer welcome at Belldale. You are a liar. I want you to leave."

"Do you, Lady Finola?"

She drew in a quick breath.

"Yes, I have learned your identity, as you have learned mine."

"It doesn't change things between us, Your Grace."

"Why didn't you tell me you were an earl's daughter?"

"Why didn't you tell me you were a duke's son?" she countered.

"I didn't think we could be friends if I did," he said. "Something in the way you spoke of the *ton* led me to believe you had a very unfavorable impression of them." He paused. "I didn't lie to you, Finola. I was Lieutenant-General Cyrus Cressley. I was wounded and forced to sell my commission and return to England. I did come to my childhood home, where a brother I was never close to wanted nothing to do with me. Margate didn't even want me staying in his house and only reluctantly allowed me use of the hunting lodge."

Cy sighed. "I found a friend in you, Finola. And then even more. I love you."

She shook her head, doubt filling her as she saw nothing but honesty in his eyes. She hardened herself, not wanting to be duped again by sweet, false words.

"Even now, when you are suddenly a duke, you still play games with me. I have been down this path before, Your Grace. Yes, I made my come-out many years ago. I was an overweight, idealistic young girl and thought I might have a chance to make a match. To become a wife and mother. To have a family I could love. And Viscount Crofton paid me special attention. Fool that I was, I thought he would offer for me."

Bitterness filled her. "Instead, it was all a game for him and his worthless, rakehell friends."

"What did he do?" Cy asked quietly.

"He raised my hopes. He kissed me—and then he laughed at me for even thinking he might want someone like me. A chubby no one, with a miniscule dowry and no social connections. This was in front of all of his friends. They chose a girl each Season and one of them pursued her, making her think she was wanted when she was not."

"This man humiliated you," Cy said, fury in those piercing green eyes.

"He did. But he taught me that no man could be trusted. I lost my self-respect that night, along with Banny, who died that same night. It has taken me years to come to find my self-worth again. I will not let you or anyone like you tear me down again."

Finola locked her gaze with his. "I will not be the fool again. Leave, Your Grace. And never come back."

She whirled and hurried into the house, slamming and locking the door. Leaning her back against it for support, hot tears flooded her eyes and poured down her cheeks as she slid down the door to the floor. Cy knocked on it, pleading for her to open it, telling her that he loved her and they could work things out. She hardened her heart and held her ground, not moving a muscle.

Finally, the knocking stopped.

He was gone.

Doubt filled her. No, not doubt. She realized that Cy had loved her. He had been a man lost when he returned to Melrose, receiving not a welcome but being shunned by his older brother. He had lost his place in the world and thought he had found a new life with her. She did recall him saying he needed to speak to her about something important tomorrow. She supposed he was going to confess he was a duke's son before they wed. She would have then told him she was a lady. It had been wrong for the both of them to hide such a secret from the other, especially after they had fallen in love.

But it was too late for them. Even if she did love him, Finola could never marry him now. He was a bloody duke. He needed to marry a woman of great charm and beauty. One who had been raised in the cradle of Polite Society and knew how to maneuver through it. The Duke of Margate needed a woman who was comfortable among the *ton*. Who could step forth and be a leader. Duchesses were women who set the fashion of the day. Held the best balls and parties. Sparkled and shone brighter than the sun.

Finola was a woman who worked for a living. Who traipsed about in men's clothing. Who had no friends or family and absolutely no social connections. She wasn't comfortable among people and only wanted to be around her dogs.

In other words, Lady Finola Honeyfield was the absolute last woman the Duke of Margate should wed.

CHAPTER TWENTY

C Y FOLDED THE clothes he had and placed them on the bed for them to be taken back to Melrose. Heaviness weighed upon his heart. Each day would now feel like this.

A day without Finola.

He had tried to convince her last night that he loved her. Cy realized in Finola's eyes that he had betrayed her, much as that viscount she had spoken of last night. He couldn't begin to fathom the cruelty Lord Crofton had shown to Finola, giving her hope of a union between them, only to subject her to embarrassment and a crushing humiliation. Worse, she had mentioned that her beloved Banny had died on that very night. How she had survived such a betrayal and come to be the lovely, gracious woman she was amazed him. Then again, it shouldn't. Finola was remarkable in every way.

Regret filled him. He wanted to apologize for what he hadn't revealed. He wanted her to give him a second chance. She was too bruised from her previous experience, though, and he doubted that would ever occur.

Bertie had waited up until Cy returned the previous evening. He saw the look of hope in the boy's eyes and hated stamping it out. Cy hadn't said a word. He'd merely shaken his head and gone up the stairs. For the first time since their arrival at the hunting lodge, Bertie had not slept on the floor next to him. He needed to do right by the boy.

And that meant seeing Bertie placed in Finola's care.

As a duke, he would no longer have time to tutor the boy each day. He intended to see Bertie educated, though. He also wanted the lad placed in Finola's care. Bertie had a way with the pups and should not be kept from the litter.

Or from Finola.

Perhaps they could lean upon one another and begin to heal.

He went downstairs and saw Bertie was slicing bread for them, as well as part of a ham Maisie had brought to them from the Melrose kitchens.

"I have breakfast for you, Your Grace," the boy said quietly, none of his usual energy and sense of fun in play. "I have also steeped the herbs for your eyewash."

Taking a seat, Cy said, "Thank you, Bertie. Servants will be here at nine o'clock this morning. They will move my things to Melrose." He paused. "I am going to see Finola and ask that she take you in."

The boy had been staring at his untouched food and quickly looked up. "But I am to stay with you, Your Grace. Father said so."

"You had done an admirable job caring for me, Bertie. The thing is, I will have a legion of people to care for me now that I am a duke. I told your father I would see that you had a profession to follow. We both know your future lies in training dogs. I know you love Finola as much as her dogs. Might I speak to her on your behalf and ask that she make you her apprentice? She wanted to do so before all this mess occurred. Is it still what you want?"

Bertie's eyes filled with tears. "It is, Your Grace," he whispered. "I love being with the pups. It just . . . feels right."

"Then I will make it so. Stay here. Help in any way you can when the servants arrive. When I return, you and I will go into Adderly. Your new clothes should be ready by now."

"Will Finola be angry that you have come again?"

Cy chuckled. "I will wager she will." He ruffled the boy's hair. "But I will willingly face her wrath on your behalf."

He removed his eye patch and then applied the wet cloth to his eyes, resting his hand against it to keep it in place as he ate. He worried Finola would not speak to him and so decided he would write to her instead. The only problem was that he had no writing materials at the hunting lodge. He would have to convince Gilly to let him into the schoolroom.

Removing the cloth, he gave Bertie a smile and left for Belldale. Cy cut through the copse but then had to give a wide berth in order to avoid the dog run. He came to the front of the house, thankful he had not been seen, and knocked.

Gilly opened the door. Her jaw dropped, and she sputtered something he did not understand.

Taking control of the situation, Cy said, "I know I am not supposed to be here. That Lady Finola has given you strict orders to slam the door in my face. I must write a letter to her, though, and I had no materials to do so. I want her to take on Bertie. You know how good the lad is with the dogs, Gilly. In my letter, I will ask your mistress to allow Bertie to stay here at Belldale and be her apprentice. Would you let me in so that I might write that letter? I fear if I approach Lady Finola, she will not hear me out."

He paused, playing on the girl's sympathies. "It is for Bertie I do this. Please."

"All right," Gilly said, reluctance in her voice. "But be quick about it, Your Grace."

Cy went to where he had schooled Bertie and removed an inkwell and quill from a cupboard. He found parchment and scribbled out a brief note to Finola.

When he finished, he found Cook standing outside the door. She had been kind to Bertie and him.

"Are you trying to make it right with her ladyship, Your Grace?"

He shook his head. "For Bertie, Cook. Not for me. I fear I have broken Lady Finola's trust. She wishes to have nothing to do with me."

"It was hard for her. Coming here after her father's death. Those sisters up in Scotland not wanting her. Sir Roscoe was good for her lady, and she was good for him." Cook paused. "I think you would also be good for her, Your Grace. Try to mend things between you."

"I am fighting first for Bertie, Cook," he told the old woman. "I am second. Once Bertie is taken care of—and Lady Finola has some time to ponder our situation—I will try again. I will never keep trying, Cook. She is the love of my life."

The servant nodded in approval. "Give me the letter, Your Grace. I will see it in her hands and make certain she reads it."

He gave her a spontaneous hug. "Thank you, Cook. I will wait at the edge of the copse. Lady Finola can find me there and give me her reply."

She pinkened. "I want what's best for Lady Finola. I think that is you."

Cy watched the woman waddle off and slipped from the house. Once more, he gave a wide berth to the back of the house and the dog run. He doubted Finola would come close to exercising the dogs near the copse, which is why he thought it safe to wait there.

He reached the edge of the woods and began his vigil.

FINOLA FINISHED WORKING with Triton and returned him to the dog run. She called to Hermes and the dog came running, eager to leave the pen and do today's work. She had him heel and was leading Hermes away from the dog run when she saw Cook coming her way. That in itself was odd. Cook rarely left the kitchens, must less the house.

"A note for you, my lady," the servant said, handing over a folded piece of parchment.

She accepted it, wondering who might be sending her a message. Usually the ones she received were sealed by the signet rings of the aristocracy. She opened it and glanced down the page for the name of its author.

Cy . . .

Refolding it, she thrust it at Cook. "Take it back," she demanded.

"I cannot do that, my lady. Because you haven't read it." Cook crossed her arms and stared at Finola, stubbornness written across her face.

"Is he here?" she asked, her voice shaking.

"He was. He left. But I promised him that you would read this."

"You had no right."

Cook's eyes flashed. "I have every right, my lady. I have watched you grow up these many years. You are the closest thing to a daughter I will ever have. I have seen you smile. Laugh. Play. And I have seen you wounded by others. I have fed you and listened to you and burst at pride with who you have become. The least you could do for me to repay me for all those years invested in you is to read the note." She paused. "Read the note, my lady," the old woman encouraged.

Reluctantly, Finola opened it again.

Lady Finola —

I know you do not wish to hear from me, but I have a final favor to ask of you. It regards Bertie.

I will have many servants to look after me now. Bertie's heart lies with you and your pups. We both know the lad has an innate sense of how to handle a dog and the way to draw the best from him or her. He also has grown fond of not only your pups—but you.

I ask that you take Bertie in and allow him to apprentice with you. I will find a tutor for him so that he might continue his morning lessons and then work with the litter each afternoon. I know I can trust you to keep him safely under your roof and care for him.

Please put aside any hard feelings you have toward me. Bertie is blameless. Do what is best for the boy.

If you agree to this, meet me now at the edge of the copse.

Cy

Finola re-read the contents again and looked up. "I will go and meet His Grace. He is asking that Bertie Briggs join our household. His Grace will provide a tutor to continue the boy's lessons and then Bertie will work with me and the dogs each afternoon. Would you please have Gilly prepare a place for Bertie to sleep?"

"I will, my lady."

Cook left, and Finola decided to keep Hermes with her. She led him away from the house and toward the edge of Belldale, where the wooded area began, dividing her property from that of the Duke of Margate. As they grew close, she recognized Cy's familiar figure pacing in the distance. He caught sight of her and came to a halt, watching as she approached.

Her heart began to ache, a physical pain in her chest, as she drew near. Cy looked so handsome. She thought of the kisses they had shared. The plans they had made for their future. It almost caused her to collapse in a heap. Instead, she pressed on, her mouth set in a firm line.

"Thank you for coming," he said when she reached him. "Will you take on Bertie?"

"Of course. He has a way with the dogs that simply cannot be taught. It is more than instinct. It is intuitive on his part."

"He would be miserable if I took him away from the dogs. Or you."

"I agree to have him come to Belldale, Your Grace, but you are not allowed to visit him there. If you wish to see him, it will have to be at

Melrose."

"I understand. Could you . . . would you send me a monthly report of how he fares?"

Finola would sooner stab herself in the heart than write to this man. A man she still loved.

"No, but I can send him to Melrose once a month and he can share with you himself how he is doing. Of course, you will be in London for a good portion of the year, with the Season and whatnot."

His brow furrowed. "Why would I wish to partake in the Season?"

She felt her face grow warm. "Naturally, you will wish to find your duchess, Your Grace. Heirs do not grow on trees."

The heat in his eyes nearly undid her as he said, "There will be no duchess, my lady. No children. No heir."

"Why not?" she asked, her body beginning to tremble, her voice shaking, her breath unsteady.

Cy gave her the saddest smile she had ever seen. "Because the only woman I wish to be in that role is you."

She flinched at his words. No, he did not mean it. She was not and never could be duchess material. He would change his mind. Cy was a man who would take his duties as Duke of Margate seriously. He would want to make certain his people were looked after and not leave that to chance. To another, distant family member or even letting the title and lands return to the crown. He would come to see all this in time.

And then he would find a worthy woman to wed.

"Send Bertie to me as soon as you would like, Your Grace," she said formally.

"We have talked. He wants to be at the funeral with me tomorrow. It is to be held in the church at eleven o'clock tomorrow morning." Cy hesitated. "Reverend Hall also agreed to perform our wedding Friday morning at that same time. In case you change your mind."

Her face now flamed, and she shook her head violently. "You were wrong to speak to him of such a thing," Finola protested.

He smiled wryly. "At the time, I thought we still loved one another and wished to wed. I even told Reverend Hall for the first time I was worried about what others thought, with us marrying so soon after my brother's death. He assured me he would make it known that he knew of the wedding arrangements before His Grace's untimely death."

Cy reached for her hand and took it. She tried to pull away, but he threaded his fingers through hers.

"We can still marry on Friday, Finola. Or the day after that. Or the day after that one. The license is good for two weeks. I know I hurt you by not sharing who I was, but I had planned to do so before we spoke our vows. I am sorry I did not tell you I was Margate's son. Or that I was brother to the new duke."

His brother had been duke for several years. She supposed Cy had not known of his father's passing and only learned of it when he returned from the war.

The thing is, Finola did still love him. She could easily forgive Cy for not telling her of his rank in Polite Society. After all, she had not told him of hers. She also realized he hadn't even considered that he was his brother's heir and that Margate's death had caught him by surprise.

But it was *because* she loved him that she could no longer marry him. He deserved a woman who would fit seamlessly into the world of the *ton* and become one of its ranking members. Banny had teasingly called Finola a tomboy, and she knew that's what she was. Not a woman of beauty or dignity or style or grace. She was the antithesis of what Polite Society would expect in a duchess.

Yet she knew Cy would never accept such reasoning. If she shared with him why she hesitated to marry him, he would convince her to do so. Finola could never allow that. It would be difficult enough for

Cy himself to step into a role he never expected to be thrust upon him. The proper wife could smooth the way for him and help him make friends and see that doors opened easily to him. She could never make those things happen because she wasn't the kind of woman a duke—or any gentleman—married.

"Let the past be the past, Your Grace," she told him. "I will attend the funeral and take Bertie home with me tomorrow."

Cy stiffened. "His things will be back at Melrose. Would you consider coming there after the funeral? Arnold told me it is expected for me to open the house and allow the mourners to come and gather."

"Yes, I can do so. Have Bertie pack his things. I won't stay long."

Cy squeezed her fingers. "Thank you for taking the lad, my lady. He worships you and would have been forlorn if kept from you."

He released her and took a step back. Finola longed to step to him. To wrap her arms about his neck and pull her down to him for a long, delicious kiss. She had to bite her lip and stand her ground so that she wouldn't move toward him and ruin everything.

"Until tomorrow, Your Grace," she said.

Finola hurried away, calling Hermes to come with her. She didn't dare turn back and look at Cy.

But she knew he was watching every step she took away from him.

CHAPTER TWENTY-ONE

C Y ALLOWED HUNT, the valet he had inherited from his brother, to finish tying the cravat. Once done, Hunt helped Cy slip into his new tailcoat, one Mr. Timmon had waiting for him yesterday when he'd taken Bertie to the village to get his new clothes, as well as pick up the last of his own clothing awaiting at the tailor's shop. He didn't care if others thought it odd that the small boy rode in the ducal carriage with him. They were going to the same place, and he would enjoy Bertie's company for the short time they had left together.

Mr. Timmon had told Cy the minute he heard that the Duke of Margate had passed, he knew the new duke would need appropriate funeral garb and had made up the sober, severe black coat. The tailor had allowed Bertie to try on his new clothes and while the boy did so, Mr. Timmon told Cy that he would need to order many more clothes.

When he questioned why he would do so, the tailor had looked blank a moment and then told him a duke needed ten times the wardrobe Cy now owned, including evening clothes for social occasions. Cy informed the tailor he would send word if anything else needed to be made up in the near future and that Mr. Timmon had his measurements to do so. The tailor asked about the Season and all that would be needed since it was right around the corner.

That was when Cy informed him he had no plans to attend this Season or any other.

His words had caused an abrupt halt to their conversation. Bertie had appeared then, and Mr. Timmon fussed over the boy a bit before they left to return to Melrose.

Mrs. Carroll had dashed out with a basket telling him she had more lemon cakes for him as she pressed the basket's handle into his hand. She had also thanked him for opening the funeral to the public, telling Cy that a majority of the villagers would be in attendance. Not for the dead duke.

But for Cy, the new Duke of Margate.

He had thanked the baker, and then he and Bertie had climbed into the ducal carriage to return to Melrose. It had felt wrong of him riding in something so grand. Cy was a man of simple tastes and the vehicle had looked to him like something the King of England would travel in.

Glancing into the mirror, he saw he looked appropriately dressed and thanked Hunt.

"It is a pleasure to serve you, Your Grace." Then worry filled the valet's face. "That is, if you wish me to serve you. I will understand if you bring in another valet."

"I have no other valet in mind, Hunt," he assured the servant. "You are stuck with me."

Hunt beamed. "Thank you, Your Grace."

Cy dismissed the valet. He didn't truly want a valet but knew a man in his position was expected to have one. If he let Hunt go, the servant would be out of a job. He would just have to get used to one and told him to think of Hunt as another Briggs, a batman for civilian life.

Going downstairs, he entered the breakfast room. Arnold greeted him and asked what he would like.

"Anything Cook makes will suit me."

Arnold signaled a footman and sent him to the kitchens and then informed Cy that the coffin had been delivered to the church for this morning's service.

"Thank you for handling those details, Arnold," he said.

"Of course, Your Grace."

As he sat, a footman pulling out his chair for him, Cy doubted he would ever hear his name again. Already, he had been called Your Grace close to a hundred times.

Besides, the only person who might have used it was no longer speaking to him.

Cy ate, looking over the London newspapers that rested next to his plate. They were a few days old. Arnold had told him the former duke had them delivered twice a week to Melrose. He supposed he better start reading them thoroughly so as to be informed.

A footman entered the room and spoke briefly to Arnold, who proceeded to come to Cy.

"Your Grace, Mr. Solway is here."

"Who might that be?"

"He is your solicitor, Your Grace."

"Have him wait in my study."

"Yes, Your Grace."

Cy finished his breakfast, which had been delicious, and refrained from rubbing his left eye. He had not done the eyewash this morning and could already tell his eyes were dry and irritated. He chuckled to himself, believing the mourners in attendance at the funeral would think his reddened eye was due to tears. No, he would shed none for Charles. If any came, they would be for the dream he would have given up.

A life with Finola.

He wasn't ready to do so just yet. Cy still held out hope that her feelings for him remained as strong as his feelings for her. That given time, Finola would see he was the same man he had been before a ducal title had been bestowed upon him.

A thought occurred to him. They had made love the one time.

What if a child resulted from that coupling?

He hoped it did—because that might be the one thing which would convince Finola to wed him. She would love a child and would not keep him or her from their father, much less all the wealth and entitlement that would come by being the offspring of a duke.

Or would she?

Turning to Arnold, he said, "Have my carriage readied. I will not be with Mr. Solway for long. And have young Bertie summoned. He will accompany me to Adderly. Be sure you allow plenty of time for the staff to reach the church, as well."

Finally, Arnold's exterior showed the faint sign of a crack. "Your Grace, might you make the boy a page? Or he could be placed in the stables. He could be trained to be a groom and eventually a driver. I know you are fond of the lad but—"

"Bertie will be leaving us today, Arnold. He will be going to apprentice with Lady Finola Honeyfield and work with her in training her spaniels. Now, tell the stables to prepare my carriage *and* summon Bertie." He paused and lowered his voice so only the two of them and not all the footmen present could hear. "And please keep your opinions to yourself."

"Yes, Your Grace," the butler assured him.

Cy left the breakfast room and went to his study. It was a room he felt comfortable in, likely because he had no sense of Charles having ever used it.

He entered, and a man with light brown hair and hazel eyes rose. "Your Grace, I am Solway. My father has been the Cressley family solicitor for many years, but he recently took a tumble and broke his leg. I work with him now and so have come to Melrose in his place."

"Are you familiar with my holdings?"

"I am, Your Grace. Quite familiar, seeing as how you are our most important client."

"You have a quarter-hour to say what you came to say."

Quickly, the solicitor ran through the list of estates owned by the

Duke of Margate and the location of each. He was informed that he owned two ships and that trade was brisk and profitable. Solway gave Cy a figure and said that was what was deposited in the Bank of England.

"Of course, you also draw yearly income from Melrose, as well. Your steward can help familiarize you with the workings of Melrose, Your Grace. You might also go through the ledgers with him and have him explain what the estate produces and what portion of that is due to you."

"I will. Anything else, Mr. Solway?"

"No, Your Grace. I plan to return to London now." The solicitor produced a card, and Cy took it. "You may write to Father or me at this address, and we will come whenever you need to speak with us."

Cy found it curious that the man would come this far and not stay for the funeral service.

"You are welcome to attend the funeral, Mr. Solway."

"I really had no relationship with His Grace, Your Grace. My time is better spent back at the office in London."

"Then good day to you."

"Thank you."

He decided that his new solicitor had no fondness for the previous duke. It caused him to wonder who might show up at today's service.

When Cy went outside, he found Bertie awaiting him beside the carriage.

"To the church," he instructed the coachman, thinking he would need to learn the man's name, as well as meet all his other servants and tenants.

In the carriage, Cy told Bertie, "Lady Finola will be at today's funeral. She will return to Melrose with the mourners and when she leaves, she will take you with her. Be sure to take all your belongings."

Tears formed in the boy's eyes, and Cy said, "Don't worry. You know how much fun you will have living with her and working with the pups. She has agreed that you can come to Melrose every month to visit and update me on what you have been doing."

Bertie now began to cry. Cy placed an arm about him. "I may need you to train a pup for me. Just think—I could be the owner of a Honeyfield spaniel trained by Bertie Briggs."

The lad smiled through his tears. "I'd be happy to do so, Your Grace."

They arrived in Adderly a short time later and after they left the carriage, he said, "Go inside the church, Bertie, and stay. I need to find Reverend Hall and speak with him."

They entered the church, and he saw the coffin standing at the front. A man in his early twenties came to greet them, explaining he was the curate.

"Where is Reverend Hunt?"

"He is still at the vicarage, Your Grace."

"Thank you."

Cy went next door and knocked on the door. A servant answered and led him to the clergyman's study. The door was open. He lightly tapped on the frame, and Reverend Hunt motioned him in. Cy entered and closed the door behind him.

"Have a seat, Your Grace. I was just reading over my eulogy."

"I wanted to visit with you before the service began. I would ask that you do not mention tomorrow's wedding to anyone." He hesitated and then added, "There may not be one. In fact, I highly doubt there will be."

"I see. If and when there is, I will be here and ready to perform the ceremony."

He liked that Reverend Hall did not press him on the issue.

"I also will not mention anything to my wife. She has, shall I say, a tendency to let her mouth run away with her. If the time comes, though, and you and Lady Finola do wish to speak your vows sometime in the next two weeks, I can summon Mrs. Hall as a witness if need be."

"Thank you. I have one other issue to discuss with you."

Briefly, Cy explained how he been tutoring Bertie every morning and then the boy had been working with Lady Finola in training her Honeyfield spaniels.

"He is the son of my batman. Bertie has become very dear to me. I would like to continue the present arrangement, with Bertie focusing on his studies in the morning and dog training in the afternoon. Do you know of any candidates who might serve as the boy's tutor? I would pay handsomely, as if the position were all day."

Reverend Hall steepled his fingers. "I have the perfect candidate in mind, Your Grace. My wife's nephew. He is finishing his university education at the end of this term and is looking for work as a tutor. The boy also fancies himself a writer. This position would allow him to earn his keep and give him plenty of time to discover whether or not he has what it takes to be a published author."

"He sounds perfect for the position. Would you write to him and see if he is interested? If so, I will contact him myself and explain the situation and salary. I could even allow him use of the hunting lodge where I stayed until recently. It is only a short walk to Belldale from it."

"I will do so, Your Grace. Thank you. It is a most generous offer."

Cy excused himself and went outside, seeing a few people starting to enter the church. He noticed Stoneham standing beside his carriage and made his way to him.

"Your Grace."

He grimaced at the address and asked, "Do you ever tire of hearing your title used over and over? As if people are thrilled to be speaking to a duke and can't help but let the title roll from their tongue."

Stoneham laughed. "I understand better than most and yes, I find it tiresome and distracting. Why don't we decide to forego using it when we are alone? I am Pierce."

"I am Cy. Thank you. You might be keeping me from going mad, Pierce."

"Shall we walk?"

They fell into step together, moving away from the church. Cy knew they had a good half-hour before the service began.

"So, you find yourself in my shoes. Suddenly a duke. At least you were the heir and not taken unaware as I was. From haberdasher to duke in the blink of an eye."

He shrugged. "From soldier to duke. I truly did not expect this. I had been gone from England a long time and assumed my brother had wed. When I arrived, I found our father had died several years ago and my brother was in extremely poor health. You would think I would have realized with Charles being so sick and without a son that I should have considered the possibility that I might become the next Duke of Margate."

"But you didn't."

"No. I was too busy adjusting to life outside the army and with only one eye to see the world." He paused. "And falling in love. Oh, I have made a mess of that, Pierce."

"Did you tell Finola of your new status? How did she react?"

"You mean *Lady* Finola? I am certain you and your duchess were aware of that fact."

Pierce nodded solemnly. "We were. That is why I encouraged you not to keep secrets from one another. I was speaking of Finola as much as you, Cy."

"I tried to tell her the day we returned from Stonecrest. She was focused on her dogs, however, and then I was called away to Melrose. My brother died a few hours after I arrived."

"So, she learned you were a duke before you could tell her you were a duke's son."

He shook his head. "Worse than that. While I was at Melrose, she took Bertie into the village to cheer him up from being parted from

Pollux. Mrs. Hunt, the reverend's wife, is a gossip. *She* is the one who shared with Finola that Margate had died—and his brother, recently returned from the war, was now the new duke."

"Ouch!" his new friend declared.

"Things went from bad to worse, Pierce. Finola wants nothing to do with me. I tried to explain how I had tried to tell her. How nothing need change between us. Yes, we would both have titles, but we were the same people we have always been."

Cy shook his head. "Nothing I said mattered. I had broken her trust. She revealed she had been hurt years earlier by a man during her come-out Season. A man who betrayed her in the worst way. Finola feels I, too, betrayed her. And in her mind, that is an unforgivable sin."

Pierce placed a hand on Cy's shoulder. "Would you like me to speak to her? Or Nalyssa?"

"No, that is kind of you to offer, but I don't wish to hurt her friendship with the two of you. If you spoke on my behalf, it would be as if you had chosen sides. *Not* her side. She needs a friend who will be loyal to her. I botched things badly. I will give her time. I am hoping that will heal the rift between us and that Finola will realize love can conquer all. I vow never to think about loving another woman except Finola, and I will certainly not wed anyone who is not her."

Pierce squeezed Cy's shoulder. "Know I am here for you. We dukes—especially those who never expected to be one—need to stick together."

"Thank you for your support." He looked around. "We should go inside the church. I invited the public, fearing Charles was so disliked that no one would attend if I did not open it up."

"You'll have a seat," Pierce assured him. "A duke always does. It is a perk of our position."

They crossed the road and went into the church, which was packed. Reverend Hall gestured to them, and they made their way up the aisle, sitting in the first row, which was empty.

"See? I told you," Pierce said. "Of course, this is the ducal pew and the duke is expected to help maintain things, such as the roof of the church he attends."

Reverend Hall caught Cy's eyes, and he nodded to the clergyman, figuring it was time to start the service. Cy did his best not to turn around and look for Finola. He had not spied her as they walked up the aisle.

He hoped she would come. He hoped she had changed her mind.

Bowing his head, he prayed she would forgive him.

CHAPTER TWENTY-TWO

Seven weeks later . . .

C Y LEFT FOR London immediately after his visit with Bertie. He had told the boy he had business in town—and he did.

Revenge.

He had spent the weeks since he had parted from Finola by learning all he could about what being the Duke of Margate meant. He had spent hours closeted with his steward, gathering information about Melrose and his tenants. He had gone through the ledgers for the last decade, back to his father's time as the duke, to see what the estate produced and how much of it. He began to do what he thought should be done by a duke, meaning caring for others on Melrose lands, but others in the area, as well.

Though he didn't have time at the present to visit his other holdings, he had written to the various stewards on these properties and had them come to Melrose, where he questioned them about the estates they managed, gleaning everything he could and promising to visit these properties in the near future.

He had also met with Reverend Hall, and they had come up with a program for improving the church. He also wanted to do things to enhance Adderly. He had even socialized some, inviting neighbors to dine with him so that he might get to know them and build relationships.

All the while he did his, he pined for Finola.

Cy decided if she were ever to move on from the wrongs done to her by Lord Crofton that the viscount would have to be put in his place.

And who better to do that than a duke?

Cy had journeyed to London, stopping at Stonecrest on his way, and spent a few hours walking the land with Pierce and Pollux. Taking his new friend's advice, he had gone to White's after he reached town, invoking his membership and becoming familiar with the club's staff. It was here where he first laid eyes upon Lord Crofton. Cy did not approach the viscount nor ask for any kind of introduction to him. Instead, he avoided Crofton even as he went to Bow Street.

This was the place Pierce had said Cy would have the most success in carrying out his plans. He learned that Bow Street runners were a type of private police force, men who investigated others and crimes which had been committed. They also found people—ones who had run away or were missing, up to ones who had become heirs to a title and needed to be located. They investigated robberies, assaults, and even murders.

Cy had met with a Mr. Franklin, who listened to Cy's request. He made certain he did not reveal his plans for revenge, merely saying he needed background information regarding Viscount Crofton, everything that could be found about the man.

Mr. Franklin had not asked why Cy was interested in the viscount and merely introduced him to the Bow Street runner who would take his case. Surprisingly, the agent was a woman.

He had been thoroughly impressed with Miss Shelby Slade. She was both attractive and intelligent, the only female runner employed by the organization. Miss Slade had asked for a week to investigate and compile information about Lord Crofton. He thought it a reasonable amount of time and agreed to the arrangement.

Cy had gone about his business, seeing his solicitor and getting a better grasp of the immense wealth he had stepped into. He spent a full two days in Mr. Solway's company, finding out the extent of his various investments, and even meeting with his banker about the accounts and monies held for him. Cy would not be the lazy duke Charles had been. He would use his position and wealth for good, both for the people on his estates and even deserving strangers.

He did not know what charitable actions he might take in London, but given time, he knew he would decide.

Hopefully, with Finola by his side.

Cy had also gone to obtain a special license so that he and Finola might wed at a moment's notice. The sum he paid to purchase it was outrageous. Yet he wanted to be prepared in case she might change her mind. If it came to pass that the license expired, he would merely renew it, again and again, never giving up hope that they might eventually marry.

He had actually enjoyed going to the Cressley townhouse, having never seen it before. His staff appeared competent and a bit curious about their new employer but kept a courteous, professional distance from him.

Now on his fifth day in town, he was breakfasting when his butler informed him that Miss Slade had arrived, and Cy asked that she be escorted to his study. Anticipation filled him, knowing the agent must have found something of interest since they were not scheduled to meet for another few days.

Cy left the breakfast room and went to meet with Miss Slade, who sat in a chair, patiently awaiting his arrival. He closed the door, not wanting their conversation to be overheard.

She rose and nodded brusquely to him. "Your Grace." She took her seat again.

When he had first met her, he had found her attire most interesting. She had been dressed similarly to the way Finola did, wearing a man's clothing, telling him it helped her move about London and other places more easily. Today, though, she was dressed in a typical gown, looking quite feminine.

He took a seat behind the desk and said, "I suppose you have something interesting to tell me, Miss Slade."

She handed him a sheaf of papers, and he accepted them as she said, "This is my background report regarding Lord Crofton. You may read it later at your leisure. I do, however, have someone I wish for you to meet with. A gentleman I have come across that has an interesting story to share with you. He is Lord Sears now, but he held no title when he was acquainted with Viscount Crofton. I think after you hear Lord Sears' story that you will have all the information you require in which to confront Lord Crofton."

"You believe I wish to confront him? I have never expressed my intentions toward the viscount."

A knowing look shone in her eyes. "A gentleman does not ask to learn everything possible about another gentleman unrelated to him unless he has something in mind. Based upon Lord Sears' account, I would say you are up to revenge, Your Grace."

Cy started to protest and then knew that would insult the runner. "Yes, I want to hurt Lord Crofton. Someone very dear to me was hurt by him."

"Are you available at two o'clock this afternoon, Your Grace? If so, I can bring Lord Sears here to you."

"That would be agreeable, Miss Slade. Would you be able to stay as I read your report now? I might have questions for you."

"Of course, Your Grace. You are currently my only case. I believe after you meet with Lord Sears, my work will be done."

Cy turned his attention to the agent's report and began reading about Lord Crofton. He learned the man was the only son of an earl and that he had two older sisters, both married with children. Viscount Crofton's mother had passed when he was a boy, and his father was in poor health now. It was expected that the earl would soon be gone, and his only son would assume his father's title.

That was important because Lord Crofton had racked up numerous gambling debts. His anticipation of receiving his father's title and the funds that accompanied it was the only thing keeping his creditors and the gaming hells at bay.

He learned that the man was four and thirty and had kept a string of mistresses until the past two years, when his debts forced him to give up the luxury. Crofton went to the occasional brothel now, where his tastes were known to be what the report termed unique.

Cy finished reading and looked to Miss Slade, asking, "What did you mean by unique, in regard to Crofton's sexual appetite?"

"I did not want anything on the page of this nature, Your Grace, but I will tell you that Lord Crofton enjoys abusing his partners. Not only verbally—but he is known for his rough play with the convenients. Women have suffered blackened eyes. Broken bones. Burn marks. A litany of complaints."

His stomach turned, thinking of the poor lightskirts who had no choice but to service such men as Crofton.

"You talk of mistresses, mentioning several of them by name."

She pursed her lips a moment and then said, "It seems Lord Crofton can no longer afford to keep a mistress, due to his financial situation. The two former mistresses who granted me an interview both spoke of his sadistic streak and were glad to be done with him."

Cy shook his head. "It appears Viscount Crofton is even more twisted than I had imagined."

Her gaze met his. "Whatever you have planned for him, Your Grace, do not hesitate to see it carried through. This man is evil personified."

"He hurt someone I love," he revealed to her. "I need him to pay for what he did to her."

Miss Slade rose. "I will leave you to your day, Your Grace. Look for Lord Sears and me at two o'clock. I can see myself out."

The Bow Street runner left Cy's study, and he returned his attention to her detailed report, reading through it again slowly to make certain he hadn't missed anything. His strong sense of justice wanted to avenge not only Finola—but those poor unfortunate women who had suffered under Lord Crofton's hand.

Hours later, Cy had gone to the drawing room, anticipating his visitors. He had told his butler to have tea brought when his visitors arrived and that he wanted absolute privacy as he spoke to his guests.

At two o'clock up and down, the teacart appeared, along with his butler and Miss Slade, who was accompanied by a man appearing to be in his mid-twenties or so. He had nondescript brown hair and eyes and was tall and gangly.

After introductions, Cy asked Miss Slade to pour out for them and once they all had their cup of tea, he looked to Lord Sears.

"Tell me your story, my lord."

Lord Sears' hand trembled, causing the cup and saucer he held to rattle. He set it on the table next to him and took a deep breath, slowly exhaling.

"Your Grace, I will preface my remarks by saying I am a different man than I was when these events took place."

"I am not here to judge you, my lord. I merely seek information regarding Lord Crofton."

Lord Sears nodded in understanding and reached for his tea again, taking a sip before speaking.

"I was newly graduated from university, a naïve young man, twenty years of age. I had flown through my coursework. Academics always interested me more than people, to be honest. I am not saying this as an excuse, merely to let you understand of my youth and inexperience."

Lord Sears swallowed, collecting his thoughts.

"Because I was inexperienced and easily influenced, I looked up to my cousin, my aunt's oldest boy. He was almost ten years my senior and from what I understood, ran with a fast crowd. I did not imagine myself to be a rake by any stretch of the imagination. At twenty, I had yet to even kiss a woman. Still, my cousin was dashing and debonair, as were his friends. The Season had already begun by the time I reached town, and my cousin drew me into his circle of friends.

"Immediately, I knew I was out of my depth. These were men who drank to excess and spent their time in the gaming hells once they left each night's social affair. I went with them to these various *ton* events—balls, parties, musicales. I then accompanied them to the gaming hells, never placing a single bet."

"And Lord Crofton was a member of this group?"

"He was not only a member, Your Grace. He was their ringleader. The head of their club."

"Club?" Cy asked.

Sears nodded. "Yes. Not a social club such as White's or Brooks'—but a club of their own creation. They called it the Epsilon Club, but Lord Crofton jokingly referred to it by another name. The Enticement Club."

The viscount then outlined what the Epsilon Club did. How they chose one woman a year, one who was making her come-out. They went after wallflowers, young ladies who oftentimes had lost one or both parents and were lacking in confidence and friends.

"I know once I arrived and became one of their companions, I was asked to dance with a Lady Finola. I did so, finding her to be sweet and unassuming. I learned that she was the prey of the Epsilons that Season. Each member of the club would pay her a bit of attention, but one member had been chosen to woo this particular prey."

He hid his shock in hearing that the story unfolding featured Finola herself. Lord Sears again reached for his teacup, his hand shaking. By now, the tea had cooled, and he downed the cup's contents. Cy knew the man was trying to calm himself and gather his thoughts and refrained from speaking.

The viscount continued to stare into space, so Cy softly encouraged, "Continue, my lord."

That broke the other man's reverie, and he said, "I could not be a part of what they were doing, Your Grace. I thanked my cousin for inviting me to share a friendship with his companions, but I told him I had received a letter that I was needed at home. I left him with the impression that my father was ill and left town as quickly as possible. My parents rarely attended the Season, preferring the country and their horses and dogs. Mama had been the one to encourage me to go to London for the Season, thinking a little town polish might do me some good."

The viscount shuddered. "Instead, I never attended the Season again. I have no idea what they did to Lady Finola. My cousin only spoke vaguely, saying Crofton would have a bit of fun with her and then put her in her place."

Rage boiled within Cy now, but his years at war helped him to keep it in check. Besides, he had no quarrel with this man.

Only Viscount Crofton.

"I have told no one this story, Your Grace. Not even my wife. I married the daughter of a local squire shortly after my return home. We have a son and daughter." Lord Sears' eyes welled with tears. "I think of my sweet girl and how I would feel if a group of bored men played such a vicious, savage trick on her."

The viscount paused. "I am not a violent man—but I would have turned so if my girl were hurt." He sighed. "It is why I have come to you today, at Miss Slade's urging."

Cy didn't care how the Bow Street runner had found Lord Sears and said, "Thank you for coming forward, my lord. My butler will see you out."

He rang for the servant and asked the butler to see Lord Sears to the door.

Once they were gone, he turned to Miss Slade. "You are right. I do not need anything further."

She nodded. "If you do, I spoke to two of Crofton's former mistresses. They are willing to meet with you—for a price. I also had a frank conversation with one of the women targeted by the Epsilon Club. While she did not wish to share her story with you, she did tell it to me and agreed I could pass it along to you."

The agent shook her head. "As for the other members of this wretched club? It has been disbanded. They moved on. Each has wed. Except, that is, for Lord Crofton."

"It is unnecessary to speak to the woman. She has suffered enough. Your work here is done."

Cy rose, as did Miss Slade. He offered her his hand.

"You have done a remarkable job in a short amount of time, Miss Slade. While I hope I have no further need of your services in the future, I know where to go if I ever have a problem which needs to be solved. I will put in a good word with Mr. Franklin regarding your work on my case."

"Thank you, Your Grace. I hope your loved one will heal, knowing Lord Crofton has been made to pay for his sins."

He thought of Finola—brave, beautiful Finola—who had been devasted by the horrible prank played upon her by Crofton and his Epsilon Club, only to leave their company and find her beloved Banny dead and gone.

Cy would avenge Finola.

He would bring Viscount Crofton to his knees.

CHAPTER TWENTY-THREE

C Y COULD HAVE asked one of his footmen—or even Miss Shelby Slade—to go about buying up the markers at the various gaming hells which Viscount Crofton had frequented. Instead, he wanted to do it himself. He didn't care if word reached Crofton or not.

In fact, he hoped it would.

He made certain to get to a London tailor Pierce had recommended to him, telling the man he needed evening clothes. Though Cy wanted them ready by the next day, a feat which should have been impossible during the Season, he discovered anything could be managed once he informed people that he was a duke. In fact, the tailor practically begged Cy to allow him to make up a new wardrobe for him. He agreed to a few items, knowing it would be wise to establish a relationship with a tailor in London, but duke or not, he preferred the bulk of his money going to Mr. Timmon. The tailor was known to Cy and had done excellent work over the years. He believed in supporting the craftsmen close to him.

Combing through the report compiled by Miss Slade, he was pleased how thorough her work was. It contained a list of debts owed to each gaming hell. He didn't want to ask how she had managed to come up with firm numbers such as these. After all, magicians didn't reveal the magic behind their tricks. He would not ask her how she had delivered the vast amount of information to him in so short a time.

Cy merely visited one of them from the list, the establishment where Crofton's debt was the greatest. He met briefly with the club's owner, saying he wished to buy up all of Lord Crofton's markers at six o'clock that evening, and asked that the man put out the word. If any owners were interested in having Crofton's markers purchased by the Duke of Margate, they should attend the meeting he would hold at this particular club.

Returning promptly at six that evening with his solicitor, the club's owner took him to a private gaming room filled with eager faces of other owners. The room's conversations abruptly ended as he explained to his hushed audience that he would be buying any marker in Viscount Crofton's name.

In gold.

A buzz erupted, and he saw everything from joy to relief on the faces of the various attendees.

"This is a one-time opportunity, gentlemen. My offer expires in one hour. If you are interested in selling these markers of Lord Crofton's to me, the line forms here."

Cy bit back a smile as men rushed to line up. The line consisted of every man in attendance.

He joined Mr. Solway at the table that had been set up, per Cy's request.

"Be quick about it," he told the solicitor. "Make certain you record the name of each gaming hell, its owner, and the amount paid to him."

"Yes, Your Grace."

He went to stand against the wall, observing the proceedings. When the final man left with his gold, Cy returned to Solway.

"Make a copy of that if you will. Keep the original one, and send the other to me at Melrose."

"Will you be returning to the country soon, Your Grace?"

"In a day or so."

Solway handed over the markers, and Cy placed them in a satchel he had found in the study of his London townhouse. He returned there now and requested water for a bath be sent up, as well as something to eat. He bathed and then shaved, taking time out to eat before he dressed himself, having left Hunt in the country. The valet had not approved of being left behind but wisely had not gone against his employer.

Tonight, a ball was being held at the Duke and Duchess of West-field's townhouse. When Cy had met with Pierce, Westfield's name was the one Pierce had provided, telling him that Westfield was a friend and could be counted on as an ally. Pierce promised to write to Westfield and tell him of Cy and urge the duke to help in any way he could.

It seemed providence when Cy arrived in town and combed through the mounds of invitations addressed to the Duke of Margate, finding one from the Westfields, inviting him to a ball which would be held this very evening. At least he had remembered to send the death notice to the newspapers, so the *ton* would know Charles had passed and that a new Duke of Margate had arrived in town.

He had written a note to the duchess, explaining that he had only recently arrived in town and would only be attending one event.

Their ball.

Since the couple lived only two blocks from him, Cy thought it ridiculous to take his carriage. The April night was cool and inviting, and he arrived only a few minutes after he'd set out, happy that he'd left his carriage at home. The roads and pavements were teeming with people in their ballroom finery.

Instead of making his way inside, he crossed the street and walked a few blocks before returning, wanting the receiving line to have died down. When he joined what remained of it, no one fell into line after him.

As he got closer to meeting his hosts, he studied them. The Duke of Westfield was an imposing man, at least three inches over six feet. His coal-black hair was slightly longer than fashionable, and his gray eyes seemed to take in everything about him. The duchess was close to six feet, unusual for a woman. She had fiery red hair and a ready smile. When he reached them, he was drawn in by her moss green eyes.

The duke offered Cy his hand. "We are two weeks into the Season and have yet to make your acquaintance, much less see you at one of the many events already held. Might you be Margate?"

"I am, Your Grace. I assume you have received Stoneham's letter."

Westfield turned to his wife. "Darling, this is the duke Pierce wrote to us about."

She smiled warmly at Cy. "It is a pleasure to meet you, Your Grace. Thank you for your note. I believe you mentioned that you are in town only briefly."

"Yes. This is the only event I will attend. I wish to be introduced to Viscount Crofton."

The duchess wrinkled her nose. "He is a rake, through and through."

"Years ago, he caused great distress to the woman I love. I am here to see that he pays for that."

Her eyes lit up. "Oh, it sounds as if a scandal is brewing. I would be pleased if Lord Crofton were taken down a notch or two. The man is full of himself."

"I do not wish to ruin your ball, Your Graces. I will confront Crofton away from prying ears and eyes. If he chooses not to accept my terms, however, I may ask you if I can address your guests and speak my truth regarding him and his odious behavior."

Westfield placed a hand on Cy's shoulder. "Stoneham thinks highly of you. No one of quality thinks much of anything regarding Crofton. I only ask that you wait until after supper before making any kind of announcement. I would like our guests to enjoy a bit of dancing and a meal before any sparks might fly."

"I can wait, Your Grace," he promised. "I am a patient man."

The duchess caught Cy's hand and squeezed it. "I would like to meet your wife."

"She is not my wife. Yet," he added, holding on to hope.

Her Grace patted Cy's hand. "I have a suspicion she will be. Sooner, rather than later. Good luck to you, Your Grace."

She released his hand, and the duke said, "Shall we go inside the ballroom? If you will let my duchess and I dance the first dance, I will then take you to meet Lord Crofton, Your Grace."

Cy followed the couple at a distance as they entered the ballroom. Soon, the orchestra was playing, and he watched his host and hostess dance. It was obvious the couple was deeply in love, just as Pierce and his duchess were.

Could he find the same love and happiness with Finola?

The dance ended, and the Westfields made their way toward him. He could feel the eyes of the *ton* following them and then landing upon him. A buzz started about the room as the members of Polite Society strained to see him and figure out who he was.

When his hosts reached him, he took the duchess' hand and kissed it. She smiled at him—and winked. The duke then kissed his wife's cheek, and she sailed away.

"Walk with me, Margate," Westfield said, his voice just loud enough to carry several feet.

The scramble to pass Cy's name through the crowd was almost comical to watch, and he found himself, along with his companion, laughing aloud.

The duke led them onto the terrace through a set of open French doors as the musicians struck up another piece.

"Can you share with me what Crofton has done?"

He supposed he owed as much to this man who had welcomed him into his home, despite the fact that Cy had informed the duke that he might do something that would cause a figurative explosion at this ball.

"This happened long before I returned to England. My best guess is five or six years ago."

Cy explained how he'd hired a Bow Street runner to learn everything about Viscount Crofton and how he'd put the pieces together after reading her report.

"I came home from the war broken in spirit, the eyesight gone in one eye. Lady Finola helped me find a reason to live again."

He went into detail about how he and Bertie had met their neighbor and had begun to help her in training her dogs.

"They wouldn't happen to be Honeyfield spaniels?" the duke asked.

"The very ones."

"I have heard of them and been considering purchasing one."

"They are remarkable—as is Lady Finola."

"Even if you had not told me, it is obvious you love her when you speak her name. What did Crofton do to Lady Finola?"

Again, he related what he had learned between Finola and Miss Slade, seeing the anger and disgust shadow Westfield's face.

"I knew Crofton ran with a group of rogues, but I had no idea the extent of their ill behavior. This is outrageous. To think they call themselves gentlemen." The duke shook his head. "Expose him if you wish, Margate. It is understandable why no lady has ever come forward to accuse him. He and his Epsilon Club villains chose their victims well. Either those women withdrew from Polite Society, as Lady Finola did, or they have never spoken to anyone of the horrors they experienced. I will support you in however you wish Crofton and his cronies to be punished."

Westfield frowned. "Come to think of it, I don't see Crofton with many friends these days."

"Perhaps the others tired of the game—or outgrew such childish, hurtful games," Cy said. "Miss Slade's report mentioned the names of the other men, saying they all had wed. I merely know that Crofton was their leader. I will be satisfied if he is the only one who suffers."

"I have a small group of close friends—all dukes, ironically. Say the word, and we and our duchesses shall give the viscount the cut direct. He will never darken another London ballroom again. Once he is removed from our guest lists, no one in Polite Society would be mad enough to invite him to one of their social affairs."

"Let me think on it this evening, Your Grace."

"You'd better think fast. Speak of the devil."

Cy glanced up and saw none other than Viscount Crofton coming their way. He steeled himself for their encounter.

"Your Grace," Crofton said as he gave a curt bow to the Duke of Westfield. Turning, he cast a venomous glance at Cy. "Who the bloody hell do you think you are?"

Maintaining his composure, Cy replied, "And whom might you be, my lord? We have not been properly introduced."

The viscount cursed low. "You know I am Lord Crofton, Margate. What I cannot fathom is why you are out to blacken my name."

"Well, since you now know one another, I shall leave you to attend to my guests." Westfield nodded at Cy and left the terrace, returning to the ballroom.

Once the duke was out of sight, Crofton glared at Cy. "I want to know what you're up to, Margate."

"I am not up to anything. If you are referring to the markers bearing your name which I have purchased this evening, it was done quite openly."

Crofton's eyes narrowed. "Yes, the news reached me rather quickly. We do not know one another. Have never spoken to each other. Why, you have only recently returned from the war and gained your title. Our paths have never crossed. I want to know why you're being such a prick—and why you chose to buy up only *my* markers."

"You are troubled at my purchasing your markers?" he asked nonchalantly.

"Bollocks!" the viscount cried. "What do you want with those markers? And with me?"

"What did you want with all those innocent women you humiliated?" Cy asked, his voice low and deadly.

That did the trick. Shock filled Crofton's face. His jaw went slack a moment. Then he steeled himself. "I haven't the foggiest idea what—"

"Don't go there, you slimy bastard," he warned. "Do not deny what you have done for years. Taking innocents and tearing them to shreds." He moved close, so close his nose almost touched that of his enemy's. "Did you think it amusing to destroy the lives of weak women? Did it make you feel strong and important? Did you ever for one minute—even one second—consider how you were destroying women who had done nothing to deserve your wrath?"

He took a step back, not hiding his disgust. "Of course not. You are a vile, desperate, little man. The term gentleman does not apply to you. I should go into that ballroom and tell the entire *ton* what you have been doing for years. How you have crushed the life out of sweet wallflowers. Shattered what spirit they had. Damaged them almost beyond repair."

Panic filled Crofton's face. "You cannot do that. You wouldn't dare. You have no proof."

"Don't I?" Cy asked, looking the viscount up and down. "Yes, my lord. I know all about your Epsilon Club. Or forgive me—should I say the Enticement Club?"

"You couldn't," the man sputtered, his face now turning bright red. "None of those women would dare come forward. If they admitted they had been a part of our games, they would be ruined."

"I would never ask them to publicly admit they had been duped by you. But I could step through those doors and make my accusations in front of all of Polite Society. I could give what information I have discovered about you to the newspapers' gossip columns. I am a duke, Crofton. You are a mere viscount. Men such as me squash vermin like you. Stomp on them until they are nonexistent."

Fear caused Crofton's body to tremble. "Please, Your Grace," he said, his tone now beseeching. "I have done nothing to harm you. I don't even know you."

"But I know someone you hurt. Deeply. Someone I hold dear. I wish to destroy you, Crofton, if only to please her."

"I will pay you," sputtered the viscount. "I will pay you."

"Pay me?" scoffed Cy. "Pay me? I own all of your markers, you swine. Close to twenty thousand pounds' worth."

"As soon as my father is dead and I am the earl, I will gladly pay you every farthing owed," Crofton declared confidently.

He knew, though, that would never come to pass. While he had visited with his banker about his own funds and investments, Cy had asked about those of his enemy's father. Discreetly, of course. And because Cy was a duke, he was able to obtain the information he sought. He had learned the earl was in dire straits.

His gaze met Crofton's. "Why do you think your father retired to the countryside several years ago?"

The other man appeared baffled at the question. "He told me he tired of town. Why? What does that have to do with anything?"

"Everything. Your father no longer had the means to maintain a household in London," Cy said. "When you meet with his banker and solicitor upon his death, you will find the truth. That he had to shutter his London residence because he could no longer pay his servants. If you went inside the townhouse now, you would discover everything of value has been sold. Paintings. Rugs. China. Furniture."

Crofton shook his head vigorously. "No. No. You are wrong."

"The same is true at his country estate. Only a skeleton staff remains in place. He is in poor health and has no reason or means to entertain others."

In this, Cy was only guessing since he believed a man such as Crofton would not have visited his only parent.

"I . . . I can wed. A woman with a large dowry."

"Even if she brought twenty thousand pounds into the marriage, my lord, it would all be owed to me. And then what would you live on? No, you would be found out during the marriage settlements negotiations." He paused. "Face it, Crofton. You have been living beyond your means for years, anticipating you would inherit a fortune—which you will not. You have taken advantage of innocents, toying with them and ruining them, emotionally if not physically."

A sob escaped from the viscount. "What do you want of me, Margate?"

"To begin with, I want you to leave London and never return. No more attending glittering society affairs. You are to lead a quiet life in the country, caring for your father until his death, and then doing your best for the tenants you inherit. If not? I shall call in your markers and when you cannot pay, have you thrown into debtors' prison."

Crofton shuddered, tears streaming down his cheeks now. Cy hoped the other man would not question the bluff. Cy had not checked with his solicitor and doubted that an earl would ever be placed in prison. But Crofton did not seem to know this. Let the thought of languishing forever in debtors' prison haunt him.

"A second thing you must do so that I will not call for you to pay your markers to me is to write a letter to each young lady you wronged over the years. For the entire existence of your Epsilon Club."

"I don't know if I could even remem—"

"You do recall every one of them," he said bluntly. "A man like you collected women's hearts as other hunters acquired their own trophies. You will write a short but sincere letter to each one and give these to me. I will see they are delivered to wherever that victim now resides. You ruined plenty of lives with your Enticement Club,

Crofton."

Cy waited a moment, letting his words sink in, and then said, "My final request is that you deliver one of those letters in person. To Lady Finola Honeyfield."

Understanding flickered in Crofton's eyes. "She is the one you are doing all this for, isn't she?"

"She is," he affirmed. "But she is no less important than the other women wronged. That is why I want you to write to all the wronged women. And hand over your apology—your sincere apology—in person to Lady Finola."

The viscount angrily swiped at his tears. "And after I am humiliated? What then, Margate?"

"I have told you. You are to retire to the country. You are to care for your estate and its people. If you are of a mind to try and change your nature and repent from your many sins, perhaps you might be fortunate enough to wed a local woman. But you are never to darken a London ballroom again, my lord. I hold your markers. I will not hesitate to call them in if I see you."

Cy studied the broken man now before him. "Do you agree to my terms, Crofton? A simple country life, repenting and learning to become a better man—or do I walk through those doors and at supper tonight tell the members of the *ton* what a wicked man you are? Of course, they will gossip about you for years to come as you languish in debtors' prison."

Another sob burst from the viscount, and he wept openly. Cy was unmoved, however. This evil man had destroyed lives. It was time Lord Crofton paid the piper.

"Yes."

"Yes, what, my lord?"

Crofton met Cy's gaze. "I will do as you ask. Write those bloody letters. And go see Lady Finola."

Cy flashed a satisfied smile. "Then if I were you, Crofton, I would pull myself together and find my hosts and thank them for a lovely evening. Go home and write those letters tonight. Every single one of them. Do not seal the one to Lady Finola, though. I wish to read it before you do so."

He flicked an imaginary piece of lint from his sleeve casually. "My carriage will be at your rooms at eight o'clock tomorrow morning. Be packed and have every letter ready. We will leave London and journey to Belldale, where you will make amends to Lady Finola."

With that, Cy turned his back on Crofton and left the terrace. Entering the ballroom, he saw it swirling with dancers. He watched them for a moment before the Duke of Westfield joined him.

"Did you have a productive conversation with the viscount?"

He nodded. "I got what I came for. After tonight, Polite Society will no longer be seeing Lord Crofton at their events. Ever. He is retiring to the country to care for his ailing father."

"And upon the earl's death?" Westfield asked.

Cy smiled. "Crofton will remain at his new country estate and make the best of it—else I will call in his markers. Twenty thousand pounds' worth at once."

"I am assuming he could not pay them or if he did, it would leave him in financial ruin?"

"You have a clear understanding of Crofton's situation, Your Grace. I will be leaving London tomorrow morning. With Crofton. The viscount will be apologizing in person to Lady Finola."

Westfield smiled broadly. "I wish you the best of luck with Lady Finola, Margate, and I hope you and your duchess will come visit us. Either at Westwood or in town during next Season, where I am certain you will wish to show off your bride to Polite Society."

"Your belief in my powers of persuasion surprises me, Your Grace," Cy said. "I only hope that I can win Lady Finola's hand."

The Duke of Westfield laughed heartily. "Oh, Your Grace, I have no doubt you will achieve everything you wish in life."

CHAPTER TWENTY-FOUR

FINOLA AND BERTIE climbed into the carriage for their visit to Pierce and Nalyssa. They had made this trip every two weeks. *And it had been what had saved Finola's sanity.*

Two months had passed since she had assumed responsibility for Bertie, and he had moved in with her and her servants. Finola had continued his lessons as best she could, devoting an hour after breakfast in the schoolroom with him, working on spelling, grammar, and basic computation skills. Then they would spend the bulk of their day with the litter, which was progressing nicely in their hunting skills.

After tea, Finola would read to Bertie for an hour and sometimes he, too, would read to her from very simple primers. She had not wanted a lapse in his education. The tutor would be arriving soon, a gentleman who was Reverend Hall's nephew. It had been arranged for him to live in the hunting lodge at Melrose. The young man would spend mornings with Bertie, his salary completely paid for by the Duke of Margate.

Finola had not seen Cy except from a distance these past few weeks, although he had sent her a few notes. They were formal and held nothing personal in them, simply informing her when to send Bertie to Melrose for a visit. This month's visit had actually occurred a week early because Cy had written that he had business which would take him to London. Bertie had gone to Melrose as expected. He came back from these visits in an exuberant state, yet he never mentioned a word about the duke. Finola suspected that Cy had asked Bertie not to speak about him to her.

Everywhere she went, though, there was talk of the new Duke of Margate. How kind he was. How generous he was. How different he was from his predecessors. The duke had arranged for a new roof to go on the church and new stained glass to be commissioned and installed. He had spent money to replace most of the roofs of his tenants' cottages and visited every single person on his land, learning their names and those of their children.

She missed him every single day.

When Lord Crofton had humiliated her, Finola had buried herself in her work, grieving for the loss of Banny, as well as that of her lost innocence. This time, however, her work with the pups wasn't enough. Yes, she still enjoyed the training of them and especially having Bertie's company while she did so. Yet nothing had been the same since she pushed Cy from her life. If not for the visits to Nalyssa and Pierce, Finola did not know how she would have the strength to go on.

Today, they would have a visit and take tea before Pierce's carriage returned them to Belldale. Although Finola had never asked Bertie anything about Cy on these trips to Stonecrest, she did so now.

"How did you find His Grace, Bertie?"

The boy looked startled at her question. "His Grace is well, my lady."

Bertie no longer called her Finola, and she knew this was at Cy's request.

When the boy said no more, she pressed further, asking, "Does it seem as if he has settled in at Melrose?"

The small boy shrugged. "I think so. This last time, His Grace put me on his horse with him and took me all about the estate. I got to meet others, even some children my own age." He hesitated and then added, "Everyone likes His Grace."

Her gaze met his, and Finola asked a final question. "Does he ever ask about me?"

Bertie shook his head vigorously. "No, my lady. His Grace asked me not to mention you. Sometimes, I can't help it, though. I'll tell him what one of the pups is doing and how you taught him the trick. Or how you're helping me learn how to train them as hunters. He never scolds me when I do so."

"I am sorry if I made you uncomfortable talking about His Grace to me, Bertie. I will not ask about His Grace again."

Finola saw the pained expression on the boy's face and turned to gaze out the window, hurt in her heart.

When they arrived at Stonecrest, Pierce handed her down, a huge smile on his face.

"You are looking at a proud new father, Finola. Nalyssa gave birth yesterday morning."

She could see the pride on his face and said, "You should have sent word to me, Pierce. I would have postponed this visit. Nalyssa needs time to recover."

"Ah, my duchess is a hardy one—and ready to show off our daughter to you." He turned to Bertie and ruffled the lad's hair. "Why, I think even Bertie might wish to see the babe."

They went upstairs to the rooms designated for the duchess. Nalyssa sat regally in bed, holding a small bundle and cooing to it softly. When she saw them, she smiled.

"Oh, I am so glad that you are here, Finola. Come meet our girl. You, too, Bertie."

She and Bertie moved toward the bed, and the boy gazed down, his eyes wide.

"She's so tiny."

Nalyssa chuckled. "She won't be for long. Mary is eating well. The doctor has been to see her and said that all is well."

"Bertie, why don't you and I take Pollux out for a nice, long walk? That will give these two time to visit properly," the duke said.

Pierce called, and Pollux came to him. Finola realized the dog must have been lying on the floor on the other side of the bed, out of her sight.

After they left the room, Nalyssa asked if Finola wished to hold the babe.

"I have never done so," she admitted. "What if I do something wrong?"

Her friend laughed. "There is nothing you can do wrong. Here, take her."

She bent and accepted the swaddled babe, bringing Mary close and gazing at her. A wave of tenderness washed over her, seeing such a tiny creature. She moved about the room slowly with the infant, talking and cooing as she had heard Nalyssa do. Finola thought what it would be like to give birth to a child of her own. She had wondered if she might be with child after her encounter with Cy and felt disappointment when her monthly courses had come. Of course, if she had been with child, it would have complicated their situation immeasurably. She should be grateful that had not occurred.

Still, holding this tiny babe tugged at her heartstrings.

A servant appeared, and Nalyssa explained that she was the wet nurse. Finola handed the babe over to be fed and then took a seat by the bed. She reached out and squeezed Nalyssa's hand.

"You look wonderful for having only given birth yesterday morning."

Laughter filled the room. "You should have seen me then. I was in labor twenty hours and was dripping with sweat by the time things ended. The midwife told me it was a good labor, however, and that I should not have a problem in the future. I hope that is the case. I am thirty years of age now. Pierce and I want to have several children while we can."

"I noticed Pollux was in the room."

"That pup has grown very dear to me, Finola. I am certain most members of the *ton* would be shocked, but he was in the bed with me the entire time I struggled to deliver. Pollux sensed my distress and did what he could to comfort me, not leaving my side during the entire ordeal. His walk today will do him some good."

"I am certain it will do Bertie good, too, seeing the pup again."

"How is it having Bertie with you?"

Finola explained their daily schedule and how the tutor would be arriving early next week to take over the schoolroom duties.

"It is remarkable that you are educating him. Very unusual for a servant."

"His Grace is the one paying for the tutor," she revealed. "I will merely give Bertie time out of his day to continue with his lessons. He is quite bright and a rapid learner. Giving him the gift of being able to read and write and do maths will help him go far in life. I can see Bertie leaving me one day and becoming a dog trainer on his own."

Though that was many years down the line, a wave of sadness washed over her.

"Have you spoken to His Grace?"

"I have not. I have seen him a few times at church. Naturally, he is sitting at the front in the ducal pew and others of the nobility and gentry are close to him. I slip inside just as the service begins and sit on the back row, then quickly leave once things conclude."

"I know we have never spoken of this, Finola, and that you must have felt betrayed by Margate. By the fact you hadn't a clue he was the heir to a dukedom. You do realize that you, too, had kept a secret from him, as well."

She nodded. "I did feel a sense of betrayal, one I had felt many years ago and told you of."

"I recall your disastrous come-out Season and the lengthy trick played upon you by Lord Crofton and his fellow rakes."

"Up until that point, I had been very sheltered. Banny was my only friend and my entire world. Losing him on the same night I was jilted by the viscount changed something in me. I only trusted in my furry friends. Nothing changed—until Cy—that is, His Grace—came into my life."

She swallowed hard. "I have actually forgiven him. Not to his face, of course, but in my heart. I know he wasn't deliberately misleading me and that he had no idea he would so quickly become the Duke of Margate. From what I gather, though, he is doing an excellent job. Everywhere I go, his name is on others' lips, and they sing his praises."

Nalyssa frowned. "Then I don't quite understand. If you say you have forgiven him and that you believe his intentions toward you were honorable, then why are you not together? I can tell you still love him, Finola. Pierce has seen Margate a few times, and he tells me Margate feels the same toward you. That he never intends to wed. What are you not telling me?"

A sob escaped her and once it did, Finola lost control. She wept profusely. Nalyssa signaled for her to move to the bed, and Finola perched upon it, allowing her friend to wrap her arms around her as she cried.

Finola reminded herself that tears never solved anything and took control of herself once more. She pulled away, but Nalyssa took Finola's hands and said, "Talk to me, my friend. I can tell you still love him and are deeply unhappy. What is preventing you from being together? Other than stubbornness—or pride."

"Neither," she replied. "I cannot be with Cy now that he is a duke of the realm. Look at me, Nalyssa. I am dressed like a lady today simply because I have come to visit with you. It is one of the few times I don a gown." She sighed. "I am a woman totally unsuited to be a duke's wife."

Nalyssa's eyes widened. "Is this the reason you will not wed Margate?"

She nodded, shame filling her.

"Does he know this?" Nalyssa demanded.

"No, we have not spoken since I agreed to take Bertie into my household. His Grace has sent me the occasional note, but I have never even replied to them. They are short and merely inform me of something, such as when he wishes Bertie to visit."

"How could you think you are unworthy, Finola? You have such a sweet nature and are so generous and loving. You have an innate goodness about you. You would make for a most wonderful duchess."

She snorted. "You really believe the *ton* would accept someone like me? I traipse about the countryside dressed as a man. I indulge in no ladylike activities, other than reading. I spend a majority of my day outside, working to train my Honeyfield spaniels to become hunters. I am the last woman who should be a duchess."

Nalyssa's gaze pinned hers. "And you think that I was considered appropriate duchess material? I, who was painted with the brush of scandal, thanks to my father's suicide? Not a gentleman in the *ton* would have me. My father gambled away my dowry, and I was left with absolutely nothing at his death. I had to reinvent myself, and do you know what? I found that I am strong. Strong enough to withstand gossip. To create a new life for myself. Yes, earning my own living."

Nalyssa searched Finola's face, and she grew warm under the scrutiny. The duchess then said, "I fell in love, my friend. Head over heels in love with Pierce. I cannot imagine spending a single moment when I did not love him. Yes, he has been an unconventional duke, especially choosing someone as me to be his duchess. But you love Margate—and he loves you. It is foolish for you to waste your lives apart from one another when you could build something solid together. Will the *ton* gossip about you? Undoubtedly. I know they have about us. Yet we do not live for others, Finola. Pierce and I live for ourselves. For each other. For our daughter now, and the family we are creating together. Only a minuscule amount of time is spent among the *ton*. The majority of our time is with each other. You should not let what Polite Society thinks prevent you from being with the man you love. If you do, you are as blind as Cy is in his right eye."

Why hadn't Finola thought of this before? Why was she letting the thought of what others believed keep her from her one, true love? Nalyssa was right. Her reasons were ridiculous to have driven such a wedge between she and Cy.

They loved one another—and she finally realized that love could conquer all.

"Your love will be enough," Nalyssa continued. "But you will not have to go facing Polite Society alone, Finola. Among the *ton* are a few other women such as me. Women who also worked for a living—and still do so. Believe it or not, they also hold the lofty title of duchess. And they are my friends. Good friends, whom I cherish and trust immeasurably."

"Duchesses . . . who are employed?" she asked, finding the concept hard to imagine.

"Absolutely," Nalyssa replied, her enthusiasm apparent. "I cannot wait for you to meet them. Hear a song Fia has composed. See a portrait Margaret has painted. They will not only become your friends, dear Finola. They—and their dukes—will be more like family to you and Margate."

Her friend chuckled. "Dukes, it seems, must be forgiven for all their sins. Even if it is the sin of wedding a most inappropriate woman. Polite Society has learned to accept these dukes also means to accept their duchesses. Our group shares close bonds of friendship and love as we knock the traditions of the *ton* upside down."

She was stunned by what Nalyssa shared.

Her friend took Finola's hand in hers. "You and Margate will fit right in with our group." Nalyssa paused. "But you must speak to the man you love. Open your heart to him, Finola. Your love—and the support of friends old and new—will allow you to start your lives together."

Squeezing Nalyssa's hand, Finola said, "You are right and reassured me that speaking up is what I must do. I have been blind. Even foolish. I must tell Cy that my feelings for him have remained unchanged and that if he will have me, I would be honored to be his duchess."

Finola only prayed that it was not too late for them to find happiness.

CHAPTER TWENTY-FIVE

Finola collected Bertie, and they went to Pierce's waiting carriage. She told Pierce farewell, and he arranged for Finola to come again the next week to visit with Nalyssa.

"Since I don't want my duchess to travel for a while, I am grateful that you have agreed to come to her again so soon," the duke said.

"I would be happy to visit her anytime. And hold your wonderful daughter."

He smiled. "I see you are as taken with Mary as we are. Mama and Pen will be coming to visit in the next few days. They will be staying long enough for you to meet them."

"Then I look forward to my next visit to Stonecrest for several reasons."

Pierce looked to Bertie. "Thank you for the tips regarding Pollux."

The duke handed her into the carriage, Bertie climbing up behind her. The boy chattered nonstop on their way home, telling Finola all about Pollux and two new tricks he had taught both dog and duke. She listened with only half an ear, though, her thoughts centered on Cy.

She needed to see him as soon as possible and tell him what was in her heart, hoping he still felt the same about her as she did him. That their love had endured the foolish separation of her making. Then she recalled Bertie had informed her that Cy had gone to town on business.

"Bertie, do you know when His Grace was supposed to return to Melrose? I simply wondered how long his business might take."

The boy cocked his head. "No, my lady. He didn't tell me. I did ask if I would be able to see him again next month. He said yes."

At this point, Finola decided if Cy were not currently in residence at Melrose that she would make the journey to town and call upon him. That bold action alone should convince him of her intentions.

She decided to send Bertie to Melrose when they returned to Belldale. The boy could inquire if Arnold knew when his employer might be returning to the country. If the butler revealed it would be soon, Finola would bide her time. If Arnold had no idea, though, then she would leave on tomorrow's mail coach. It came through Adderly a little before noon each day.

The carriage began to slow, and Finola felt good about the decision she had made. Cy would soon know her true feelings.

The vehicle's door opened, and a footman handed her down. She gasped.

A grand carriage stood in front of her house, one just as elaborate as the one she had just exited. She hoped beyond hope that it was Cy's carriage but didn't know, having never seen it before.

She called up a thanks to the coachman for returning them to Belldale and then found Bertie's hand, squeezing it tightly.

"Is that His Grace's carriage?" Bertie asked softly.

"We will soon see," she told the boy, moving them toward the vehicle.

Suddenly, the door to the carriage flew open, and Finola stopped in her tracks. Her heart began to beat violently against her ribs as she saw who climbed from it. A man who had caused her immeasurable grief.

Viscount Crofton.

Quickly, she wheeled, releasing Bertie's hand to rush to the house.

"Wait, my lady!" called Lord Crofton.

Finola froze at the sound of his voice and then turned, determined to confront him after so many years. She marched toward him and when she reached him, slapped him hard, stunning herself and the viscount.

His gaze met hers. "I suppose I deserved that," he began.

"There is no supposing to it, my lord," she said coldly. "You did me great injury many years ago. I only wish I would have been mature enough then to recognize you for the loathsome creature you are. But I am a different woman from that meek, cowed wallflower you knew. I determined after I left you that I would become strong. That I would never make the same mistake again. I have built a good life for myself, my lord. I am content, which is more than I can say for you."

She paused and studied him a moment. "The years since our last encounter have not been kind to you, I see. Your late nights of drinking and love of food are showing. Where once your belly was flat, a paunch now sits there. Your eyes are bloodshot. Your hairline receding. You were nothing but your looks and charm. With your looks fading, you and your Enticement Club will not be able to bamboozle poor, unsuspecting young ladies. I wish now that I had spoken out against you back then. Yes, I would have ruined my reputation by doing so—but you and your friends would also have been ruined."

Finola paused, the blood pounding in her ears. "I have no idea why you have come to Belldale, but I want you off my property. Yes, my lord, *my* property. Sir Roscoe left me the house and estate so you can see, I am managing quite well on my own."

Finola turned to leave, and Lord Crofton called out, "Please. Wait, my lady."

The use of the word *please* intrigued her, having never heard it pass the viscount's lips. She whirled, facing him once more. "I will ask why you are here, my lord."

He pulled a folded piece of parchment from his pocket and handed it to her.

"This, Lady Finola, is my written apology to you. I also wish to speak it to you in person."

A wave of emotion flooded her. Her throat constricted. She willed herself not to cry in front of this man.

"My letter states things more eloquently, my lady, but I will say this to you now."

Crofton paused and then dropped to his knees, thoroughly shocking her.

"I—and the Epsilon Club—did a great disservice to you, my lady. To other innocents, as well. The club was all my doing. I fully regret what was done to you and the other women we mislead. No, duped. I will have to live with that regret the rest of my life. I do not come to be absolved of my sins. I do not ask nor beg for your forgiveness because you should not give it to me. I know I destroyed your life that night. You are much stronger than I ever believed a woman could be, though. You have risen like a phoenix from the ashes. I recognize the name Belldale because it is home to Honeyfield spaniels. I understand that you are the one who trains them. You have reached a pinnacle of success few women—or even men—do. You did this even though I tried to break you in spirit, merely for the fun of it.

"I am sorry for what I did all those years ago, Lady Finola. I will never do it again. I am leaving London and Polite Society permanently. I will retire to my father's country seat. I must learn to live with the pain I have caused and try to move forward and become a better man."

Tears brimmed in her eyes as she said, "I do forgive you, my lord. What you did was awful, destroying the lives of so many, but you seem repentant now. Perhaps you have matured. I know it is wrong to hold a grudge. Things such as that fester. They eat up a person's soul. Get up, my lord."

Lord Crofton came to his feet and said, "I do not deserve your forgiveness, my lady, but I thank you all the same for it. You are a better person than I ever hope to be." He paused. "And you deserve every lasting bit of happiness you might find. I bid you good day."

As the viscount left her and headed toward the carriage again, Bertie swiftly came to Finola's side. She wrapped an arm about the boy as they watched Lord Crofton ascend into the carriage. To her surprise, Cy then climbed from the vehicle and called up directions to his coachman. The driver nodded but did not start up the carriage.

Then Cy turned and called out, "Bertie, come here. I have need of you."

The boy scrambled to the duke, who placed his hand on the small boy's shoulder and bent, talking to him a moment. Bertie nodded several times, and then Cy rose.

Looking to her, Bertie said, "Don't worry, my lady. I will be back tomorrow."

The driver leaned down, offering the boy a hand. Bertie took it and was propelled into the seat next to the coachman, who took up the reins and flicked his wrists, starting the vehicle.

As it drove away, Cy came to her. Finola swallowed, emotions welling up inside her, overwhelming her so that she couldn't even speak. Her eyes filled with tears.

He reached her and took her hands. "I heard everything you said to Crofton. You were magnificent, my lady."

Then he raised her hands, and his lips brushed against her knuckles, undoing her. Finola burst into tears and fell against Cy, who wrapped his arms about her.

"There, there," he comforted, stroking her hair.

Her tears dampened his shirt and waistcoat as she clutched him, inhaling his familiar scent.

Raising her head, her gaze met his. "I was such a fool," she said, barely seeing him through her tears.

"You were no such thing. You were a young girl, treading the shark-infested waters of the *ton*. A charming, handsome man paid attention to you. You had no way of knowing what games a man such as Crofton played."

Finola realized Cy thought she was talking about being duped by the viscount and shook her head vigorously. "No, Cy. I mean now. Pushing you away. I was foolish to throw away what we had."

"You do not have to say that, my lady, simply because I brought Crofton here to apologize to you. You owe me nothing. I merely wanted to see a wrong righted. I know his apology comes years too late, but—"

"Stop talking and kiss me," she commanded, yanking on his cravat until his mouth slammed against hers.

She wrapped her arms about him, holding tightly. Still, he lifted his mouth from hers, confused.

"Wh—"

"I love you, Cy," she said simply. "I never stopped loving you. Yes, I was surprised when I learned you were a duke. But that is not why I separated from you." She smiled wryly. "After all, I had not been totally honest about my own identity."

"Then why would you wish to keep us apart, Finola?"

She sighed, hearing him call her by her name once more, knowing how right it felt.

"Because I did not see myself as good enough for you. I am the last woman Polite Society would envision a duke marrying."

Wonder filled his face. "You did this . . . for *me*?"

"Yes," she admitted. "I did not believe I was good enough to be a duchess. Your duchess. I—"

Her words were cut off as he took her mouth. The kiss was demanding, seeking everything from her.

Finola was more than willing to give all to Cy. To the man who held her heart. She answered his kiss with everything she had. Her love for him poured from her—and it was returned. She knew without words being spoken that this man, this former army officer, now a duke of the realm, loved her. Truly loved her.

When Cy finally broke the kiss, they were both breathless.

"I love you," he said, panting. "I will always love you. And in my eyes, you are the perfect woman to be my duchess. Yes, you might not fit the mold for what other dukes seek in their wives, but Finola Honeyfield, you are the duchess of my dreams."

"Then we should make those dreams come true," she told him. "Can you ride to Chichester and beg the bishop to issue another license? I cannot wait three weeks for the banns to be called."

He beamed. Releasing her, he withdrew something from his inner coat pocket.

"What's this?" she asked, her heart beating rapidly.

"This, my love, is a special license I obtained from Doctors' Commons while I was in London. I purchased it in the hopes you might change your mind about marrying me. I intended to renew it every time it expired. For as many months—or years—as was necessary."

Her fingers toyed with the hair on his nape. "You were willing to spend that much money on the hope I would someday consider wedding you?"

"I would spend every farthing I had if it would bring you to me," Cy said, taking her in his arms again and kissing her hungrily.

This time she was the one to break the kiss. "When do you wish us to wed?"

"I would say now—but I do not see a clergyman or any witnesses standing about." He laughed. "And I would have us climb into my carriage and head into Adderly to see Reverend Hall, but I told my coachman to drop off Lord Crofton in the village and then stay until he puts the viscount on the mail coach tomorrow morning."

Finola stroked his cheek. "That was awfully impressive. You finding him. Convincing him to come to Belldale and issue an apology to me."

"I knew despite how successful you have become, you still hurt from that time so many years ago. I wanted him to stop plucking new victims. Rest assured, he will never darken a *ton* event again."

"How did you do it, Cy?"

He grinned. "Do you really want to keep talking about Crofton? Or might you be interested in saddling Autumn and riding into Adderly and marrying a duke?"

Finola kissed him over and over. "Yes, marriage to a duke sounds like a wonderful idea."

"Bertie is at the inn there, along with my footman." He framed her face. "I believe we can steal Bertie away for a bit, though, so that the lad might see us wed."

Cy led her to the barn and readied Autumn. He mounted the horse and then reached for Finola, bringing her up and nestling her against him.

"We are actually going to do this," she said, smiling.

"We are. When we leave Adderly, we shall be husband and wife."

Cy kissed her, a sweet kiss full of sincerity and love.

The trip to Adderly only took a few minutes. It would have been shorter, but Cy stopped the horse halfway there to kiss Finola some more. They reached the church and found Reverend Hall just outside its doors, polishing the handles.

He set down his cloth as they approached. "Do I have a wedding ceremony to perform, Your Grace?"

"You do," Cy said, confidence brimming in his voice. "We need to retrieve Bertie from the inn. Does the lad count as a witness?"

"He is welcome to attend the ceremony," the clergyman said, "but witnesses need to be of legal age. I can fetch Mrs. Hall."

"Do that," Cy said. "We will also bring a few others to witness our nuptials."

Cy threaded his fingers through hers. "Shall we?"

They walked to Mr. Timmon's shop first and then called to invite

Mr. Simon and Mrs. Carroll to the ceremony. Cy gave a coin to a boy they passed, asking him to tell Doctor Addams to hurry to the church. Finola laughed as the boy took off running.

By the time they doubled back and crossed the street to the inn, people were flooding the streets, Bertie one of them. The boy ran to them, a huge smile on his face.

"Is it true, Your Grace? You are marrying Lady Finola?"

"I am. We were coming to get you," her fiancé said. "We couldn't wed without your presence. Come along."

Bertie ran ahead of them, joining the others who were entering the church. Although Finola would have liked to have Nalyssa and Pierce witness the ceremony, she was happy to wed Cy now.

"Stay here," he said. "I will go and see if everything is ready."

Mrs. Hall came out from the church, carrying a small bouquet. "These are for you, my lady. We don't want a wedding without flowers now, do we?"

She gave Finola the bouquet and then said, "It is so nice to see you in a gown, my lady. You look lovely. You should wear one more often."

Cy came out and obviously overheard the woman's last remark. "I think my duchess looks lovely no matter what she wears, Mrs. Hall." He cocked one eyebrow. "And no doubt she will look beautiful in nothing at all."

Mrs. Hall gasped. "Your Grace!"

He gave the woman a boyish smile. "I am simply looking forward to my wedding night."

The woman turned, her face beet red, and fled back into the church.

Cy laughed. "Everything is ready inside." He glanced about. "It looks as if everyone in the village who has heard is already inside, the exception being Dr. Addams. I see him coming, though."

Glancing over her shoulder, Finola saw the physician galloping down the main thoroughfare on his horse. He pulled up near them and looped the reins around a post.

"I hear there is a wedding ready to take place. I wouldn't have missed this for the world. Congratulations, Your Grace. Lady Finola. I will see you inside."

Cy caressed her cheek. "I am sorry we did not have time to have the marriage contracts drawn up. We can see to those immediately, though. Know I will always take care of you and any children we have."

"I never doubted you would," she told him.

"I will tell you now that I want everything in writing, love. You and I can sit with my solicitor as he draws up the marriage settlements to make certain he gets everything correct. Belldale will remain your property, and all that is within it. The same goes for your Honeyfield spaniels."

His words stunned her. "That is most generous, Cy."

He brushed a soft kiss against her lips. "You do not have to change who you are, Finola, because I love you just as you are. And that means I expect you to keep working. Just because you will be a duchess does not mean you should stop training your dogs. It is what makes you happy, and you are bloody good at it."

A warmth began to glow within her. "You do not mind a duchess dog trainer as your wife?"

Kissing her again, he said, "Not only do I support your endeavors—but I expect a healthy discount from you on any dogs I purchase from you in the future."

She saw the teasing light in his eyes. Love for this man spilled from her, and Finola grabbed his lapels, pulling him down for a lingering kiss.

Cy was the one to break the kiss, and she saw the emotion on his face. "Are you ready?" her betrothed asked. "To begin our adventures as husband and wife?"

"I will always be ready for you, Cy."

He kissed her lightly and then escorted her inside the church. A hush descended over those gathered. They walked up the aisle, and she saw nothing but smiles on the faces of the villagers. Her own smile was wide, reflecting her utter happiness at the turn of events. She had awakened this morning as Lady Finola Honeyfield, an unattached woman of small but independent means. The day would conclude and see her become the Duchess of Margate.

With the love of her life forever by her side.

They reached the altar, where the waiting Reverend Hall greeted them.

"I am most pleased to perform your marriage ceremony, Your Graces."

"Did you give him the license?" Finola asked.

"I did, my love."

"Then I suppose we should begin," the clergyman said jovially. He gazed out at the gathered crowd and said in a sonorous voice, "Dearly beloved, we are gathered together here in the sight of God, and in the face of this congregation, to join together this man and this woman in holy matrimony."

Finola glanced up at Cy, and he smiled down at her as Reverend Hall walked them through the steps of the ceremony. When it came time to produce a ring, Cy turned, calling up Bertie. The boy bounded toward them, opening his palm. Cy plucked the ring from it, Bertie grinning from ear to ear, bouncing with excitement before he returned to his seat.

"It is but a simple gold band," Cy said softly, "but I can always replace it with something else."

"It is perfect," she told him.

As he placed the wedding band on her finger, Finola knew she would never remove it. Not in life. Not in death. For she and Cy were always meant to be together.

EPILOGUE

The next morning . . .

C Y AWOKE AND for the first time in his life, he knew utter contentment.

Finola lay nestled in his arms. His wife. His life. The mother of his future children.

And the woman who had saved him in every way.

They had returned to Melrose after their impromptu wedding yesterday afternoon, promising the town's citizens they would be invited to a wedding breakfast the next week. They had told Bertie he was to go ahead and return to Belldale and that he should exercise the pups as usual tomorrow morning, putting them through their paces afterward.

When the boy asked when they would arrive, Finola told him that she would be taking the day off to celebrate her marriage with her new husband. She assured Bertie that she trusted him implicitly, and there would be a return to a more normal routine the day after.

Cy knew it would be important for Finola to keep up her training with the pups, but it might prove more convenient to move them to Melrose sometime in the near future. These were all things that could be discussed later.

Now, he wanted to make love to his duchess.

The room was still dark, the heavy curtains keeping out any sunlight. He relished Finola's warmth against him and inhaled the scent of lavender, which always clung to her. Slowly, he began stroking her bare back, the delicious curve the most marvelous thing he had ever felt.

She began to stir, and he kissed the top of her head. Her palm began caressing his chest, and then she playfully tweaked his nipple, sending a surge of desire through him.

"Are you too tender for us to make love again?" he asked, concerned because they had done so thrice already. Once upon their return to Melrose. Again after they had eaten a leisurely supper in bed. A third time during the middle of the night when they had reached for each other hungrily.

"I will never tire of your touch, Cy."

He kissed his wife long and deep, amazed this beautiful creature was finally all his. As his hands roamed her curves, he said, "With the candle now burned out, I wish to see you. Might I open the curtains?"

"Only if you are gone but a moment. Any longer and I cannot forgive you."

He kissed her, his mouth feeling the curve of her smile. Cy then threw back the bedclothes and made his way to one of the windows and tossed back the curtains, Strong sunlight poured into the room. Turning, he saw Finola had pushed herself to a sitting position, her long, cinnamon-brown hair tumbling about her.

He took two steps toward her and froze.

No. It couldn't be.

"What is it, Cy?" she asked worriedly.

He moved to the bed, a slow smile spreading across his face. Perching on the bed, he framed her face in his hands.

Gazing into her eyes, he said, "I see you."

"Of course, you see me, you silly goose. You opened the . . ." Her voice cut off abruptly and her eyes widened. "Do you mean . . . that you can *see* me? With both eyes?"

"Yes. Yes. Yes!"

Cy kissed her everywhere. Her brow and nose. Her cheeks and mouth. The sensitive spot just below her ear. Joy filled him.

He made love to his beautiful duchess with enthusiasm, kissing—and seeing—every inch of her. They both reached their peak together, and then he collapsed atop her, quickly rolling to his back so that she was astride him.

"How can this be, Cy? I don't mean to question a miracle but . . . how?"

"I think a visit to Dr. Addams is in order. Also, I would like to go to Stonecrest today and share our good news with Pierce and Nalyssa."

"Oh, you do not know since you have been gone. Nalyssa had the babe. It is a healthy girl. They named her Mary."

He kissed her hard and fast. "And I hope we have made our own babe this day. You will be a wonderful mother, Finola."

Her palm cradled his cheek. "You will be the best of fathers because you have so much love in your heart."

Cy rang for hot water, and he and Finola washed. He had already told her they would be sharing the duke's rooms, though all her clothing would be stored in the duchess' bedchamber. She could dress there.

"We must see about getting you a lady's maid," he said.

"Do I really need one, Cy?"

"I think my duchess should have one. Maisie would be a good choice. While you don't often wear gowns, there will be occasions now when you do, such as when we entertain our neighbors for our wedding breakfast next week. That reminds me, you will need to sit with Cook and work out a menu for the occasion."

"We have other things to discuss."

"I know," he said. "We can do so after we see Dr. Addams and are on our way to Stonecrest."

Cy had sent two footmen for Finola's things, and she went to her rooms to dress. He followed her, playing lady's maid to her and helping her don her undergarments and a gown. She was then valet to him, kissing him between each piece of clothing he put on. Once dressed, they headed downstairs for breakfast.

Arnold looked pleased at their arrival, and Mrs. Arnold also appeared in the breakfast room.

"I am happy to give you a tour of Melrose today, Your Grace," the housekeeper told Finola.

"We need to save that for tomorrow, Mrs. Arnold," his duchess said. "We are going to Stonecrest today to share our good news with the Duke and Duchess of Stoneham."

"If you will have the coachman ready the carriage, we will leave directly after breakfast," Cy informed his butler.

Soon, they were on their way, with Cy having told the driver to first stop at Dr. Addams' house.

This time when Cy knocked, the servant who answered the door recognized him and curtseyed.

"How are you today, Your Graces?" she asked. "I hear congratulations are in order."

"Thank you," he said. "Might Dr. Addams be available?"

"He is, Your Grace. Let me take you to him."

Finola hung back, and Cy took her hand, lacing his fingers through hers. "I want you with me to hear what Addams has to say."

They were led to the examination room he had previously been to, and the servant disappeared, promising the doctor would join them momentarily.

Cy took the opportunity to kiss his bride.

He broke the kiss and grinned. "I will never tire of kissing you, my love."

"That is good to hear—because I feel the same," Finola said pertly, kissing him.

Hearing a throat being cleared, they sprang apart, and he saw Dr. Addams had arrived.

"Ah, the newlyweds. What might I do for you today, Your Graces?"

"I can see again, Dr. Addams," Cy informed the physician.

A pleased and knowing look appeared upon Dr. Addams' face. "If you will sit on my examination table, Your Grace, I would like to look at your eyes."

Finola took a seat in one of the available chairs as Cy climbed onto the table. Dr. Addams intently studied Cy's eyes and then stepped back.

"It is as I suspected, Your Grace," the doctor said. "It could be a combination of two things. You and I—along with your army doctor—had discussed the pressure which might have built up on your optic nerve. Time has passed since the bullet struck your head, and the swelling most likely has totally subsided. That in and of itself could be the answer to the riddle we have been asking regarding your sudden blindness. With the eye relieved of the pressure, it allowed your vision to return."

"And the other factor?" Cy asked.

"We had also discussed the strain you had been under. Being forced from all that was familiar to you, into a new life. I believe the strain you were under was also affecting your sight. Or lack of it. Finding a bride, one you obviously love, has lifted the curtain of depression, uncertainty, and sorrow which you were feeling."

"You were saying happiness was the cure all along?"

Dr. Addams smiled broadly. "Once again, I don't think we need to question things too closely, Your Grace. Your eyes look fine to me, and you are seeing clearly. I would continue the eyewashes you have been doing, but you can taper off when you find you have no more need for them. I think they would help give you some relief for now."

The physician added, "Congratulations, Your Grace, on your marriage and having your eyesight fully restored."

Dr. Addams then turned to Finola. "Your Grace, I believe your eyewashes played a definitive role in His Grace recovering his eyesight." He tried to suppress a grin and failed. "Along with the love you have for one another. I would be most grateful if you would share the herbs used and the ration of each. I am always looking to add to my knowledge in order to help my patients in their recoveries."

Finola smiled radiantly. "I would be happy to do so, Dr. Addams. I will write out the specifics and send them to you. Perhaps you might like to call on us tomorrow for tea, and I will have it ready for you at that time."

"I would appreciate it, Your Grace," said the physician. "Good day to you both."

Cy and Finola returned to their carriage, and he pulled her into his lap, kissing her leisurely the entire way to Stonecrest.

When they arrived, they were met by Pugh, the Stonecrest butler.

"I know we are unexpected visitors, but if Their Graces are available, my duchess and I would like to visit with them."

Pugh gave them a welcoming smile. "Of course, Your Graces. Please, come in."

They were led to Nalyssa's sitting room. The French doors were open, and Pugh went through them, announcing, "His and Her Grace, the Duke and Duchess of Margate."

Cy and Finola stepped through the doors, seeing Pierce and Nalyssa sitting at a table in the sunshine. Both rose and embraces were exchanged.

Pierce clapped Cy on the back, saying, "You sly fox. You did it."

The four of them sat, and another pot of tea was brought out as they caught their friends up on the events of the last twenty-four hours.

"It would have been nice to have you at our wedding," Finola said. "But it was so spontaneous. Fortunately, Cy had the foresight to purchase a special license, making the wedding possible."

Cy shared what Miss Slade had found and how he had brought Lord Crofton back with him from London.

"He apologized in person, as well as giving me a letter of apology," Finola told them.

"Did he sound sincere?" Nalyssa asked.

"As sincere as someone such as the viscount could be," Cy said. "Of course, with the threat of being exposed and humiliated in front of all the guests at the Duke and Duchess of Westfield's ball, he had little choice."

"As long as you hold his markers, you have leverage over him," Pierce pointed out.

"I do not know if he can change, but being forced to remain in the country and trying to rebuild his father's estate should make a man of him," he said.

They spoke of the wedding and how there would be a wedding breakfast the following week. Nalyssa assured them that she and Pierce would attend.

"I will be up for traveling by then. It will only be a few hours away from the babe. Or we could even bring Mary and her nurse with us," she mused.

"Speaking of Mary," Pierce said.

Cy looked over his shoulder to see a nursemaid bringing the infant to her mother.

The duchess said, "No, give her to the Duke of Margate. I think he might enjoy holding a babe."

He accepted the swaddled newborn and looked down at her. Mary opened her eyes and stared with curiosity at the man who held her. A wave of tenderness rippled through him. If he could feel this for his friend's child, what would it be like to hold his own flesh and blood?

"I believe you are seeing her with both eyes," Pierce said. "I note that you are no longer wearing your eye patch. When did your vision return?"

Holding out a hand to his wife, Finola took it.

"It came suddenly," he explained. "This morning. We have just come from Dr. Addams, and he said it could be a few things. I don't question it. I merely celebrate it."

Nalyssa smiled. "I think it is love which cured you, Cy. It took finding your soulmate and lasting happiness to bring about this miracle."

Cy squeezed his wife's fingers and gazed down once more at the newborn in his arms, who still studied him with interest.

"We will do our best, Mary, to give you a playmate as soon as possible," he told the babe.

Pierce and Nalyssa laughed at his declaration.

But Cy was looking at Finola as he said it, seeing her love for him reflected in her eyes.

"I look forward to the children we will have, my love," he said softly, knowing their lives were only just beginning.

About the Author

Award-winning and internationally bestselling author Alexa Aston's historical romances use history as a backdrop to place her characters in extraordinary circumstances, where their intense desire for one another grows into the treasured gift of love.

She is the author of Regency and Medieval romance, including: Dukes of Distinction; Soldiers & Soulmates; The St. Clairs; The King's Cousins; and The Knights of Honor.

A native Texan, Alexa lives with her husband in a Dallas suburb, where she eats her fair share of dark chocolate and plots out stories while she walks every morning. She enjoys a good Netflix binge; travel; seafood; and can't get enough of *Survivor* or *The Crown*.